DATE			

SUCH WAS THE
SEASON

BOOKS BY CLARENCE MAJOR

Such Was the Season
My Amputations
Emergency Exit
Reflex and Bone Structure
NO
All-Night Visitors
Inside Diameter: The France Poems
The Syncopated Cakewalk
The Cotton Club
Symptoms and Madness
Private Line
Swallow the Lake
The Dark and Feeling
Dictionary of Afro-American Slang
The New Black Poetry

SUCH WAS THE SEASON

A NOVEL BY
CLARENCE MAJOR

Mercury House, Incorporated
San Francisco

Copyright © 1987 by Clarence Major

Published in the United States by
Mercury House
San Francisco, California

Distributed to the trade by
Kampmann & Company, Inc.
New York, New York

The lines from "November Cotton Flower" from CANE by Jean Toomer, are reprinted by permission of Liveright Publishing Corporation. Copyright 1923 by Boni & Liveright. Copyright renewed 1951 by Jean Toomer.

Manufactured in the United States of America

Library of Congress Cataloging-in-Publication Data

Major, Clarence.
    Such was the season.

    I. Title.
PS3563.A39S8   1987   813'.54   87-7760
ISBN 0-916515-20-6

> . . . dead birds were found
> In wells a hundred feet below the ground—
> Such was the season when the flower bloomed.
> Old folks were startled, and it soon assumed
> Significance . . . .

—Jean Toomer, *Cane*

1

Last week was a killer-diller! I don't know if Juneboy brought good or bad luck. First news he was coming down here came from Esther. She called me one night from Chicago, where she lives, oh bout a week fore he was to get in. She said, "Annie, my son Adam is coming down there to speak at Spelman bout his research at Howard University Hospital."

I said, "What kinda research, Esther?"

She said, "Annie Eliza, I done told you bout Adam's research so many times, I swear you don't never listen to nothing I say."

Then I said to my baby sister, "You tell that boy he better stay with me when he gets here, I won't stand him staying in some hotel or with nobody else."

It had been many a year since I had seed the boy. He had to be in his mid-forties by now and I hadn't seed him since he was bout eighteen. All the other childrens come down from everywhere they done scattered to, for funerals and sometimes for weddings and when babies is born in the family, but not Juneboy. He swore when Scoop was shot that he would never set foot again in the South. Everybody in the family knowed how Juneboy felt.

Well, his coming anyway, even for this lecture business, was a kinda homecoming and I was looking forward to seeing him all growed up, but I couldn't imagine he was all that Esther made him up to be. I sure didn't know he was a doctor. Guess I thought he was still in school. Anyways, Esther was just always trying to make it sound like her kids had complished as much in life as mine.

Maybe his homecoming was a way of coming down to earth, finding out bout us, his peoples. I hoped so.

1

But there was no way to know the whole time he was here was gon be so, so full of all kinds of unexpected things happening. That whole business with Renee. Senator Cooper's mess. And Jeremiah's incident. Seems like every minute of every day — and he finally stayed eight days — something upsetting was going on. And the moon was full part of that time, too.

Then Juneboy hisself called me, the day after I talked with his mother, and told me, "Aunt Annie Eliza, thank you for offering to put me up." He said he sho appreciated it and that he was looking forward to "a reunion with all the folk."

I ast him bout this research he was talking bout. He said, "I'm working on a cure for sickle cell anemia with a group of other pathologists. We hope to find a way to break the hereditary chain." He said, "The interest at Spelman is more social than scientific."

Well, I member thinking while he talked, that he sho talked like a educated man, but then there is these street hoodlums too that can talk real smart, so smart you'd think they knowed something bout everything.

I ast him how was his wife, cause I forgot he was divorced. Then he told me, and I membered Esther telling me. So he would be coming down by hisself.

Though I have a guest room, I always give family guests my own bedroom, and I sleep on the couch out back. Juneboy was family.

Well, child, there was just three or four days to get the house cleaned up and you shoulda seed me rushing round this place of mine, sweeping and vacuuming and dusting and polishing and scrubbing. Everybody say my place is spic and span all the time cause I keep it that way. But they don't know how underneath things there is dust. I was after the hiding dirt, you see. Momma always taught us girls to be clean. Momma kept a clean house. Esther and Kathy like me in this respect. They real partickler. Prudence was like that too all her life.

I called up everybody — Ballard, Donna Mae, Jeremiah and DeSoto, Kathy — everybody I could think of and told them Juneboy was coming down Thursday morning, April tenth. He was flying in direct from Washington, D.C. I told them what he told me: he was gon go straight to Spelman and talk to the social peoples first then take a taxi out here to my place. Spelman just there on Leonard Street Southwest. I told Juneboy I could drive my old Chevy to Spelman and get him. He said no, no it wont necessary. I offered to pick him up at DeKalb or Hartsfield, whichever one he was coming in to. But no, he said the peoples at Spelman was picking him up. So I told everybody so nobody felt like they done let Juneboy down by not picking him up at the airport. He had his own plans already pretty much worked out.

Homecoming. That use to be a big thing, a custom in our family. Nowadays only time folks get together is, like I say, when somebody dies or somebody marries or has a baby. But we Sommers use to all go down to Monroe to see Momma and Poppa when they was still living. We did it in the spring, in the first week of May. Back in them days country folks round Monroe was still marrying by stepping over the broom. At them homecomings everybody was feeling real good. We all helped Momma cook up a lot of fried chicken and made potato salad and we ate watermelon and drank lots of ice tea. Sometimes the menfolk would sneak off and drink whiskey but we womens just pretended we didn't know. We singed a lot of happy songs too, songs like "Oh, My Little Soul's Gon Shine," and "Ain't No Grave Can Hold My Body Down," and "Every Time I Feel the Spirit."

We started going back to Monroe a year after Prudence moved up to Chicago. It was our way of getting her back, and we here in Atlanta—Kathy, Ballard, Esther, and me—we too got ourselves back down there. You see, Rutherford never left Momma and Poppa. Then Esther left Scoop and Momma and Poppa took her kids for a while and she went up North to stay with Prudence. Prudence helped her find a job and she been up there ever since.

That first homecoming was real special. I member it better than I member yesterday. Poppa was in good spirits. The fried chicken tasted real good and it was crispy. The watermelon was sweet. The grace said at the table was short so peoples got to eat fore they food got cold. All of our childrens was either not born yet or real little. Poppa, who's real name was Olaudah Equiano

Sommer, talked Indian talk and we all laughed. He was proud of
his Cherokee relatives. He told us a story bout his father, a
important man in the Cherokee Nation, who helped collect
money to send colored familes to Liberia. You see, back then a lot
of Negroes still wanted to go back to Africa. Olay—that's what
folks called Poppa—another time told us how his father made
good luck come to the tribe. Grandpoppa built hisself a big bird,
a hawk or a eagle. He made this thing out of wood, you see. Then
he painted it all the natural colors it was spose to have. He kept it
outside the Nation, out in the forest. Nobody knowed bout it
cept Grandpoppa hisself. Everyday he took hisself out to this
giant bird and he rubbed it with special oils he made from plants
and he spoke a secret language to this bird and, after he did this
over and over for a very long time, the bird started to talk back to
Grandpoppa. He ast Grandpoppa what he wanted, told him he
could make a wish, and, if the wish wont selfish, the bird told
him he could make it come true. Grandpoppa had to get up on
the bird's back and make the wish while sitting up there with his
eyes closed. Grandpoppa told the bird not to worry: The wish
wont gon be one with self-interest in it. So the bird told
Grandpoppa to go on, get up there, and make his wish. He did
and he wished the best of everything for the Cherokee Nation,
no more war with the white man, no more war with the Creeks.
Grandpoppa prayed that the Cherokees would not have any
more trouble with the Chickasaws or the Confederates. He
prayed for one thing and another for many hours. Then he
stopped and the bird told him his wish was a good one and that it
would come true, told him to go on back to the tribe and he
would see for hisself. He did and at first he looked round but
couldn't see how anything was changed. He looked and he
looked for days but nothing looked different. Grandpoppa began
to think the bird had played a trick on him so he went back to the
big bird and told him he couldn't see change. The bird laughed
and said change was everywhere, change for the better, there in
the Cherokee Nation, and that he only had to learn how to see it.
The bird told Grandpoppa to go on back and try again. This time
he began to notice how peoples was smiling and speaking kindly

to each other and how even the little bitty children wont fighting over toys or nothing. The mommas making corn mush looked happy and the boys going out for the rabbit hunt looked just as happy. This noticing that Grandpoppa was doing went on for days, and before long he started believing the bird's magic had worked.

I member being so struck by that story that I dreamed about it over and over for a long time.

So homecoming was a time of happiness, storytelling, a time when we all come together and membered we was family and tried to love each other, even if we didn't always do it so well.

Now, Juneboy was having his homecoming, coming back to the South, and, like I said, nobody had any idea what a mess everything would be while he was down here staying with me.

★   ★   ★

I been living here in this same house in East Point for thirty-six years, ever since my husband Bibb bought it with his soldier money, back in 1947. I was the first mongst us children to live in a house I owned. Momma and Poppa course owned the house we growed up in. Me and Bibb planted the trees in the backyard. The big one out front was there when we came. Just as sho as the Chestatee River pours itself into the Chattahoochee, I'll be here in this house till the day I die. It's been a good place and peoples like to visit me. They tells me they feels comfortable here in my house.

I didn't spect Juneboy till round midafternoon. I was straightening up the back room, just a humming, "Somebody Knocking at Your Door," when I heard the doorbell ring one time. I likes visitors who ring only one time. I can't stand peoples who lean on the doorbell like they from the country and ain't never seed a doorbell before.

I went up there to see if it was Juneboy. But it wont. It was that little boy, Edgar Lee, who runs errands for me. He wanted to know if I needed anything from the store.

I didn't need nothing just then.

Then a half hour later, while I was trying to see what was happening on one of my soap operas, the doorbell ringed three times. It made me a little mad but I didn't want to go to the door mad if it was Juneboy.

And it was him. I could see him in that growed up face of his and in that smile. I was seeing him through the screen door but I could see him good enough.

I opened the screen door. "Lord, have mercy! Land sakes," I said. "Boy, look at you! All growed up and fine looking, too."

He hugged me and kissed my cheek. I held onto my wig so he wouldn't upset it."

"You're looking well, too, Aunt Annie Eliza."

"Well, don't stand there in the door letting the flies in, come on in and make yourself at home. You home now, boy."

I led him on in.

"House looks just like I remember it. So neat and pretty."

"Just like your momma keep house, huh?"

"Yes."

We laughed together.

I led him on back to the back and turned to look at him again. "Just let me look at you a minute."

I stood real close so I could see his eyes. He still had them same eyes. I knowed them since he was a baby in a stroller. He was Juneboy all right. Even with that old ugly beard!

Juneboy come just a blushing so I stopped looking at him. Then he held a box out to me. "I brought you a little something."

I took the box and just started ohing and ahing all over the place, acting like I was real surprised but I wont. Not that I spected a present.

I sat down at the table and put the box on it. I looked up at Juneboy. I was like a child at Christmas time. "Can I open it, Juneboy?"

"Sure. It's yours. Open it."

I carefully pulled the ribbon off, lifted the tape off the edge of the paper, and got the box out. At this point I was already trying to guess what it was. I figured it was a blouse or a set of dish towels, maybe a old lady's dress. The box was lightweight, you see. My mind was trying to talk to me, saying, "Annie Eliza, don't spect much, now. You not a child at Christmas time. It's the thought that counts."

Then, child, I opened the box and wouldn't you know it, it was one of them wall hangings, real pretty one, like Indians maybe made it. That's it right there on the wall. It's made with heavy rope and beads. It don't spose to do nothing: just hangs there like it's doing. It's got its own way, you see. I knowed it probably didn't cost Juneboy very much, maybe it was real cheap, but it was the thought. I made such a fuss bout it, kept right on raving bout it till I noticed he looked embarrassed. I didn't want him to think I was making fun of his present to me. He sensitive. So I stopped and ast him if he wanted a cup of tea and I ast him if everything went all right at Spelman.

He said, "It was like trying to make an egg stand on its end. The time of year, the season, was wrong. I worked at it, I worked hard at it, Aunt Annie Eliza. I told them what I dream of discovering and they listened as well as any audience can, but I felt sqre, in the end, that I had not reached them, they had not understood. Not a single face in the audience gave off that certain light of recognition."

I didn't know what the boy was talking bout but I knowed enough to know he felt like he was a failure with that audience and maybe it was his fault and not theirs. I was ashamed of thinking: maybe Juneboy didn't know as much as he thought he did.

Then I got out some tea. I use Lipton. Renee buy all them fancy teas but, the way I figure it, Lipton just as good as any you can get and you don't have to pay all them high prices.

Juneboy sat there looking real serious, like he had something on his mind. Then he started talking, "You know, I've come here because of the lecture they asked me to give at the university, but I have another reason for returning to the South, especially to Atlanta. I have been suffering spiritually, longing for something I think I lost a long time ago. Aunt Annie Eliza, as old as I am, I should have resolved so many questions that I haven't managed to. Who am I? Where did I come from? My first questions, and they are still unanswered. I've been running from my early self, and now I want to stop. Somehow, I am hoping that I can get back in touch with that little boy I was, looking up into my mother's and father's faces and discovering the world. I tried to become a different person and I guess I succeeded. But now I need to find that earlier self and connect it with the new self that I am now. It's funny, I don't think Lauren ever had this conflict. When I see her, she has her problems but they are not the same as mine — and we grew up together, had the same experiences, cried together, laughed together.

"I think back hard and try to remember my father. I loved Scoop so much and felt his pain so deeply. Aunt Annie Eliza, do you understand what I'm trying to say?"

"Sho, Juneboy. You want to get to know your family down here. That's real nice. I'm gon take you to meet everybody, and — "

"Thank you. But it's not just meeting them, it's — "

I couldn't help myself, I cut him off cause I thought he was talking crazy talk. I said, "Juneboy, how was your flight down?"

He gave me a scared look, like he done seed a ghost.

" — There was definitely something wrong with that flight, Aunt Annie Eliza. I thought surely any minute we were going to be hijacked. It was like there was something in the manner of the hostesses and you could see it in the faces of some of the passengers. When the pilot talked to us over the intercom, his voice was shaking. He said he had something important to tell us, but he never got around to saying what it was. Then he called out the name of one of the passengers and this tall hostess found the man because he hadn't responded. She got him up on his feet. He was sitting across the aisle from me. She told him the captain wanted him to come up to the cockpit. Meanwhile, we hit some rough clouds. There were funny buzzing sounds from the middle of the aircraft, probably from where the wings join the body.

"I watched that man the captain wanted — his name was Joseph something, some kind of eastern European name. I watched him get up and saw the strain in his face. He was like a man either going to his execution or to the most glorious event of his life.

The hostess walked just behind him. He had the grimness of determination. Even when I could no longer see his face, it showed in his shoulders and in his movement. So, curious about what was going on, I got up and followed them, pretending to go to the toilet. It worked out just fine. Somebody was in the toilet so I had an excuse to stand there just outside waiting for it to be free. The cockpit door was open, so I got to watch what was going on in there. Joseph's back was to me but I could see the face of the captain. I couldn't see his copilot. The captain was looking up into Joseph's face. I couldn't hear what he was saying because of the hum of the airplane, but he had this awful pleading expression. I do believe the man was about to cry or was already crying. He clearly was at the mercy of the passenger Joseph."

I brought the tea to the table and got two cups and poured it for us while Juneboy went on telling his story — which, mercy me, was making me feel nervous, not bout what happened but bout Juneboy hisself.

"Then the thing that convinced me, Aunt Annie Eliza, the thing that clinched it for me, was when I saw the captain hand Joseph a little package. Joseph put it in his pocket. He kept shaking his head, saying something to the captain. The captain also went on talking, looking up at Joseph — obviously begging him to do something or not to do something.

"Even when the toilet was free, I continued to stand there watching the exchange. Nobody noticed. I was discreet. I saw that Joseph was about to end his business with the captain. He was pulling away, turning, attempting to come back to the cabin. He was half turned. Without using the toilet, I returned to my seat so I could see his face as he came down the aisle. He was coming down, disappointed but also with a sort of bittersweet victory glowing in his eyes. No hostess escorted him back. He returned alone. Then, just before he sat down, he gave me this look. He looked at me with this twisted smile, the smile of a man who is thinking of suicide. The smile said this but it also said that he thought I had no idea what was going on inside of him. I thought the airplane might explode in midair, to tell you the truth."

I ast Juneboy why.

"Because right after Joseph returned to his seat the captain came over the intercom again and said, 'Fasten your seat belts because we may be entering the worst weather in my experience.' But looking out the window we all could see that it was a sunny and clear day. We were probably at that moment flying over Winston Salem, North Carolina. I looked down and saw a lot of green stretches that looked like they might be tobacco fields."

I couldn't even imagine what Juneboy was talking bout and why he told me this. He sho scared me. Then I recollected that Juneboy always had a vivid imagination ever since he was little. Then, child, I just decided to put my fear of him outta my mind. I was gon enjoy his stay with me if it was the last thing I did.

* * *

While we drinked our tea Juneboy ast me bout everybody. He wanted to know if his Aunt Kathy and Uncle Donald was okay. He ast bout Donna Mae but I noticed he didn't ast bout her father, Ballard. I told him everybody was excited bout seeing him after all these years. He looked like he was pleased.

I was kinda overcoming my fear of him, you see. Esther told me some years ago that Juneboy wont right in the head. Had something to do with the time he spent in service. The doctors discovered he had some ghosts or something living in his brains. Nobody knowed what to do for him. I member feeling real sorry for him and I also member thinking the ghosts got there cause of his sadness due to the way his father died.

All of this, I thought, was probably why his marriage didn't work out. Esther had told me that the girl Juneboy married, this Margaret Anthony—funny I member her name, maybe cause it sounds like Mark Anthony—was a real sweet girl. Esther liked her a whole lot. She was the only gal Juneboy ever took up with that Esther liked. This Margaret Anthony was a lady and she had education behind her.

Now, the first day, when Juneboy and I both thought he was gon be here in Atlanta just three or four days, I was trying to

figure how to best get him round so everybody could see him. I
still have confidence in my car. I could drive the boy where he
wanted to go. I knowed Renee was having some kinda big dinner
party Friday night. Well, I figured Juneboy might not be interested in that. He sho wanted to see his cousins — my boys,
DeSoto and Jeremiah, and Donna Mae. I knowed DeSoto saw
Juneboy in New Haven, Connecticut, at least one time when he
and Whitney took a trip up North driving around one summer.
When he came back, DeSoto told me how Juneboy always
regretted not being at his father's burial. So, I sorta thought I
might end up having to drive Juneboy to the grave site where
Scoop lay resting his old no good soul.

Not that I minded, mind you. I member the last time I seen
Scoop. It was that time when Juneboy was down here, at eighteen
years old. I fixed dinner for Scoop and Juneboy then. I used the
good tablecloth and the fine china and the best silverware. Scoop,
being a street man I never approved of in the first place, probably
never preciated the trouble I went to. But I did it for Esther's boy.
Esther is my favorite sister. Kathy is too religious — she makes me
just want to fall on my knees and pray for the rest of my life. She's
a year and a half younger than me. I can't stand too much of
Kathy and that husband of hers. Yet I'm stuck with them, being
right here in the city. Esther followed Prudence North. Prudence
is dead.

We finished our tea and just as I was taking the cups to the sink
I was so embarrassed cause it suddenly came into my mind that
all the while the television with my soap operas been on. I didn't
know it but maybe I had been listening to them with one of my
ears and it made me feel sorta guilty.

I went and turned it off but the show had ended.

★   ★   ★

When DeSoto got off duty he came by to see Juneboy. DeSoto
was the only one of us who had seed Juneboy growed up. They
was real friendly, joking round and stuff.

I started making the supper for us that night while I listened to them talk bout the time in New Haven. Seem like Juneboy musta took DeSoto and Whitney for a night on the town cause the things they kept remembering sounded pretty much out of my sense of the way peoples ought to live. There was some kinda balloon they was chasing all over the town, seem like. Then they was in a tavern drinking beer and the balloon was gone and probably busted somewhere. Then they said something bout this old couple that went out to a cliff in they car and tried to kill theyselves but changed they minds at the last minute and backed the car up. I don't know why they got into the things happening in New Haven. Maybe Juneboy's professor was the man in the car and the woman was the professor's wife.

One thing was clear, DeSoto and Juneboy sho liked each other and that—right off—made me feel less scared of Juneboy.

After a little while DeSoto took Juneboy away with him. Probably out to some bar somewhere. Mens!

I tried picking up on what was happening on "General Hospital" with Luke and Laura and the Quartermaines and Jimmy Lee and the rest of them when my stomach started hurting like I ate something poison. I never had such a pain fore then like that. Girl, I thought I was gon die. I kept thinking, "Now, what did I eat that got me to hurting so bad?" And I couldn't think of a thing. For breakfast all I had was Cream of Wheat. For lunch I ate a piece of chicken, the breast, from last night. Couldn't a been the chicken cause I cooked it fresh, like I said, just the night before. I was hurting so bad I could hardly get myself stretched out on the couch. Other than the Cream of Wheat and the piece of chicken all I had was coffee and tea and I ain't never been sick from coffee or tea.

I finally got myself stretched out there but the pain was so sharp I couldn't even concentrate my mind on "General Hospital." My body was talking to me something powerful. I sho wont having no labor pains. Specially since I hadn't been nowhere near no man in that respect in many, many years. I ain't had no use for all the bother that goes with being like that with mens. Oh, I tried it one time after Bibb's death, but it didn't work. Just one time. It wont worth it, child. I might as well had a been shelling peas or shucking corn.

Now, this pain. It was like something growing inside me and not just growing inside me but taking over my whole body, you see. I felt my hands, one with the other, and I couldn't feel nothing but the pain, like it had become me. And there was this feeling of swelling, I mean a giant swelling inside me and not just a swelling inside me but a swelling that was me itself, a swelling that had taken the place of me, my body was it. I member wondering if it was my arthritis gone all the way to the limits but it wont the same kinda pain I know as my arthritis pain. It was this other, much bigger thing. I'm shame to say I even wondered if it had something to do with Juneboy's coming but I couldn't figure how that could be since all he did was kiss me on the cheek. But you know, in the olden days they use to say even just a kiss on the cheek by a hootchy-kootchy man could cast a spell on you. The hoodoo mens and ladies used to be afeared something terrible. But that was nonsense in this day and age and besides, Juneboy wont nobody but Juneboy.

When I felt like I swelled as big as I could get, I couldn't move and I wanted to get up and go look in the mirror but I couldn't get off my back cause I had sort of turned into a big round spongy thing, like.

It musta stayed on me, all this pain, being me, for over a hour, maybe two. Then it slowly just on its own started creeping away, like it was leaving through my fingers and out of my toes and by way of my mouth and eyes and ears. I was like a balloon with the air being let out of it slowly, you know what I mean.

So, by the time DeSoto brought Juneboy back I felt fine. Well, almost like it hadn't happened cept I felt the shakes like I think maybe drunks feels the morning after they been through they cups.

It was a good thing I had already made supper earlier in the afternoon, knowing Juneboy was coming. I ast DeSoto to stay for supper with us, so he called Whitney to let her know he wouldn't be home. I ast Juneboy if he wanted to watch the early news. He did, so I turned the channel to the station with the five-thirty news. When I walked close by Juneboy I didn't smell no liquor on his breath so I was happy but I couldn't figure where he and DeSoto went off to, so I ast him. He said DeSoto took him up to Martin Luther King's tomb. Then they drove round some. DeSoto knows Atlanta so I guess he was just refreshing Juneboy's memory. But Atlanta done changed so much since Juneboy was down here last time. I think even the house they lived in — even the whole neighborhood Scoop and Esther lived in when Juneboy and Lauren was little — is gone and a park is there with a expressway running through it.

I told DeSoto and Juneboy bout my pain but I didn't make no big fuss over it specially since it had gone. All DeSoto ast me is if I took something for it. I didn't tell him I couldn't even get myself up for two hours. One thing bout pain, that one and other kinds, is it tells you you living — you know you living.

I had cooked a pork roast for Juneboy and some turnip greens and baked potatoes. We musta ate dinner early that Thursday evening. The pork roast was done just before they showed up.

While we ate Juneboy started telling us bout being in Poland recently with what he called a delegation of other pathologists. He said something bout visiting some of they universities over there and talking to medical students bout sickle cell. Then he told this story bout being at the airport ready to leave Poland and the Polish police stopped him and took him outta line and made him sit with some Arabs till everybody else was on the plane.

Then, he said, it was while he and the Arabs was sitting together that he got to know these Arabs and they found out who he was and told him they was gon invite him to speak on the same subject in they own country. But you see Juneboy and the Arabs was real mad, sitting there like that with no reason.

And sho nuff the Arabs did invite him to come to Algiers, he said. In Algiers he visited the Casbah and said it was stinking and the peoples were very poor and sick.

He met some Frenchman over there who was staying at this same big fancy hotel where Juneboy hisself was staying. This Frenchman was going round treating the Arabs like they was still his subjects and one time one of them in the travel agency threw his passport on the floor rather than handing it back to him and another one came along and kicked it across the floor just as the poor Frenchman stooped to pick it up. That struck me as real mean.

Juneboy talked so much his food was getting cold.

I could tell now Juneboy was just trying to impress us. I still didn't believe the boy was all he was getting hisself up to be. I wanted DeSoto to stop asting Juneboy so many questions. I started looking at the television again, but I couldn't stop hearing they talk.

I gave in. I ast Juneboy what the older women, women my own age was like. I could play his game too.

"The older women are hidden behind veils and are kept inside. They are in sharp contrast with those young ones in skirts who work in offices. One feels the slush of time in Algiers. It's a tough question. The revolution restored the old order but what do you do with it—especially in its new form?

"And, you know, the cops were gentle. I sensed it. They carry their weapons with a carelessness I admire. They don't seem ready to sling at the first nervous twitch. At the airport, old Arabs sleep stacked against each other in cold, marble corners, waiting for flights that may never come. One feels they live there. Nobody forces them to leave the shelter of the airport.

"There in Algiers one must prove one's words, one's possessions, one's intentions, one's past."

"God, Adam," said DeSoto, "you've been in some strange and crazy places."

After DeSoto was gone, and after dinner, Juneboy and me watched a movie. It was one with Richard Widmark and Lena Horne. He was the town sheriff and she was the town lady. They was in love with each other. I was shocked that they would show a black woman like that on television all wrapped up with a white man. Everybody knowed that it had been going on for hundreds of years but to see it on television—where you don't spect the real world to show itself—was shocking. I was personally shocked.

2

Like Juneboy, I didn't want to go to Renee's dinner party. All them fancy politician peoples make me nervous. I'm just a plain down-to-earth common sense person and besides I don't understand none of all that high talk they put on. Course Jeremiah, my oldest, been round them since he was at college. You should hear him talking high and mighty with them bigshots. Sho, I'm proud of him but Lord knows he shouldn't drag his poor old momma into situations where she just end up feeling embarrassed. And poor Juneboy, he just wanted to watch some television.

. Sometime I know I am too hard on Renee. It's just that that gal is so spoilt that it upsets me to see some of the things she do. Seem like all she can think about is mink coats and diamonds and big pretty cars and giant television screens and Lord knows what else. Tried to give me one of her used mink coats a couple of years ago. Child, you should have heard me carry on. Renee, I said, it's so thoughtful of you, honey, and you know I do preciate the offer but my friends would think I'd lost my mind if they saw me in a expensive coat like this. Everybody I know know I can't afford mink. Might think I stole it or something. She turned just as red as a big old ripe apple. She one of them red childs anyway, you know, with freckles and them gray cat eyes and all that nappy red hair that she don't never know what to do with.

Anyways, she wont about to spend almost a half a thousand dollars on a catered dinner party for Atlanta's Negro royalty without having some deep dark plan to her own advantage. That child wouldn't know how to do anything for anybody but herself if you paid her. You can see that by the way she treats them children of hers. I feel so sorry for little Curtis, Jane, and Jo,

16

sometimes I just break down and cry. They got everything material they need and ain't ever gone a day hungry like a lot of the children round here but they ain't got the most important thing—a caring and loving mother. Why, when I was bringing mine up I never once let DeSoto and Jeremiah sass me and stay up late the way she lets them children do. I even seed her give Curtis some beer when he was hardly a year old.

They wanted me and Juneboy over there by six, they said. It was Friday night and Jeremiah had got hisself a substitute to preach the sermon at his church, First Christ Church over on Decatur. He never missed preaching his own sermons unless something really important got in the way or he was down sick. When I ast him why not have the dinner party on another night he come just a talking bout Friday being the best time for Renee. Seems everything has to be her way.

I told Juneboy he better get dressed, then I got out my best wig from the hat box under my bed. It's blond but kinda red too. When I was young my hair was like that, so it looks real natural on me. DeSoto says it makes me look young enough to be his sister. Well, I ain't shamed of wearing a wig like some of the ladies I know at church. The good Lord don't say nowhere in the good book that it's a sin to pretty yourself up, if you can. Two summers ago when I went up to Chicago to see Esther, she says to me, "Annie Eliza, take that ugly thing off your head, makes you look like one of these here street hussies."

I told her she never been able to tell me what to do and she wont bout to start at sixty-three. I used to change her diapers and when she tries to get smart with me I remind her. It puts her in her place. I wore my wig all over Chicago, strutting my stuff just as pretty as I pleased.

I stood at the mirror adjusting the wig. I could hear Juneboy in the bathroom running water in the face bowl. My alarm clock on the bedside table said five-thirty. We could walk to Jeremiah's in fifteen minutes. His house was the biggest and the prettiest in the whole neighborhood and it was three blocks down in what they call a cul-de-sac. That's a French word. It means dead end. Jeremiah bought the place five years ago from the last white family to move outta the neighborhood. Paid a hundred and fifty thousand dollars for it, but if you ast me that place ain't worth all that much money. God knows ain't no place on this good earth worth a hundred thousand dollars. Sho, it's big and it's got so many rooms you can't count them all and keep a clear head and it's got fluffy carpets and giant television screens in all the bedrooms and antique furniture everywhere. The whole place was designed by some fancy designer who charged them more money than most people round here make in a lifetime, but I wouldn't give you a hundred dollars for it. It wasn't Jeremiah's money no way. All them church ladies bought that house. I never seen so many ladies in love with one plain old man!

★ ★ ★

It was a warm spring night as Juneboy and me walked down to Jeremiah's. I'd been worried some bout Juneboy's pearance, I mean him going to this big dinner party with these high class peoples. You see, I didn't want him to embarrass our side of the family. Esther's children never had the privileges my boys had. They didn't have a proper father. I mean, they were sorta raised here and there first by Momma and they no-good father and his crazy sisters. Then Esther took them up to Chicago but she had to work all the time. They didn't come up with good strict home training. That's the only way children learn good manners. Now I'm not blaming Esther. God knows she tried the best she could, but she was only sixteen when she got pregnant with Juneboy. By the time the boy was three, Lauren was born. That no-good gambling man of hers. I never knowed if Scoop was his real name or not. Didn't sound like no proper name I ever heard. Anyway, I was pleased to see Juneboy so dressed up in a nice tweed jacket and slacks. I figured we might get through the evening without embarrassment.

On the way over there, we walked past a house with a driveway that showed a view of my backyard in the moonlight. Juneboy come just a telling me bout a time he membered when he and my boys was playing together when they was little out back of the house. Bigger than Jeremiah, he said he had Jeremiah locked up as the bad guy and he made Jeremiah stand gainst that old tree like he was tied to it. DeSoto was spose to be helping him keep Jeremiah gainst the tree. I ast what Jeremiah spose to be guilty of and he just laughed and said it was all just a game but when they played Jeremiah was always the bad guy, you see. I had no memory of them playing like that. I did member DeSoto picking on Jeremiah though and I use to fuss at DeSoto for giving Jeremiah such a hard time all the time.

Jeremiah's driveway was full of Cadillacs and Mercedes-Benzes and they had them parked all up and down the block. Four of them Cadillacs belonged to Jeremiah. He always say they belong to the church and to God but I never saw the church or God driving them. That boy of mine is a killer, I tell you! We could see all the lights in the house was on. I told Juneboy what a shame it was that that gal was so wasteful. He just smiled. As we walked up the long winding driveway, I told Juneboy bout the time Renee hired the two-day a week maid to come in full-time to feed the childrens because she was too lazy to get outta bed before twelve. That was back fore the youngest one, Jo, was walking. Thank God, Jeremiah put his foot down, one of the few times! He told that gal if she wanted a full-time baby-feeder she had to get herself a job and pay for the service. But he don't take a firm hand with that gal the way he should. She just one of them nigger gals spoiled something you wouldn't believe, and, child, so full of herself she can't smell her own stink. And all just cause she comes from the Wright family. You know the Wrights is one of the biggest and richest Negro family in politics in Atlanta. My boy gets invited to all they big gatherings and most of them go to his church when they bother to praise the Lord at all. I let Juneboy touch the door bell just so I could watch the surprise in his face when he heard all them bells in there making all that music as though angels was coming down from heaven. But wouldn't you know it, the poor boy was so unused to such class he just didn't pay no tention to it the way polite people with the right kind of background would have. I could hear them bells in

there making all that sweet music and I just gave praise to the
Lord that at least one of my boys had made it big in this world.

Little Curtis opened the door.

First thing I heard was Renee's big mouth — and she was way
back in the kitchen. It wont the first time Renee done this
catering thing. She had her kitchen full of them folk from the
catering service. Little Curtis (named after Bibb's brother) told
me he didn't want no kiss from me when I ast him to give
Grandma a big kiss. That boy is so mannish, just like his father
when he was little. Then he ran on off somewhere to play with
his tanks and Star Wars. (When I was bringing up DeSoto I had
the hardest time keeping them from all them sinful toys like
cowboy guns and all that old violent stuff.) Seemed like every
television in the house was on and each one on a different
channel and the record player in the living room was on too.
That's what I disliked bout coming here: always so much
confusion.

Then little Jane with her pretty self came running down the
hall to meet us. I took her up in my arms and kissed her. She said
the mayor was in the den and that the kids was combing his hair
and tickling his belly.

Sho nuff, in the den, there was our mayor, Dr. George
Watkins-Jones, short and fat and black as ever, stuffed into the
usual expensive striped dark blue suit, sitting deep in the couch
before the giant screen of the television. Three of his grand-
childrens was all over him — pulling at his necktie, unbuttoning
his shirt, asting him all kinda silly questions; and all the while
him looking like he trying to concentrate on whatever was going
on on that television screen. I looked round at the television and
there was Mr. Mayor hisself up there on the screen.

I said, "Good evening Mr. Mayor," but he didn't hear me. I
don't even think he looked in my direction till he couldn't see
hisself on the television anymore. When the Pepsi commercial
came on, he looked at me and lifted a hand by way of greeting
me. I never did like that kind of casual greeting from nobody. It
shows disrespect. I knowed George fore he was mayor and seen
him many times since, maybe as many as ten or fifteen times,

usually here at Jeremiah's or in church or at one of them dinner parties they give over at Lee Anne's and Congressman Fred Wright's place. I said, "Good evening Mr. Mayor," and he called me Annie Eliza like he always did.

"Mr. Mayor," I said, "This is Dr. Adam North, my nephew — my youngest sister's oldest child."

Juneboy, like a real gentleman, went over and shook the mayor's hand but the mayor didn't stand up.

I put Jane down on the floor cause she started wiggling and she ran off toward the kitchen.

DeSoto, still in his police sergeant uniform, came in from the dining room and kissed me on the cheek just as I was bout to sit my weary bones down in the armchair (the one Renee spilled red wine on last Christmas). I was watching the suspicious look the mayor was giving Juneboy. Then I thought maybe the mayor was afeared Juneboy might assassinate him. It struck me as funny and I laughed. The mayor's bodyguard was nowhere round and that was strange.

While DeSoto stood between me and the screen picking his teeth with a toothpick (a bad habit he's had since high school), I pretended I was watching the television — which I couldn't even see — just so the mayor wouldn't think I was paying mind to what he was saying to Juneboy. He ast Juneboy what he did and Juneboy told him nicely bout the research he was spose to be doing, he said, into sickle cell anemia. The mayor sounded real interested and ast Juneboy all about it and Juneboy talked up a storm like he knowed everything in the world bout this Negro disease. He used big words too, words like hemoglobin. Juneboy told the mayor some organization done gave him a grant, which is money, and Juneboy let the mayor know that he was spending a year spending his money from the grant peoples at Howard University Hospital. Then the mayor told Juneboy bout this cousin of his who had sicklemia and I got the impression the mayor didn't think this thing called sicklemia was as bad as sickle cell. And Juneboy agreed. Then the mayor wanted to know where Juneboy lived normally. He said "normally." Juneboy told him he taught internal medicine at Yale University. I kinda laughed to myself.

Then the mayor wanted to know if Juneboy was married and had children and I heard Juneboy say he was divorced and had two boys which is the truth. You shoulda seed the look on the mayor's face. He's a God-fearing family man with many grand-children, two sons, and three daughters, and everybody can tell you our mayor ain't got no time for people who divorce. It's sort of like they ain't serious bout life. He squinted his little old red ape eyes and frowned with them deep lines between his eyebrows and you could see he was gritting his teeth behind that tight mouth. He kinda pushed one of the kids away from messing with his face. Said to Juneboy, "Sounds like you already made a mess of your life, young man. I admire the work you're doing in sickle cell anemia research but what we Black people need are strong, lasting Black families." The mayor went on and on, I tell you, reading the boy, so much so I felt sorry for poor Juneboy. Mayor Jones said it was a crime and a sin to leave a wife and two children. Juneboy started sweating as he tried to explain that his wife left him. The mayor paid no tention to the claim; he just went on preaching at the young man bout what was good for Negroes. (He didn't say Negroes. He said Blacks but I don't like the word Blacks, never did. You can call me old-fashioned if you want, I don't care. Back in the sixties when all the kids started using Black I tried for a while to take it up but it just didn't feel right on my tongue cause my generation, you see, always thought of Black as a bad word. You called somebody black back in the thirties and forties when I was coming up, you insulted them something terrible.)

DeSoto walked out the way he came and that seemed to break the spell for some reason. The mayor stopped talking and just stared at the doorway DeSoto left by. The minute DeSoto left he stuck his head back inside the room and said, "Come here, Momma, I want to talk with you."

We went in the dining room and DeSoto took me by the arm and pulled me into the corner by the cupboard. He started acting this way, like a movie tough guy, round the time he started on the police force. I never did like it. I said, "DeSoto, I'm your mother. Don't pull on my arm like you think I'm some gal you met somewhere on the street."

"Sorry, Momma. Didn't mean no harm." He gave me that old winning grin. "I just want to talk to you about—" he nodded his head toward the den "—that man. I don't care if he is the mayor, he got no right to lash into Juneboy like that. Juneboy is our guest. My first cousin!"

I told DeSoto to calm down.

"It ain't fair, Momma!"

"I know, I know. But you can't deny that the mayor is right about divorce. The mayor is just trying to talk straight Christian talk to Juneboy. Lord knows he probably ain't been nowhere near a church since he was little when Esther used to make him and Lauren go—"

"Momma!"

Then I heard the front doorbell and the kids running up the hallway and the door opening and Reverend Baldridge-Hawkins' big laugh. Then Jeremiah came up from the basement where he has a bar and a pool table and all those video games. Kissed me on the cheek and already he was reeking of booze. Everything seemed to be happening all at once. The front door sounded again and a whole bunch of peoples was up there coming in.

I just wanted to find a corner and hide.

3

Everybody and his uncle was there that night. Back in the den with the mayor was his wife and that old civil rights lady Margy Jeanne Wright, who always be on television news talking bout what's wrong with our city. I like Michelle, the one who wants to be a actress, better—and Michelle is prettier. Ain't got them big buck teeths like her sister and brother, Margy and Ellsworth. Ellsworth was standing in the dining room talking with Councilwoman Sandra Valerie Wright. No doubt planning some strategy, as they say. She always talking bout organizing people. Sounds like communist talk to me but peoples say she highly respected. Councilman Cherokee "Jimmy" Barnswell had with him some young floozy with one of them real short dresses hitting bout halfway cross her thighs. She kept smiling through all that makeup caked on her face. She looked like somebody dressed up for a scare party. The councilman seemed deep in one of them business discussions with my son Jeremiah. The mayor's daughters—Rosa, Ruby, and Lena—was just wandering bout the house like nervous tigers in a cage.

Renee? That Renee was fussing with the kitchen help and directing the setting of the table and keeping the kids going round from room to room carrying the salted nuts and stuff. These Wrights, you know, is Renee's side of the family. The great old man, Congressman Mitch Wright, died back in the sixties— stricken down with a heart attack while addressing a group of civil rights peoples. People still member him though and they tell me he's now in the history books and his grandchildren, Michelle's and Margy's and Ellsworth's kids, have to read on him in school right along on the same page where they read about the great Dr. Martin Luther King.

24

Well, I wandered round a bit, sneaking a glance at these folks and more, but pretty soon I got settled in my corner on the old chair by the white telephone and Jeremiah's old Siamese cat, French John, came and stationed hisself on my lap like he thought I was his natural bed. I never cared for cats but they always seem to head straight for me.

Just as I sat down, wouldn't you know it, Congressman Fred Wright came over and spoke. I was honored. He's so handsome with those pretty eyes and that light brown skin. He got nice straight teeths too. In good health for a man his age. Keeps his weight down. And don't wear his hair long like some of these fancy peoples try to do, trying to look like movie stars! They say Fred is a real close friend of Jimmy Carter. Now there's a man I like! Anyways, Fred ast me how I was doing, ast bout my arthritis. I didn't tell him how bad it was being lately cause I don't wants to bend peoples' ears with my troubles the way my sister Esther do. Child, all you want to do is get away from all that complaining! So I just told Fred that I was feeling tolerably well for a gal as old as I was and laughed and he laughed with me. Then I noticed him eyeing my wig and I got real worried. Maybe it was crooked or something and, child, I tell you I wanted to get away from him real bad and go to the bathroom to look in the mirror to make sure. When I saw his pretty wife, Lee Anne, coming I saw my chance and jumped up and met her halfway and spent bout five minutes telling her how pretty she was — and she is cute as can be with them big brown eyes and that sweet, sweet smile. I told them they was such a handsome couple together, then scused myself and put the cat down and went up the hallway to the closest bathroom. But the door was locked, so I went on round and up the winding stairway to one of the ones up there.

I locked the door. The wig was all right but it dawned on me that my girdle was too tight and that was why I was feeling so uncomfortable. I knowed I'd been gaining weight lately and it's true I hadn't been inside of this thing in months and it was killing me and I decided to take it off right there and hide it in the kid's dirty clothes hamper. I could pick it up tomorrow. Well, girl, it was so funny, trying to get outta that God-awful thing, I had to laugh at myself right there in the bathroom. I pulled and pulled and pulled. I yanked and tugged. But that thing didn't want to come off. I couldn't figure how I'd gotten into it in the first place. Well, you know, I tend to swell. Part of my arthritis problem, I guess. I swell at night a lot more than in the daytime. And I'd put that thing on when it was still daylight.

After bout — oh — heck, a half hour, I got it down past my hips and put that old thing in the hamper. But I'm embarrassed to tell you that the minute I was ready to go back to the party, or rather back to my chair downstairs, I stumbled against the face bowl and my teeth fell out. Fortunately they didn't break. You see, I hadn't been wearing them but bout a week. New ones made up for me, but I hadn't got use to them yet. I must have had my mouth open and they just plopped right outta my mouth and into the face bowl. After I saw they didn't break, I broke down laughing so hard at my foolish old self, I thought I'd die from heart failure.

★   ★   ★

I knowed what to spect: Only the most important peoples was to be seated round the main table. It was always done that way. If you ast me, it was the way I liked it. Many a years I held my plate on my lap and was not too proud to do it here. When I use to work in the homes of white folks, cooking and scrubbing and taking care of they babies, many a nights I sat in the kitchens eating with my plate on my lap. But that wont the problem. Renee and Jeremiah just plain didn't have enough chairs and the table wont nowhere near big enough for getting everybody round that table, big and long as it was. Even the Last Supper had its limited guests, you know.

Renee was running round fussing over the seating arrangements and Jeremiah was going through the house trying to round up all them who was spose to be at the main table. The noise and confusion was making me sick. You know, at my age, I just don't think a person should have to put up with so much that tears down your nerves.

I didn't even have to tell Renee I would be sitting in my favorite chair in the corner by the white phone just inside the living room off the dining room and holding my plate on my lap. She knowed from past experience what I was going to do. Besides, in that spot I could hear what all the bigshots was saying without having to talk with them. I'm not a educated woman so I don't know a lot of big, fancy words. I'd just as well sit back and listen. I understand most of what I hear them saying but that's enough for me. I'm not running city hall!

Naturally, the children got they food at a separate table in the kitchen, that is, Curtis, Jane, Jo, and the other real little ones like them. Don't ast me who they was cause I couldn't tell you all the names or who all them belong to. With so many peoples round I lose track. But Margy and Michelle was there at the big table.

While the peoples was getting settled down round the table, with the mayor at the head, I went to find DeSoto. His wife, Whitney, had come and was there in the den with him sitting on the couch already eating. I said something to Whitney bout her pretty dress but DeSoto was so busy watching television, if a bomb had dropped on that house that boy wouldn't have heard it. He can't eat without television. He'd starve to death if there was no television in this world. I looked at Whitney. She was so pretty and she looked so intelligent I just thought how proud I was to be her mother-in-law. She's a secretary for a big law firm uptown on Piedmont. I forget the name.

Frank Petit—boy they call Frankie—and Russ Glen and that radical young woman, Penny Gruerrin was all in here with them, in the den I mean. They'd decided, I guess, to eat they supper in here where the television was. I understood why DeSoto and Whitney was here—cause, like me, they ain't got big educations—but I couldn't figure why Mr. Glen and Miss Penny Gruerrin and Frankie was here like this, why they hadn't been given a place at least close to the main table. Then I figured maybe they didn't care for the mayor and the Wrights. But that didn't make sense. Nobody made them come. Well, I just pretended I wanted to see what was on that old television screen and stood there like some dummy for a minute or two looking at it like I was interested, then I went on back to my chair.

I sat there looking at Renee's seating arrangement. Lord, you wouldn't believe it but everybody was sitting just where I predicted in my mind they'd be. I know that girl's mind: ain't lived with it all these years for nothing. As I said, the mayor was at the head. She'd put herself at the other end. On the right side, down there to the right of the mayor, was Mrs. Jones, just as pretty and sedate as she could be. (Sedate is a word Renee loves to use. I'm sure she don't even know what it means.) Coming up this way toward me, next to her was Fred's wife, then Fred hisself, and to Fred's left was Reverend Hawkins, and squeezed in between Margy and the reverend was a empty chair and Cherokee Jimmy's floozy. Now, over to the left of Mayor Jones was Juneboy (Dr. Adam North, said Renee, when she introduced him to the dinner guests round the table!). Next to Juneboy was my son Jeremiah. (And believe me, child, I was sure hoping Jeremiah would keep Juneboy under control so he wouldn't embarrass us — our side of the family.) Sandra (I wouldn't call her that to her face, her being the widow of the great Mitch Wright) was next, between Jeremiah and Lena, Mitch's sister. Webb, her husband hadn't come. He wont in politics anyway and I hear tell he's a alcoholic and they children run in the street with drug addicts. Finally, squeezed in at the corner was poor Michelle. Onliest folk here with any elbow room was the mayor and Renee herself. Looking at them squeezed round that table I sho nuff was glad to have my big chair all by myself and like I said I never minded eating with my plate on my lap.

Jeremiah ast everybody to bow they heads and he spoke in that deep preacher voice he gets when he in the pulpit. I call it his sermon voice. He said, "Gracious Lord, Almighty God, Generous One, Holy Father, please hear our thankfulness, as we thank you, in this hour of plenty, listen to our gratitude, accept our sincerity when we say we give praise to you for the food which we are about to eat, we give praise from deep within our souls, knowing full well that people are starving in Africa, the land of our forefathers, people are starving in Asia, people are starving in South America, people are starving in the streets of America, and in Europe too. So, Dear Lord, we express our gratitude to You for the warmth of this fine company and for the nourishment of our bodies that this food will bring about. Amen."

We all followed Jeremiah in saying amen. The amen was okay but not strong like the feeling you get in church from the amen corner, but, then, these folks was politicians, not all of them real strong churchgoing folks.

Then I reckon I noticed for the first time that Cherokee Jimmy wont at the table. I knowed he and Jeremiah was the best of friends, but I also membered that Renee wouldn't have given that man the time of day or a drink of water if he was dying in the desert. So what had she done with Cherokee Jimmy? I didn't dare try to guess. He sho wont in the den with DeSoto and them. Could he have left even before dinner? My guess, at the time — before I knowed what happened to him — was that he was in the bathroom and he'd be coming in any minute. I knowed he wont welcome to sit by the mayor — he wont important enough — so the only other place would have been in the empty chair by his floozy. I tell you true, I got a little scared about his being away, being that it was the night of the full moon. You know what I mean, child.

Well, them catering peoples started bringing the food out long bout now, right after Jeremiah's blessings and thanksgivings, and everybody started talking all at once and real loud. They quieted down only when the mayor was talking or when Sandra was talking. You see, they respect her cause of her dead husband being so famous and all. They got kinda quiet when Fred had something to say, too. But the rest of them just babbled on and on like they didn't want to hear nothing nobody else was saying.

The catering folks stopped by me on the way to the table and served my plate like I was somebody too. You wouldn't believe the food, you just wouldn't believe it. For starters — that's Renee's word — they brought out a platter of some sort of Japanese kabobs with water chestnuts. Strong ginger taste. Then another strutter brought out a equally large platter of shrimp balls. Renee explained they was Cantonese. And, honey, piping hot. Burned your mouth! Then another one of them big platters came out full of deep-fried pastries. Middle Eastern, Renee said. Samosas or samoka, I forget which. All this stuff was too rich for my poor old stomach so I only took a pinch of each one cause the taste was good. Just between you and me, you know I can't be eating nothing that's going to pull my teeth outta my head. You laugh, but I'm serious. Can you imagine the embarrassment! Me with my teeth stuck in a deep fried piece of pastry?

The catering folks brought the second course out. Steam was pouring up from all these platters. If my life depended on it, child, I couldn't tell you what all that Renee had ordered as I looked on all that stuff moving round the table. Some of it looked too strange to me, so I said to the catering people, "No thank you."

The second course was a bunch of big bowls of salads and soups — some kinda Mediterranean fish soup, a French onion soup, and one little bowl of something I never seed before. Renee called it "bulgur and parsley" salad. I looked it up later in the cookbook DeSoto gave me for Christmas.

But I was watching more than I was eating. And listening too. Somebody said something bout my one-time friend, Dale, properly now known as State Senator Dale Bean Cooper, Jr. This is when Renee coughed, that kinda cough she coughs when she's bout to say something she thinks is important. But all she said at this point was that later on she had a nouncement to make and it concerned everybody at the table and also concerned Senator Cooper. Well, everybody got down into they soup bowls with silence and you wouldn't believe how the mood of the dinner party changed so suddenly. It was like everybody felt right off like they had been tricked or something. But they had no way out. They had to wait and see. I knowed what was going to happen cause I know Renee, but I wont bout to open my mouth.

But old prettyboy Congressman Fred Wright changed the subject and in his prettyboy way, he said, "Now, listen, you all, this is supposed to be a friendly dinner — as far as I understand.

And I would just as soon cut the political talk right here and now. This is supposed to be fun time . . ."

"I never said that," said Renee.

"Never mind," said the congressman. "It's bad for the digestion to talk politics at dinner."

Meanwhile, as they say, the show went on: platters of roast beef and Yorkshire pudding, onion stuffed ham heavy on the pepper, veal cooked in lemon sauce, and a huge — I mean, huge — roast goose stuffed with fruit, was brought out. And then! Lo and behold, they brought out some sort of ham dish cooked in mustard sauce, and then a spinach cheese pie. Child, I have no idea how folks — rich or poor — have any room for all that rich food. All I could think of was what my Momma used to say, "Think of all the poor peoples starving in China." Or, as Jeremiah says in his sermons, "Poor folks — by the millions — are starving in Africa!"

Now Congressman Fred Wright had his own story to tell. He always do when there be folks round him. He can't help hisself. But as he went on and on about something I didn't listen too close cause my food was getting cold. Anyways, I learned a long time ago that these Negroes who run this government — just like any other government — ain't putting the butter on my bread. Now, Jeremiah might tell you a different story. But there is times when I'm not so sure bout him either.

Anyways, I guess you know that there is this family connection between the Wrights and the Joneses. You see, Mitch Wright's oldest sister — I guess I never knowed her name — was married to the brother of the mayor's father. All of them folks is dead now.

The next thing I know the mayor had turned hisself to Juneboy and ast him bout his father. You could see this embarrassed poor Juneboy, Scoop being a no-count person. The mayor wanted to know what kinda business Juneboy's father was in during his life.

Poor Juneboy was at a loss for words. It was my Jeremiah who spoke up and told everybody bout old Scoop. I heard things that night bout Scoop from my own boy I never knowed nothing bout before. Now, course it all makes sense. Bibb died when the boys was so young it was only natural for them to look to other mens for examples of what to be like. I never did prove of Scoop, you know. But he was round, and what could I do? Bibb had died and we was still in grief and, although my baby sister had done gone North, we still thought of Scoop as family, even if he was just married-into family.

Jeremiah said, "He had a great capacity for enjoyment. I remember him with respect and admiration. He was a kind of father to me after my father died."

I looked at Juneboy's face. It was straining, child. It was like maybe Jeremiah had done got something good outta Scoop that poor Juneboy never had a chance to catch on to. I don't know. It was just a guess. Lord knows, I don't know nothing for sure.

Then, child, Juneboy blurted out, "So you are the guy who stole my father!" And I wont bout to laugh till everybody else laughed. But Jeremiah looked at his first cousin and waited for him to go on. I could tell Jeremiah wont in no manner of way bothered by the joke. It came clear, by the way Juneboy was eating his food, that he wont gon say no more.

Jeremiah knowed the cat had Juneboy's tongue now, so he went on and told the mayor and us, "Scoop taught me about money and about people. I used to go around with him when he collected numbers. (I know you don't know about this, Momma.) People looked up to him like he was a god. It might have been seeing the way he was looked up to that later gave me the idea of going into the service of God. I know that sounds really strange, not having a man of the church as a mentor. But Jesus himself, I understood, even then, would not have excluded Scoop. Jesus was an outlaw."

★   ★   ★

We was all pretty far long with eating when outta nowheres came the missing member of the party, Cherokee Jimmy.

Jeremiah jumped up, making a big fuss bout Cherokee disappearing like that and just at dinner time, but he was joking, teasing him bout being out back of the toolshed, and everybody laughed and somebody said it was all right for the councilman to go out back like that just as long as he was by hisself and everybody laughed again. Then Renee pointed to the empty chair for Cherokee Jimmy Barnswell and stuck him between his floozy and Reverend Hawkins. I thought in due time old Cherokee Jimmy might tell where he had been all that time but he never said a word bout it.

I looked down the table at Juneboy. Nobody but Jeremiah was talking to him. I knowed that boy shouldn't a been invited to sit at the table. These folks was just too high class for him. He was a ragweed among lady's slippers.

Renee ast Cherokee Jimmy if he knowed anything bout something she called a Tomato Conspiracy. She said she and a friend had some information bout crooked wholesalers. Cherokee Jimmy got real mad and told her it was just a rumor. Jeremiah spoke up too, saying it was gossip and nonsense. He said there wont nothing to it. Then Renee herself got all red and mad. You could see it.

"However," said Jeremiah, "Renee must find some wrongdoing somewhere out there in that big evil world."

Mayor Jones laughed. "But it's the function of the police, not that of citizens."

Everybody laughed too, but real nervous-like.

When the catering folks finished clearing way the dishes and bringing out the dessert—caramel bananas in rum, ice cream with butterscotch topping, apple pie, pecan pie, and a big old raspberry pudding—Renee stood up and ast everybody to give her they attention. She was bout to make her nouncement.

4

"You all know we, as family and friends, don't get together nearly as often as we should. Oh, we have our Christmas parties and our New Year's parties, and we celebrate when somebody is elected or reelected to office, state or national, and we see each other sometimes in church on Sunday mornings, but as a family and as people who are supposed to care about each other, we just don't seem to have enough time to show enough caring. Well, that's one reason I asked you all here to dinner tonight. I have another reason too . . ."

As Renee talked I was looking at the back of her head, sort of. She was facing them down the length of the table. I could see most of they faces. They all looked real nervous and all of them—cept Juneboy, who didn't know any better—kept they eyes on they dessert.

Renee kept right on talking, even with nobody looking her honestly in the eye. She said, "Some of you may have already guessed my other reason. It's not surprising and I am sure you won't be surprised, given the history of my family. I'm a Hicks now but I was born a Wright, and politics is in my blood just like it was in the blood of the great Congressman Mitchell Wright. He was my uncle, as you all know. He and my father loved each other as much as any two brothers ever could. Daddy wasn't as great and as famous as Uncle Mitch but he was a good man and lived an honest life and always treated his family well. He worked hard and we never went without the things we wanted. My daddy bought me a brand new car for getting straight A's my senior year in high school. He was good to us all like that. And he came from the same flesh and blood as Uncle Mitch. In his way, my daddy, Bob, as you all call him, was as political as Mitch.

In fact, Momma told me many times that Uncle Mitch used to come to Daddy for advice. Uncle Mitch would fly in from Washington and Daddy would pick him up at Hartsfield or wherever he was coming in at. Sometimes Uncle Mitch flew into Morris. That was when he was on an army carrier. Daddy would drive any distance to pick up his brother. Stone Mountain — wherever! Momma told me . . . "

As Renee talked her silly heart out, I noticed folks come just a twitching, maybe cause Renee was speaking bout her mother, poor Betsy. Everybody knowed Betsy was in the crazy house and wont likely to ever get out she was so out of her mind. Seems to me they put Betsy away going on something like twenty years ago. She down in Milledgeville.

"Momma told me everything." She said these words like they was spose to have a lot of meaning. I hadn't thought bout Betsy much in all these years. I member her all dressed up one time back when she was just beginning to go out with Bob. I myself musta been bout twenty-two cause Bibb and me couldn't have been married at that time more than a year or two. Mitch wont even running for Congress yet. He was big in local politics though. I forget exactly what kinda title he had in them days. But he was fresh outta college and the mayor — white back then — was always turning to him for advice when it came to the colored folks and what they wanted and didn't want. I guess that's how Mitch got to thinking he knowed what was best for all colored folks. For some reason when I think of Betsy I see her in that bright pink dress she had when she and Bob was together in that awful place we saw them once. Place called Tiny's Little Red Rooster in Marietta on a dirt road out where some colored shacks stood by a cornfield. Bibb and me went there not knowing what to spect. There was this old sinner man singing nasty songs bout what he was gon do to some gal when he catch her. He said stuff that no child of God could stand to hear: real ugly filth — stuff bout how big his thang is and what he plan to do with it. All kinda filth came outta his mouth. He talked about going up side the woman's head if she spent his money. He sang

another song bout how some gal broke his heart but that old
nigger never had no heart to break if you ast me.

Guess I got carried away. The point was Betsy in her pink
dress. I'm glad I member her that way, in that cheerful dress.

Renee said, "Momma told me everything I needed to know
about Daddy." Somebody cleared his throat. Renee took a sip of
water from her glass. Then she said, "My other reason for asking
you here is to ask for your support. You see, loved ones and
friends, I aim to challenge Senator Dale Bean Cooper, Jr., for his
seat in the Georgia state senate."

There was a lot of restless foot scraping under the table and
some rusty throat clearing and somebody knocked over a glass of
lemonade.

The mayor raised his fist and aimed it at her. He shouted,
"Now, listen here, young lady! A woman with three little children hasn't got any business leaving them and going off into a
man's world dabbling in politics! You hear me? Look at me when
I talk to you, so I know you're listening! Where'd you get such a
foolish thought from anyway?"

"I've been planning it for—"

"And what about Jeremiah? Who's going to take care of
Jeremiah?" asked Lena Alexia Wright-Webb.

Jeremiah wouldn't let Renee answer. He said to Lena, "If my
wife wants to run for the senate I'll give her my full support. If
she wins and has to spend a lot of time away from home, with the
Lord's help, I'll wash the dishes and mind the children, do the
laundry, and if I need more help I'll pray for it, and, with some
luck, I might get it. Now, that's how I feel about the whole
matter."

"Still," said Fred, "it's not so simple. We have commitments to
keep. One of them is to Cooper, who's been loyal to the Democratic Party and the state during the entire period of his public
life. Besides, most of the people you see sitting around this table,
Renee, have already promised Cooper their support next
November. Now how can you expect us to back away from that
promise?"

"Plus you have no experience at all in politics." This was Councilwoman Sandra Wright. She kinda held her nose real high like she smelled something rotten as she spoke.

"That's not true. You people forget I campaigned a lot for George and you, too, Sandra. I worked for the governor, too. Most important of all, I served one year on the city council — and I did well."

I could tell the child was bout to cry. I hoped she wouldn't. I didn't want to see her with her silly self in public office but somehow I didn't want her to lose face before these bigshots either. Anyhow, she got that thin high whine in her voice and I just prayed for her from that moment on.

Fred wiped his mouth and looked down the table at Renee. He'd turned kinda purple in the face. He said, "Renee, tell me, what is meant when somebody speaks of senatorial courtesy?"

"What?"

"Senatorial courtesy."

"Listen, Fred. I'm not a schoolchild and I resent your treating me like one. I'm an adult and I demand you treat me like one. I'm a woman and a mother and a wife. I deserve more respect than I'm getting here tonight."

The mayor said, "Fred didn't mean any harm, Renee. We're all thinking in your best interest."

Sandra said, "If you're serious about running for the senate you could wait a year or two, support Cooper till he runs for another office. I've heard he has his eye on Congress. Meanwhile, you'll gather more experience and be all the better prepared to challenge the person you'll be up against two or three years down the road. Besides, if you ran against Cooper now you would lose — and miserably. That wouldn't help your chances in the future."

Reverend Hawkins spoke, "My guess is Dale would be delighted to have Renee here running against him."

Just about everybody, I guess, laughed. I did, too. Like I say, me and Dale knowed each other for many years and use to be pretty good friends back in the days fore Bibb died and fore Dale became a bigshot.

Renee got real mad. "I resent the smug, condescending atti-
tude you people are showing me. I certainly expected more—"

"Now, now," said the mayor.

Margy said, "I'd vote for you, Renee."

"Me too," said Michelle.

"Thank you, Margy. Thank you, Michelle." Renee looked
kinda proud and angry too but like she was saying sour grapes
when she looked round at the others. "I expect we of the
younger generation will have to just take power since our elders
don't intend to support us."

"Now, just wait a minute," said Congressman Fred Wright,
turning red beneath his freckles. "You can get all the support you
deserve right here in this room, but you've got to be reasonable
first. Sure, we'll support you in every way that makes sense but
you've got to realize, Renee, that public life isn't something you
decide to do overnight like, say, going away for a weekend."

"A person's got to start somewhere." Renee seemed now to be
talking to someone outside the dining room. She sorta looked
toward the hall to the den. Faintly, from in there you could hear
the television. Sounded like one of them variety shows where
you have a lot of people talking real loud and not saying anything
too important—just a lot of stuff to make folks laugh.

Then, just when I thought Renee was going to sit down and
finish her dessert, she turned, came toward me, and then went on
by me out to the kitchen. We all sort of started picking at our
dessert, that is, them among us that hadn't finished eating.

I could hear Renee out there shouting at the hired help. You
could hear pots and pans and dishes crashing like somebody was
trying to fight they way through a whole room full of them
things.

5

Saturday morning I got up the usual time, early with the sunrise. Juneboy started moving round bout eight. While he was in the bathroom I went in my bedroom to get me some clothes for the day. (I was sleeping on the couch in the back — I guess you'd call it a back parlor — which is the room I do most of my living in anyways.) I turned on the set to watch "Good Morning Atlanta." I always start the day off watching the news and I like the peoples on that show.

Juneboy and I had some Cream of Wheat. I offered to cook him some eggs and bacon but Cream of Wheat was all he wanted and that was fine with me since that's what I eat most mornings. Sometimes I have myself a sweet roll but Dr. Limerick, he always after me bout the sugar. I got a sweet tooth like my Momma had. It's in the blood.

I ast Juneboy what he thought of the party. He laughed and said it was fun and the food was good. He said he thought Renee would make a good politician. I didn't say nothing to this. I finished my Cream of Wheat first while he was still talking bout Renee's little speech. He thought it was some good talking. I still didn't say nothing.

Me and Juneboy had a busy day cut out for us already. I wanted to take him by to see his cousin Donna Mae. You member her? My oldest brother Ballard's oldest daughter. After Corky died, Ballard moved in with Donna Mae and her no-count husband and they children. The children all growed up now. But I knowed Ballard would be at his shop (he runs a dry cleaner's over near Kathy's house, in Southeast Atlanta). We'd stop there on the way so Juneboy and Ballard could see each other. Last time Juneboy saw Ballard musta been when Juneboy was eighteen that time he came down to Atlanta for something or other, I can't remember. It musta also been the last time Juneboy saw his daddy alive. Bringing Juneboy and Ballard together was worrying my mind while Juneboy and me ate our Cream of Wheat. I couldn't member that they liked each other. Ballard is this big old tall hateful quiet man, who ain't never had much use for peoples in the first place. Juneboy, you know, is kinda shy, kinda sensitive. Being so different from each other didn't seem to promise much. Then all these years in between . . .

At one o'clock my sister Kathy and her husband, Donald, were coming to my place to see Juneboy, and later that night, DeSoto and Whitney wanted Juneboy over to they place for dinner. DeSoto was to pick him up and bring him back.

We finished breakfast and got started. My old green Chevrolet took ten minutes to warm up even on a warm morning like that one was. But it gives me less trouble than Jeremiah's Cadillacs and all them other fancy cars.

We had to get all this done today cause tomorrow I was to take Juneboy to Lexington to see his father's grave for the first time. I knowed Juneboy was trying to overcome his resentment of the South and to find a way to come back to us, his family. Well, he had his body back where he started but who knows where his head was. He wanted to see Scoop's grave and I was gon take him to it. It was the least I could do for Esther's boy. Lexington is bout two and a half hours away by car.

There wont no parking space in front of Ballard's Spic and Span cleaning establishment so I had to park on a side street. Me and Juneboy walked back to the little shopping center where the shop was. Some Negro in a truck had his radio up real loud right in front of the shop. The usual bunch of no-good Negro mens was gathered in the lot talking Saturday morning talk. Seem like all my life I've seen them and yet, for the life of me, I can't figure out what's so important to talk about like this, in parking lots and in barbershops and on street corners. Oh, well. Bibb never was one to hang out on corners. I was lucky.

Ballard was in the back. His clerk, Mary Ann, opened the gate and we went on back. She knowed who Juneboy was so she came

on back with us for the reunion. She had this old silly grin on
her face that looked like it was a mask made outta wood. I had
told Ballard I was bringing Juneboy to say hello, that we couldn't
stay long (knowing he wouldn't a wanted that anyway). Lord, I
felt so scared. It surprised me: how scared I felt. I had no idea
what would happen. Rumor was Ballard never liked Scoop's kids
cause Scoop—so Ballard thought—was sweet on Corky. But I
know Scoop wont—that was just a lie. You try telling Ballard
that! Yet it wouldn't a been right for Juneboy to come here and
not see his uncle.

We reached the back and there was my brother Ballard at his
little desk doing paperwork. Too cheap to hire somebody to do
his paperwork. His little glasses was down on his nose, bout
halfway, the way he always wears them when he's working like
this. Ballard had his cataracts removed last year. Mine was taken
out three years ago. I knowed he was seeing a lot better these
days. But when I told him this was Juneboy he took off his
glasses and frowned at Juneboy. You have to know my brother to
understand. He frowns at everything. Ballard came into this
world frowning at everything in it. The harder he frowned the
more interested he was in what he was frowning at. He kept on
looking at Juneboy. For that time while they was just looking at
each other, I thought I was going to get sick. Then everything
changed. Juneboy rushed over to his uncle and hugged him right
tight. Ballard kinda bristled. I don't think no other human being
had touched him since Corky died. Everybody been scared of
touching Ballard. I never liked it. But Juneboy didn't know no
better. He just didn't know that peoples don't touch Ballard. Yet
it worked out all right. I watched from a distance. I member my
hands got all sweaty and my throat got dry. All I could think
about was how much everybody had suffered, how much my
brothers, my sisters, my momma, my poppa, Juneboy and Lauren, me and Bibb, my sons, everybody, all the others, had
suffered, and was scared, like Ballard. I knowed Ballard was
scared. He been scared since he was a little boy, my big brother,
but he's brave, too. And he carries on.

Well, I was happy the meeting went well and I got Juneboy outta there fast as I could fore something went wrong.

When we got to Donna Mae's, Buckle let us in. He was drunk as usual. A little man, I can't see for the life of me where he puts all that liquor. In the thirty or so years since I've knowed him — all the time he's been married to Donna Mae — I never once saw him sober. They tell me nowadays he takes his bottle to church with him. It's the only way Donna Mae can get him to go. Five feet away from him, you can smell the liquor. His eyes was red and almost closed when he tried to smile at me and Juneboy. First thing he said to Juneboy was: "You don't know me, do you? You don't member me, do you?" Well, you see, Juneboy was just a little thang when Jim Buckle married Donna Mae. Wont no reason why he should have membered Donna Mae's husband.

But I could tell Juneboy suddenly membered old Buckle the minute Buckle said that remembering stuff to him. You could see he membered him some kinda way. He hugged old Buckle.

Just at that minute, Donna Mae came out from the bedroom into the living room where we was standing there at the door. She was all smiles and went straight to Juneboy and gave him a big hug. He hugged her back. Now, when Juneboy and Lauren was little, it was Donna Mae, herself then a teenage girl, who used to babysit them for Esther — specially after poor Esther had to go to work cause old no-count Scoop was off somewhere in trouble with the law or some other kinda nonsense.

You could tell Buckle been watching television cause it was on loud and clear there in the room. Some kinda sports game or something like that. Now, a man with politeness and good manners would have turned that thing off but he didn't. Donna Mae ast us to sit and stay a while.

Buckle sat in his favorite armchair, facing the set, with his whiskey glass in his hand. He did try to make conversation with Juneboy, who was on the couch, but he couldn't keep his eyes off the sports game. After bout five minutes, Donna Mae got up and turned the set off and he sort of frowned but she gave him her warning look. Buckle now was asting Juneboy bout his research. I guess somebody told him Juneboy was some kinda research

person working at a university up North. Juneboy told him bout
the work he was doing on sickle cell but I bet you anything you
want to bet that Buckle didn't understand a word the boy was
saying. Now Donna Mae works in the office of a factory where
they make dresses and shirts so she's used to being round peoples
and she knows how to type and file, so she was interested in
Juneboy's work. But Buckle, uneducated and drunk all the time,
had no way to understand. Too many years out there sweeping
the floor at Hartsfield International.

I stole a look at poor Juneboy. He looked like he was real
frustrated with Buckle not understanding. Then I saw him give
in and like Buckle anyway. His face changed and he smiled at
Buckle who wont a bit interested in Juneboy's work.

Outside on the street a kid yelled at another kid.

Then Buckle said he wanted to show us his new car. Me and
Juneboy followed him and Donna Mae downstairs to the rec
room where Buckle got his own private television he watches
dirty movies on after Donna Mae go to sleep at night. She told
me all about it. It's a nice room all right and Buckle got a
frigerator down there too in a side room. It's where he keeps his
liquor. Poor man. He led the way through the rec room over to
the door to the garage. In the garage there was this shiny big new
white foreign car just as bright as a Easter egg. I don't know what
kind it was but it sho looked like it cost a pretty penny. Buckle
was like a fool as he opened the door and stroked the velvet seat
covers and stroked the woodwork of the dashboard. You could
tell he was waiting for Juneboy to be impressed and to say
something. He kept looking at Juneboy like he was specting him
to speak any minute. Juneboy finally said, "It's a very nice car,
Buckle."

Well, it was too chilly in there for me. I was feeling my
arthritis. So I told Donna Mae and Buckle I was going back
upstairs where it was warm. Donna Mae laughed at me.

Then Buckle said he had something to show Juneboy. I
knowed what he meant.

Donna Mae and me went back upstairs. We talked about her
work at the factory and bout how expensive car insurance was

and about my arthritis and her recent operation for gallstones.
She told me Billy, her oldest son, had finally found a job driving
a truck, but Doug was still out of work. She ast bout Kathy and
Don, and I told her they was going to stop by at one today to say
hello to Juneboy. I told her that DeSoto was going to pick up
Juneboy round six and take him out to they place. Juneboy was
having supper with them so I wont going to cook nothing
tonight. Whitney was planning to cook roast beef and make
macaroni. She would send me some by DeSoto when he
brought Juneboy back.

Then Buckle and Juneboy came up and I could tell that
Juneboy had not drunk any of Buckle's liquor by the way Buckle
looked so disappointed. I was happy bout Juneboy turning
Buckle down. It was another good sign.

Donna Mae said she would try to get Doug on the phone so
he could come over to meet Juneboy. She knowed that Billy was
at work today so there wont no point in calling him. When she
finished talking with Doug, she hung up and started telling me
bout her factory problems again. Her boss had a lawsuit gainst
him, some big case she wont spose to talk about but she figured
we wouldn't tell nobody so she told us anyway. She said she felt
real mixed up and sorry to be on the wrong side.

Then Doug came in and looked all sheepish when he saw
Juneboy, who stood up and met him and shook his hand. Doug
looked at his own hand like something had happened to it. That
mighta been the first time anybody ever shook that boy's hand
like he deserved respect. Doug still had a big head full of woolly
hair. Nobody can get that boy to cut all that mess off his head. He
look just like a big old dog. And he twenty-five years old!
Anybody twenty-five years old ought to by then have some sense
and know how to look decent. His pants was wet on the front like
he done peed on hisself. When Donna Mae ast him bout it, he
said he was washing his car when she called. His father told him
to sit down.

He was kinda shy bout it but he sat on the couch by Juneboy
and ast Juneboy where he lived up North and what kinda job he
had. Juneboy told him bout the sickle cell work but I didn't

listen cause I'd heard it all before. I told Donna Mae bout poor Renee last night and Donna Mae shook her head.

Doug ast his father what was the score and Donna Mae didn't let Buckle answer. She said, "Y'all can find out tonight on the news. That set ain't going on long as we got company."

Buckle said, "Now, Donny, you don't know. Juneboy hisself might like football. He might want to know the score too!"

"You want to know the score, Juneboy?"

"I don't mind, but I'm not dying to know it."

"In that case," said Donna Mae, "the set stays off."

After bout a hour of sitting there with them I stood up and said we had to go cause it was going to be such a busy day for Juneboy. Kathy was coming at one.

Donna Mae said, "It's only eleven. Y'all don't have to run so soon."

I told her we did.

Then they all walked us out onto the sunny front porch. Juneboy kissed Donna Mae's cheek and shook hands with Buckle and Doug.

I turned the car round in the middle of the street and saw them up there on the porch waving at us as I drove us on down the quiet street.

Kathy and Donald got to my place at ten after one. Juneboy was out back watching some old movie with lots of dancing in it. Fred Astaire, I think. They was just coming from church. I swear, they go to church more than Carter got liver pills. She was dressed in a black dress like somebody just died and Donald was in his eternal blue suit and red necktie. Kathy and me never had a lot in common. I go to church on Sunday but it would kill me to go every day and night like she do. She don't always make Donald go with her but most times she do, when he ain't too tired. He work real hard. He ain't got the strength he used to have when he was young so he come home pretty tired out these days. He's been at the Parks Department for thirty years. He cuts tree limbs and takes care of lawns and works with a crew that do a lot of heavy work like making walkways and building fences. Stuff like that.

Well, I took them back to see Juneboy. He had changed into
blue jeans, which made him look a lot younger than he was.
Juneboy got up and kissed his aunt on the cheek and shook his
uncle's hand. Then he went over and turned off the set.

I felt a little nervous cause I didn't know what to spect. But
Juneboy acted like he was glad to see them. I made some tea and
brought the pot out to the table. We was all sitting round the
table. It's my real dining room, since I don't ever use the big one
in the middle of the house less I have a lot of peoples, very special
folk, over for some real big affair and that ain't happened since
Jeremiah got his doctorate in religion.

Donald was telling Juneboy bout when he — Juneboy — was
real little, a time Juneboy couldn't member. It was when Esther
and Scoop first got a telephone. Lauren, being quicker than
Juneboy at learning how to answer it and talk into it, was always
running to answer the phone when it ringed. One time Donald
and Kathy was at Esther's and the phone ringed. Lauren, with her
little chubby self, ran and picked up the receiver. Juneboy, sitting
in his little chair, looked seriously up at Donald and said, "I bet
you wish you could do that, don't you?" and, course, everybody — Scoop, Esther, Kathy and Don — laughed so hard nobody
ever forgot. The thing became a family joke bout Juneboy.

While they was talking I went in the kitchen and took one of
my arthritis pills. My hands was hurting something awful.

Well, they ast Juneboy bout his job and his marriage. I guess
Kathy just plumb forgot that Juneboy was divorced. Then she
looked embarrassed but not for long. She smiled that big child-
ish smile of hers then ast him if he had a girlfriend and what was
her name and if he was serious bout her. He said he had a
girlfriend and her name was Kirsten Steinkoenig. Well, we all
knowed that wont no name of some colored girl. You see, Esther
had already told me Juneboy was involved with this white girl he
worked with at Yale University and that he was lonely down in
Washington without her and that they both was flying or driving
back and forth from Connecticut to Washington, D.C., just so
they could be together. But you see Kathy didn't know none of
this or she had forgot I told her. She looked real surprised when

she heard that name and said, "Now, Juneboy, that must be a white girl. Is she white?"

Juneboy said, "Couldn't be whiter, Aunt Kathy."

"Go on with yourself," Kathy said, grinning. "Is she nice?"

"Very nice, Aunt Kathy."

And so the talk went on like this for bout a hour or so. Then Juneboy and me walked them to the door and said good-bye. They wont likely to see him again fore he was to leave for Washington, D.C., on Wednesday morning.

DeSoto came for Juneboy at six and brought him back at fifteen minutes after ten. I was lying on the couch watching a Saturday night comedy. I forget which one.

Juneboy sat at the table after he made hisself a cup of tea and told me bout the evening with Whitney and DeSoto. He talked for quite a while but I was only half listening, with the television on and all. I was tired.

I reminded him that we had to get up early in the morning.

That night I dreamed I was a little girl again and in church and all the folks was a shouting and whooping, asting the Lord for forgiveness and suddenly the church (this was in Macon) filled with a bright light, a light so bright it could not have come from nowhere but the bosom of God, straight out of His chest, but you couldn't see Him. Somebody shouted that the light was blinding them and called for mercy. My heart beat so fast I thought I was going to have a heart attack.

I turned over and was in another dream but I'm shamed to tell you this one. Oh, I trust you, I'll tell you anyway. Juneboy was in this one, but he looked like Jeremiah. He and Renee was wrestling on a bed together and pretty soon they started doing you-know-what. I don't know why I had such a dream. I ain't dreamed about that sort of thing in years, not since Bibb died. Even after Bibb's death I never thought of another man. There was only that one time bout five years after Bibb was gone to rest eternally that I had anything to do with another man. I never wanted the boys to have to put up with any other man coming round. So this dream really surprised me — and scared me a little bit too. I woke and had trouble getting back to sleep.

I still couldn't get poor Renee outta my mind, the way she ast all them bigshots to support her stand for office and the hurt she got for herself when she did this thing. You had to admire the child for her courage, standing up like that and saying what she said. I laid there in the soft darkness, just thinking bout her. In many ways she was a lot like her momma, poor Betsy.

I went back through my memory of the time I went down with Renee to Milledgeville to see her momma. She had never gone down there by herself. I knowed she went with her daddy, Bob, before she married my son. She got Jeremiah to go with her many a times. I went down with her that one time cause Jeremiah was too busy. My, that musta been three, four years back.

Renee did the driving. I hates to drive. I don't do it if I can help it. So we was in Renee's car. I just looked at the landscape. It was in the fall. The leaves was all yellow and gold and rust-colored and the sky was a bright, bright blue. It was a pretty drive, seeing the horses and cows grazing in pastures alongside the road. On the way, I was scared, maybe as scared as Renee. I hadn't seed Betsy since they put her way. I didn't know what I was gon say to her, what she might say to me. Was she gon be a total fool? Maybe she would just say nothing, maybe just look at us, or me, or stare at the floor or some wall.

We got to the gate. It was like a prison, down there. The sun was burning high, burning everything. It was a day you don't want to remember, a day of no hope. I figure there be peoples like Renee, who might want to drag up such deep memories, but for us, for real forward-going folks, we would say no.

A guard came out and met us in the sunny parking area. It was a dry and ugly place. I member it well. No sign of life. Then another guard came and opened the big doors. You never heard such a clanging and banging in all your life! Then we was led inside.

Inside there we was. It was a waiting room. And we waited, and we waited, and we waited. You know the story. We waited a long time.

Then — God forgive me — they brought Betsy out. First of all, I did not want to see her and second of all, once I saw her, I knowed for sho, I had no use for seeing her now or in the future! All I could think was, "Poor Betsy!"

Then the minute they left her with us she started talking talk that made sense, and, child, I tell you, there just wont no avenue, no road, no highway, no getout, no way.

The first thing Betsy said to us — and keep this to yourself — was this: "I have to pretend that I am crazy in order to stay here. I am not crazy," she said.

Betsy wont all that crazy. Renee said she was gon get her momma put into a private crazy house pretty soon. Poor Betsy. I member her telling me bout how smart Renee was when she was a little girl. Think of that. Ain't that wonderful?

Betsy started crying while she was talking to us. I don't know exactly what set her off. Maybe it was just seeing her daughter. I gave Betsy my handkerchief and she blew her nose in it and I told her to keep it.

I couldn't understand why Betsy wanted to stay in the crazy house. Her guard, a colored lady bout my own age, told Renee, "Young lady, get your momma outta this place. Ain't nothing wrong with her. She wasting her life here. They work her to death and they beat her half the time. If she any crazy, this place done it to her. But believe me, she ain't no crazier than your average peoples walking around outside."

Renee just nodded her head and I could tell Renee didn't believe the guard and she didn't believe Betsy neither. Renee stubborn like that. Bullheaded child.

Renee ast Betsy bout the food they gave her and Betsy said it was all right, that she didn't have much taste for food nohow.

The guard woman said the food was something terrible. Not fit for a dog to eat.

Renee ast Betsy if they gave her clean clothes.

Betsy didn't answer.

The guard lady said the patients got clean underwear once a week. On Monday. They also got clean dresses on Monday.

I wondered why Betsy was in a state institution and not in a private one where they say peoples gets treated better. I don't member Bob Wright being that cheap!

Well, we stayed there with Betsy bout a half hour fore another guard lady, this one white, came and told us the visiting time was up. During the whole time mostly what Betsy said over and over was: "I have to pretend that I am crazy in order to stay here. I am not crazy."

Poor thing! Now, this is just between you and me. If Renee gets elected she gon get her momma outta that place and into a private one where they take care of peoples the right way.

6

Cause I'd promised Juneboy to take him out to see the grave of his father, the next day, Sunday, we was up bright and early for the long drive up north to Lexington, which is where his father was killed in a gunfight with a white man at a gambling table in the back room of a gas station. They buried Scoop in Lexington cause it was cheaper than bringing him back here to Atlanta where he was born. His momma, Miss East Coast Clardia, was old by then and had no money anyway, and all of Scoop's three sisters—Zora of Magazine Point, Alabama, Honey Dripper, and that Cherokee one, the youngest, Selu—wont nowhere near Atlanta by then. Folk said Zora was out in California, Honey was up North maybe in Philly, New York, or Chicago.

So Jeremiah knowed I wont going to be in church for his sermon this morning. Even with the weather being warm and all, I still had to let my old hundred-year-old green Chevrolet warm up. I got up way fore Juneboy and made some coffee and, from my back window, watched the sun come up. I do this most mornings these days. Sometimes I never even go to bed, I just fall asleep on the couch in the back room, watching television, and stay that way to bout five, when I wakes up and make coffee and wait for the sun.

When I had the coffee cup to warm my hands (which is good for my arthritis) I stood at the window, waiting for the first light. I couldn't keep from thinking bout Friday night and poor Renee and that whole affair but I didn't want to think about it too hard. I try to stay outta other peoples' business. When I heard Juneboy stirring, I put my cup down and went to the bathroom and put in my teeth. I washed my face and combed my hair and took my arthritis pill. Then I went back to the kitchen and poured a cup

51

for Juneboy. I left it there on the counter so he could get it when he came out. I figure most peoples like me. They don't want nobody rushing in on them fore they got they eyes wide opened.

I turned on the television, forgetting for a minute that it was Sunday morning and there was no news but just church with all the preachers talking on every channel. I turned it off. Jeremiah had a series of sermons they televised from his church bout three years ago. I watched a few of them but I don't think television is any proper way to respect or praise the Lord. It's got too much sin behind it to have a clean face.

I cooked Juneboy some eggs and bacon and made some toast and sat with him at the table while he ate. I myself just ate a sweet roll. I was kinda shy bout asting him bout his personal life so when he started asting me questions, I was happy cause that at least broke the silence with him just making chewing noise. He said, "Aunt Annie Eliza, you must be very proud of Jeremiah . . ." and here he stopped a minute, then said, "and, uh, DeSoto . . ."

I told him they complishments had made me a very happy mother. I told Juneboy I was mighty proud of DeSoto. You know DeSoto is smart. And gots lots of interests. He studied law enforcement. Course, Jeremiah got his doctorate in religion. Everybody knows bout this.

I told Juneboy bout the time I took a course called "Better Health" at Beulah Heights. Learned all bout how I was spose to be taking estrogen and progesterone cause of menopause; learned more than I wanted to know bout my own body! He wanted to know if the kids round here in the East Point area get encouragement to go on to college after high school. He hadn't seen much of it up North.

"Shoot, what you talking bout?" I said. "Boy, all these kids round here got strong examples everywhere they turn. We got a Negro mayor, we got Fred in Congress, and on the state level we got lots of Negroes." I told him bout all the kids I knowed in the neighborhood, kids who'd growed up round here, running errands for me, delivering papers. A lot of them was doing well at Morehouse or Spelman or Emory. One boy who delivered my newspaper for five years is now a doctor with his degree from Emory and he got a practice up on Peachtree Street and most of his patients are rich white folks.

Well, I could have talked bout the neighborhood all morning but we had to get started, so when he finished I cleared away the dishes and got my cloth coat and my knit cap and he helped me get into the coat just like a perfect gentleman. You never would a believed his daddy died the way he did: The boy had such good manners.

It was a real pretty drive that time of year, going out of the city, and, once we got out past Scottdale on seventy-eight, which is the best way to get to Athens and Lexington, I rolled down the window and the air was fresh and the morning smelled so good. It'd been months at least, since I'd been out this way. I couldn't member the last time I'd taken my old Chevrolet out on the highway like this. It felt good, even though I never was one much for driving. I smelled parched peanuts in the air. The sun was coming up real strong and melting the dew on the trees and shrubbery alongside the road. We was still driving through rich neighborhoods though, big old weeping willows and cucumber trees and umbrella trees and magnolias in front yards. These was the rich folks who lived outside Atlanta. The mayor knowed a lot of these peoples; they'd helped to put him in office.

By the time we'd been on the highway bout a half hour I come just a smelling a whole world of fresh blooming dogwood. I got a holly and a big old sweet bay in my backyard but I hadn't smelled dogwood like that since I was a little girl on our farm in Monroe, where all of us childrens was born. I was going to drive through Monroe after Loganville. I was trying to member the last time I'd been there. It sho was since the funeral of my youngest brother, Rutherford.

Well, the Chevrolet was holding up all right as we drove on through Loganville. Just on the other side of Loganville I drove into one of them rest stations and turned the engine off. Near where we stopped was one of them picnic tables. On it, eating crumbs was two yellow-chested warblers. I hadn't seen warblers like them in a long time. In my backyard I sometimes see myrtle warblers and them cerulean ones and all kinds of sparrows and once in a while I see a blackbird of some kind but can you imagine how excited I was to see them yellow-chested warblers! They mighta been what they call a magnolia warbler. I've forgot so much that I use to know. Anyways, I held Juneboy back, said, "Hush. Don't move. Look at them." I gave him a look. He was smiling. I think that must a been the first time I seen him smile that good since he was a little thing on a tricycle and I was babysitting for my baby sister just after she and Scoop broke up. We watched the yellow-chested warblers strut and peck till they flew away. They flew away together. Well, almost. One sort of looked up at us standing there and jerked his head round a few times, getting his eyes on us the right way. Then he made the decision. He took off and in no time to speak of the other one, probably the female, took off after him.

I went on up the path to the ladies' room. You member how not so many years ago going to the ladies' room for us colored folk wont so easy as all this. Most often when we was traveling on the road like this, we had to use the bushes. Inside the toilet, there was two other women. One on the stool (judging from the smell), the other one doing up her face. She was white and bout my own age. I saw her look at me through the mirror when I came in. Her smile was kinda plastic—you know, stiff. I smiled back at the lady and she said something bout how nice the weather was and I agreed with her.

I did my business and left. Lexington is bout eighty miles from Atlanta. We'd come only bout nine so far. I didn't know if I wanted to stop in Monroe or not. The family home was still there but Rutherford's illegitimate daughter, Sue Mae, owned it now, now that Momma, Poppa, and Rutherford hisself was all dead. Seeing it, I was sure, would bring back some good memories but maybe too many bad ones. Sue Mae had fought us in court after Rutherford's death and won. Just as I was thinking bout Rutherford, Juneboy said, "Aunt Annie Eliza, let's stop in Monroe. I haven't seen Grandma's and Grandpa's house since I was about six or seven years old."

I thought about him when he was that little. I could see Esther carrying him round by the hand. He was little for his age. Well, I could stand seeing the house, even if it hurt. I couldn't very well tell my nephew no, could I? But I was hoping he wouldn't want to see his Uncle Rutherford's grave, too! You member Rutherford, my youngest brother? Lived with Momma all his life cept for the brief time he was with hussies like Sue Mae's mother. She lives in Athens now.

We younger ones called Rutherford "Ruth" cause we couldn't say Rutherford. When he growed up his friends called him "Ford." Okay. We'd stop at Monroe, drive by the house. I told Juneboy I didn't want to see Sue Mae, so we wouldn't be able to go inside. He understood.

We drove by Walker Park and came into Monroe in no time. You have to drive on through town to the other side and a ways out fore you come to our old place. The main drag through Monroe hadn't changed a bit since I was little, leastways I couldn't see no changes: drugstore, clothing store, the cafe, the usual places, and the courthouse. I drove slowly through town. Didn't see nobody I recognized walking along the sidewalk. Course, most of the peoples I member from growing up days is all dead now.

We came to the dirt road where the house stood under a old, old sweet bay tree. The pepperwoods and the one sausage tree was all still there in the front yard. The grass hadn't been cut in some time. There was a black Buick in the driveway. Musta been Sue Mae's. Juneboy ast me to stop but I didn't want to stop right in front of the house so I drove on up a ways and parked. He got out and walked back down the road. There was no way Sue Mae would recognize him. She had never seen him and probably wouldn't have knowed who he was if he had a told her his name. He would have had to tell her his momma's name fore she might have placed him in her mind. Juneboy musta been every bit of five when Sue Mae was born. I watched Juneboy through the rearview mirror. He was walking like he wont too sure bout what he was doing. All dressed up in that silky blue suit and with that red necktie, he sho didn't look like nobody from round these parts. Just as he reached the yard, Sue Mae's teenage gal, Bitty, came out on the front porch. I could hear the screen door slam. She stood there looking at Juneboy.

Juneboy took a tiny camera outta his pocket and snapped a picture of the house. I guess he just wanted it. It sho didn't look like much as houses go but it looked a lot better than it did when I was little. Ruth had fixed it up a lot after Poppa died.

Juneboy came back and, wouldn't you know, ast me to show him Grandpoppa's (my poppa's) and Uncle Ruth's graves. My heart just sunk down to my stomach. I swear, child, I didn't want to get all them feelings moving inside me again. Ruth hadn't been dead more than a year. Juneboy was informed like everybody else but he didn't come down for the funeral. Too busy I guess. But then everybody in the family knowed he hated the South and everything in it and for years swore he would never set foot inside it again. Esther said he believed the South killed his father. If you ast me, that man kilt hisself with his wicked way of life. But you know you can't go telling the son of such a man a thing like that. I membered what he told me bout him wanting to get in touch with his roots, on Thursday right after he got in. And I guess wanting to see Ruth's and Poppa's graves was part of this need Juneboy had inside hisself.

I drove him out to the old colored cemetery where both Ruth and Poppa was. The minute we got out I wished I had brought some flowers for my brother's and daddy's graves. I used to drive down here right after Poppa died and place flowers on his grave. Roses usually. I did that a lot for bout three years. Then I started coming down bout once a year. Sometimes Kathy came with me. Once when Esther was down from Chicago, us three sisters went together with flowers. Course we was all at Ruth's funeral. I'm shamed to tell you, but I never went back to Prudence's grave after the funeral. She'd been like a mother to me and it was too painful. She's buried right here in Atlanta. Momma right here too, beside Prudence: "Here lies Eva Mae Sommer, wife of Olaudah Equiano Sommer, mother of Ballard Sommer, Ruther-ford Sommer, Mrs. Katherine Sommer-Benge, Mrs. Annie Eliza Sommer-Hicks, Mrs. Prudence Sommer-Platt, Mrs. Esther

Sommer-North, May Her Soul Rest in the Bosom of God." I
like to think of Momma and Prudence like they was when they
was alive, so I don't go out to the graves.

The reason Momma and Poppa ain't buried in the same
cemetery is a long story. Us children fought over Momma's site.
Those of us who wanted her in Atlanta, for the convenience,
won. Now that she is here I don't think any of us go out there
cept Kathy and maybe Esther when she come down here. Ballard
is too stubborn to go anywheres but to work and back home. I'll
tell you bout that man someday.

You know they say Rutherford killed hisself. Sue Mae found
his body. He was slumped over in his old car. Had been shot
through the head. The gun wont none anybody had seen before.
That's why we don't believe he did it hisself. It was on the seat
beside his body. This happened six months after Momma died.
It's true he was depressed after she died but he wouldn't a taken
his own life. I just don't believe it.

I led Juneboy through the little cemetery till we came to
Poppa's and Ruth's graves: side by side, father and son. (Ballard
says he wants to be buried beside his wife, Corky. She died some
ten years back, maybe twelve.) Rutherford's headstone was so
new it looked outta place in this part of the cemetery where
nobody new had been put down lately cept him. The cemetery
was surrounded by little chinquopins. At the back side there was
a couple of old toothache trees. While Juneboy took pictures of
the graves, I watched a woodpecker back on one of the tooth-
aches knocking a hole in the body, kinda low where it was thick.
I'd never seen a pecker do that to such a small tree. I burst out
laughing at how silly he looked pecking at that little old tree.
Juneboy thought I was laughing at him and he ast me what was
the matter but when I told him he just looked annoyed with me
like he thought I was the one who was silly. A mighty nice wind
was coming up and some of the morning haze was going fast.
Looked like we was going to have ourselves a tolerable day.

We drove on. You have to swing a little northward going
toward Athens. Me, Kathy, and Esther went to high school there
but only for a couple of years. Back then we thought of Athens as

the big city. Compared to Atlanta, a country circuit rider wouldn't even stop there. But it's still pretty big times compared to Monroe, doodly-squat Monroe. I drove right on through Athens and picked up seventy-eight again. Gas was getting low so I figured I'd stop in Crawford at the old filling station there this side of town. After gas (which Juneboy insisted on paying for) we had only three miles to go before getting into Lexington.

You sorta come down into Lexington on a curving road and you start seeing the stores along this main street and the court-house is on your right and then there's the bus station, and so on. I hadn't been here since, gosh, I was maybe sixteen. Had no reason to. Didn't know a soul here. I still membered where the colored cemetery was though. Momma musta brought us here for somebody's funeral but I can't member whose. I never came down here with Esther. Esther and Scoop divorced twenty-eight years before his death and she had remarried and probably completely forgotten Scoop as anybody whose grave was worth visiting. Yet he was Juneboy's and Lauren's father.

It took only a minute or two to get through the city itself and we was going on up out of town on the highway. I knowed exactly where I was spose to stop but a lot of new houses was all along the road and everything looked different. But I figured I'd recognize the place on the road. It was just after a hill, just a little ways down. I don't know how to tell you the rest of this. I stopped at the right spot, more or less. I membered a colored family's house right there on the left side of the road. That's how I knowed the spot. Across the street from this old unpainted house, with a crape myrtle in the front yard that had a tire tied to it with a rope, was spose to be the weed path that led up longside a cornfield to the little cemetery where I'm sure Scoop was buried. He was shot the year a president was shot and they put a new president in office. That's how I member.

I still can't find the words to tell you what we saw and how I felt and how Juneboy musta felt. There was no path longside a cornfield. There was no cornfield. Right where the path and the cornfield was years before was a big housing project. You know the kind. You see them all over Atlanta.

I started crying, child. I surprised myself crying like that. I looked at Juneboy and told him the truth. He took it pretty well. He didn't cry. Maybe he cried later but he didn't shed a tear when I pointed to where the weed path once was.

Juneboy said, "Aunt Annie Eliza, let's drive up in there and you show me where you think the cemetery was."

I drove up there and parked in one of the parking spots reserved for the tenants. A whole lot of Negro childrens was running round playing in the parking lot and I saw a few women looking out the windows at us. Me and Juneboy got out and I tried to figure out where I was in relation to the highway down there. I membered exactly where the weed path had been, so we went over there first. I looked down to the highway to try to judge my distance.

Juneboy said, "Is this where the footpath was?"

I told him it was, indeed. But what I couldn't figure for sho was how long it took to walk from the road up to the cemetery without doing it again.

Juneboy said, "So let's go down and walk back up."

We did and stopped when I felt like we had walked the right distance. "This is it, this area right here, all around here." We was standing in a parking lot, not the one we parked the car in but one a bit south of it, around one of the buildings, on the back side. The ground was all concrete now and twenty-one years ago it had been the colored cemetery and Juneboy's father was down there now, with a lot of other colored folks, under concrete. It was the saddest thing. Nobody could come here to lay flowers on any graves and lucky for us, I guess, we hadn't brought any. I watched Juneboy looking round at the ground with such a, such a . . . I can't describe his expression. It reminded me of that face of the Indian on a pony you see on television, looking for the ancestral burial grounds and all he can see is these hamburger stands and gas stations.

"I'm sorry, Juneboy."

He touched my shoulder and said, "No need to be. Thank you anyway for bringing me."

I felt awful, just awful.

"In a way," Juneboy said, "it's a fitting burial for Scoop. It's like he has lent his flesh and spirit to the continuation of the culture. The little kids playing in those parking lots are the ongoing spirits of all those silent souls down beneath the concrete. Scoop's spirit reaches up through the hard surface and spreads like the branches of a summer tree."

* * *

We got back before midafternoon. First thing, Renee called. Said she needed my advice. I told her to come on over. Like I said, I had my differences with Renee but she was my daughter-in-law just the same. She felt she could get true advice from me where she couldn't get it from nobody else. Besides, the only other woman she could turn to was in the crazy house.

I made some coffee and Renee and me took our cups and went out into the backyard and sat on the bench. It sho was hot for a spring afternoon! The temperature musta rose at least ten degrees since that morning when Juneboy and me was driving down to Lexington. I thought Renee was gon complain again bout Jeremiah and his church ladies but she come just a talking bout something else.

". . . and a friend of mine — I can't tell you his name yet — has asked me to help him investigate a big wholesalers scheme that apparently has local government consent, at least the consent of some members of state government."

"What you talking bout, Renee?"

"It has something to do with greenhouse vegetables and fruit. That's all I know, so that's all I can tell you. He wants me to join him in exposing the corruption."

"Renee, you trying to get yourself kilt?"

"Of course not, Momma. My friend says joining him can help my campaign. I came here to ask you your opinion, but I'm hearing it even before I've asked. It's true, I am scared of the whole thing. It sounds dangerous. People who meddle in these sorts of things often end up face down in the river. We both know that. You think I should stay away from it?"

"My advice is yes: stay away from it, child, unless you ready to die. You hear me?"

"I hear you, Momma. But I'm not so sure I want to stay away or can afford to. If I have principles — "

"What good your principles if you dead?"

She just looked at me like I had disappointed her and I guess I had. I hadn't told her what she wanted to hear.

I membered Renee's father, Bob, was just like that. Bob would come to you and say, "Annie Eliza what should I do about such and such?" and you give him your opinion and he gives you back this old stubborn face and then he'd go off and do what he was planning to do in the first place, which didn't have anything to do with the advice you just gave him.

He got it into his mind once he wanted to preach, said the Lord had called him, and the man went round for months telling everybody he was gon build his church on a solid rock, a unshakable rock, and it would be a beacon for the pure in heart and all the children of God. Betsy couldn't do nothing with him during that time. The man was plumb crazy. Didn't have a pot to pee in and him talking bout building a church on a solid rock. Besides there wont no solid rock closer than Stone Mountain and I knowed durn well that white folks wont gon let Bob build his church up there. But he did get something together.

He got hisself one of these storefronts, you know. Place had been a grocery store so it still had mice and roaches. Well, he worked and he worked at it, got the place cleaned up and moved benches in and painted and polished it and found a old piano and built hisself a pulpit and put up pictures of Jesus and Mary and Joseph and angels. He did all this getting ready while he was still holding down his regular job too! He sho prettied up the place. Everybody was surprised. Even Betsy kinda gave in, thought maybe Bob had got the calling. He placed ads in the Saturday papers and he opened his doors. Well, the ad ran and nobody came. He ran the ad the next Saturday and still nobody came. This went on, and course he was paying rent on this storefront and, fore long, with the church still empty, he went out and tried to round up peoples on the streets, in cafes, in beauty shops. He

would go into a beauty shop where there was a bunch of womens
with they heads up under the dryers and where some of them
was getting they hair straightened and he would preach a little
sermon, just to give them a sample of his style, and then pass out
this piece of paper with the name of his church and the address
on it, and there was also some little message from the Bible right
there on the page. (I knowed the printer who printed it for him.
His name was Joe Brown. He used to print advertisements for
Ballard. He printed the wedding nouncements for everybody
and he printed nouncements for folks when they had a baby in
the family.) Bob went to shops and into the parks too and talked,
specially evenings and Saturdays. Betsy was bout to lose her poor
mind she was so worried bout him. His big brother, Mitch, was
embarrassed. You see Mitch loved Bob very much and always
tried to help him. There wont nothing Mitch wouldn't do for
Bob, his baby brother. From the beginning, Mitch protected
him, even in schoolyard fights, and always helped him land jobs
when he needed jobs. Well, even with all of Bob's effort, nobody
came to his poor little storefront church. It just sat there empty as
the look in a work-mule's eyes. And fore long, naturally, he had
to close it up and give up his dream of being a preacher. This
happened bout a year fore Renee was born.

But Bob had gone round asting everybody he knowed what
should he do, should he preach or what, and peoples told him
no, no, no, but he always went and done exactly the opposite of
what everybody told him. The man was stubborn as a jackass.
Right after he failed as a preacher he got this notion into his head
that he wanted to serve humanity in another way. He would be a
musician and make peoples happy with his music. He bought
hisself a saxophone. And, child, his playing was so hard on the
ears everybody in they neighborhood started complaining, but
Bob kept right on trying to play the saxophone. He went out and
got hisself some lessons but he didn't stay with them very long
cause he disagreed with the teacher. The teacher believed in
playing one way and Bob thought his own way was better so he
stopped taking the lessons and went right on trying to teach
hisself to play his own way but better. This went on for a number

of years, this business with the saxophone. Mitch tried to get Bob weekend jobs playing with bands round town and even in other states but nobody was interested in Bob's music after they listened to him for the first five minutes. Meanwhile, Mitch had his political life to think about and his family, so he sorta gave up on Bob's efforts in music. At this point poor Bob came close to killing hisself.

Well, seeing Renee's stubbornness, I guess, got me thinking back on Bob. He might have made it had he had even a little sense of humor bout hisself. That's the trouble with Renee too. She can't laugh at herself and just let life be.

7

That Sunday night after Juneboy and me had supper we got dressed up and I drove us to First Christ Church round eight. Jeremiah had already told me he was gon talk bout "Women's Rights and the Word of God." I was lucky to get a parking space right in front of my son's church.

Right inside the outside doorway was a big picture high on the wall over the doors to the inside. I hadn't seen it before. It was new. It was a picture of Christ with lots of little children gathered round Him. Christ was sitting on a rock and holding out a apple to one of the children. In a basket at His feet was a big bunch of grapes and on the ground there was lots of other fruit. But this apple Christ was holding looked more like a tomato than a apple. Under the painting was a sign that said: Eat Lots of Fruit and Vegetables for a Healthy Body and Holy Mind.

All the deacons and the sisters was gathered together up front on opposite sides of the pulpit. Jeremiah hadn't come out yet. That boy, he's a mess. He just likes to wait till the last minute, then makes his grand entrance like he thinks he's a movie star or a king. When me and Juneboy got seated, up front, row three, near the middle, I looked round on the sly to see who all was there. I saw my sister Kathy but Donald wont with her. There was Donna Mae and Buckle. You could count on him having his bottle with him. He looked like he had already finished most of it. Over yonder to the left was Cherokee Jimmy, Russ Glen next to him. Two or three rows behind them was that radical woman Penny Gruerrin with some man I never seed before. DeSoto and Whitney was only a seat in front of us. Whitney was wearing that same dress she wore Friday night. I know that girl can afford to buy another dress. Now, you tell me what's wrong with her? Also

on the left, but closer to the front was Councilwoman Sandra
Wright. Fred was no doubt already back in Washington. I was
surprised to see Ellsworth sitting next to his momma, Sandra.
Next to him was Michelle but I didn't see Margy. I wondered if
she was sick. Lena was there, not far from them. But Webb wont
next to her. Probably down there at the jailhouse bailing out one
of his drug addict children. You see stories bout them children
getting busted—that's the word the young folks use—in the
newspapers all the time. I looked for the mayor but he sho wont
there.

I was so busy looking round looking for faces of peoples I
knowed I didn't even see my handsome son when he came out in
his velvet preacher robe. I heard him clear his throat at the
microphone before I saw him. He introduced the new choir
leader, Brother Ben Smith, a short fat man with a bald head but a
big sweet smile. My son sat down in his velvet chair while
Brother Smith told us to take out our songbooks from the backs
of the seats in front of us and told us which page the first song
was on. I took a songbook for myself and gave Juneboy one.
Brother Smith said he wanted us to praise the Lord tonight along
the lines of Reverend Hicks' sermon. He told us to turn to,
"Sister Mary Wore Three Links of Chain."

The choir was upstairs in the choir loft back of us. Brother
Smith lifted his arms and gave them the cue. A burst of young
voices sweeter than you can imagine, like sounds pouring down
out of heaven:

> Sister Mary wore three links of chain,
> Sister Mary wore three links of chain,
> Sister Mary wore three links of chain,
> Glory, glory to Her name.
> She cleanses me of all my sins!

The congregation slowly picked up and started following the
lead of the choir, specially here at the chorus:

> She cleanses me of all my sins,
> All my sins She takes away,

All my sins She takes away,
Glory, glory, to Her name,
She cleanses me, cleanses me . . .

And we singed the other four verses, the one bout going up on
the mountain top; the one bout Mary and her boy child; the one
bout being saved; and the last one, which gets real loud with the
shouting and the happiness of the soul feeling all that heavenly
glory, just singing Her name over and over. Oh, there's no feeling
like it!

Then we singed the one bout hypocrisy and Sister Hannah. I
hadn't singed that one since I was a child in Monroe. You know
it? Goes sorta like this:

Look out Sister Hannah,
Look out Sister Hannah,
Look out how you walk on the cross,
Your foot might slip
And your soul gather moss.

Hypocrite dress very fine,
Hypocrite dress very fine,
Hypocrite ain't walking God's straight line.

Then Brother Smith changed the mood by getting us to sing
one of my favorite songs, "I Got Shoes." I growed up on that
song. It makes me tremble from my toes up to the roots of my
hair. I feel good all over when I sing it and hear peoples singing
it. Member it?

You got shoes, I got shoes,
All God's children got shoes.
When I get to Heaven gon put on my shoes
Gon walk all over God's Heaven!

And the other verses, you gets a good congregation singing
them and you never heard such glory in your life! "I got a derby,
you got a derby," and, "I got a robe, you got a robe," and, "I got a

crown, you got a crown," and, "I got a harp, you got a harp." You can just hear the folks fore my time, my momma's and poppa's generation, seeing they earthly burdens lifted, flying way to heaven, wearing shoes every day just like white folks.

When Brother Smith finished, he blessed the choir and the congregation and turned and gave praise to my son, then stepped aside and Jeremiah got up and went into his pulpit. I can't tell you how much my heart swells with pride every time I see him step up there into that pulpit. Jeremiah waited till the peoples got quiet again. He's like that: very dramatical, you know. His eyes be lowered when he's being dramatical. Funny thing, peoples do get quiet when they seeing him being quiet. The hush is so loud you can hear it.

Then he spoke. "Brothers and sisters, tonight our theme is Women's Rights and the Word of God. This is a subject we need to talk about.

"When you think of the women in the Bible, of course you think of Mary, Mother of Jesus, and you think of Mary, mother of James, and Mary, mother of John, and Mary, sister of Lazarus and sister of Martha. You think of Rhoda. You think of Lydia. You think of the wife of Solomon.

"Well, my beloved brothers and sisters, I want to direct your attention to Mary of Magdala. We are looking at the Gospel of Matthew. In the Gospel of Matthew, we read in chapter twenty-seven, verse fifty-seven, that the body of Jesus is already en-tombed. Mary from Magdala and the other Mary are there, waiting in front of the tomb, waiting for the Resurrection of their Lord, the Son of God. Now, you talk about faith. Think about it. These two women, sisters, had the words echoing in their minds: 'After three days I shall rise again.' But think about this Mary from Magdala. I have seen women of faith in my time. I have lived with women of faith, women of strong, strong belief, women of courage, so much courage you would have to wear dark, dark glasses not to be blinded by that courage — so strong it is. Brothers and sisters, I am talking about women with courage, with faith, with deep, deep conviction, women who want to help us all, to save us all, to help us enact the word of God, women who see the Light. My own mother, right here among us tonight — many of you know her — is such a woman. For many years now, many of you have worked with her for the greater good of womankind. But I need not remind you; you have your own memories, your own good faith. The faith of Mary of Magdala is the kind of faith I'm talking about, the kind of faith I have seen in my years in this community.

"But tonight I wish to speak of yet another woman of faith: my own wife, also a beloved friend among many of you — Renee Wright-Hicks. Mrs. Renee Wright-Hicks! To many of you, simply Renee! And that is the way I am sure she wishes for you to know her, simply as Renee! As Mary of Magdala believed in the faith of the blood of Jesus, knowing that it was a sign, and not the end, but a positive sign, Renee has made a commitment to your own interest, to our district. Today many of you heard her announce her candidacy for a seat in the state senate, heard her on radio and on television. She proposed to unseat State Senator Dale Bean Cooper, Jr. Now, you know as well as I know, Senator Cooper is a fine man and a gentleman, one who has done the best he could do. But is his best really, in the eyes of the Lord, the best we deserve?"

Jeremiah waited a minute to listen to the congegation agree with him. That boy of mine sure is smart. If he put his mind to it, he could be the president of the United States of America!

He was going on with his sermon and I was sure proud of him, "Don't we deserve better?" He cupped his ear like he couldn't hear too well. We, the congregation, told Reverend Jeremiah we was on his side, that we thought Renee would be better for us than that old man Cooper. But *you* know what I think? I personally think Renee got bout as much sense as a piece of driftwood lying in the mud. All that gal thinks about is clothes and stuff and if she gets a pimple on her face she weeps like a stupid child for days. She so vain, Lord, you wouldn't believe nobody like that possible on this earth — not no colored person, leastways.

". . . the Pharisees, you know, blew the whistle on our Lord. They saw the faithful sisters there at the tomb and thought,

'Now, these women are women of faith, they believe that dead body is going to rise up and come out of that stone tomb in three days.' So they got themselves on over to Pilate's office as fast as they could make tracks. This is the government we're talking about. Remember the government? All of them have a lot in common! The Pharisees reminded Pilate that this guy Jesus had been—in their opinion—an impostor, just a dude going around pretending to be the true Son of God.

"So today, as in the ancient past, we have to be aware of the Pharisees running to Pilate putting the bad mouth on those among us who would follow the teachings of Jesus, those among us who would serve the people and the public interest. Make no mistake, there are Pharisees among us.

"But we do not want to spend more time than necessary being careful, watching for the Pharisees. They are not worth all of our time; we need mainly to be aware of the possible danger they represent. Then once we have them in focus we need to go ahead with the business of doing unto others as we would have them do unto us. The Golden Rule is the best rule. We need the faith of Mary of Magdala and the faith of the other Mary and the philosophy that is the Golden Rule."

"Amen," said the congregation.

"Now, the scriptures tell us that Pilate gave orders to have the grave guarded by his soldiers so that the believers in Jesus would not steal the body of the Lord from the tomb. Now why do you suppose the Pharisees would even think such thoughts about the followers of Jesus? The Pharisees were displaying their own wickedness."

"Amen," said the congregation.

"The Pharisees so mistrusted the believers that they assumed there were among them those who might try to remove the body and hide it so that the people would think that Jesus had risen—as he promised—on the third day. You see the evil in their minds? You see how they visit that cynical view of life on the followers of Jesus? It's what *they* would have done! But it was a view coming from a posture where there was no faith in anything except evil and moral corruption. Say hallelujah!"

The congregation said, "Hallelujah!"

I was so proud of my boy, watching him preach like that.

"So brothers and sisters, faith of the quality of that shown by the two Marys is the faith we want today in our political life here in Atlanta and for women both in politics and in private life. We need women in politics! We need women in the home! Women need the right to control their own bodies, to make decisions about their own futures, publicly and privately. It is a curse before God that the issue is still before us after thousands of years of female oppression."

"Amen."

"But you know Jesus rose on the third day just like he promised and it didn't matter that the soldiers of Pilate were there. That was how strong faith was!"

"Amen!"

"Now, in the scriptures we learn that, when the Sabbath had ended, Mary of Magdala and the other Mary went to the tomb to see the miracle they knew was about to happen. How could they do otherwise, given their strong faith? The minute they arrived at the entrance, the earth beneath their feet shook and, we are told, an angel, messenger of God, appeared. This angel, stronger than any mortal man or woman, rolled back the rock the soldiers had laid at the entrance to the tomb. And you know what? Something funny happened. That angel was so sure of his mission, the rightness of it, the unwavering rightness of it, that he took himself a seat right there on that stone. Probably crossed his legs, too. Just sat there sure as he could be. Mary of Magdala and the other Mary looked at this angel in amazement. They thought he looked like lightning. Now, try to imagine lightning in the form of an angel. It's not so difficult. In a way, an angel has to be lightning, unearthly, striking a connection between Heaven and Earth.

"And you know something else? Those soldiers guarding the tomb almost wet their pants. I mean they were scared enough to throw down their weapons and run till their legs turned to jelly. But they took the easy way out. They dropped right there in their tracks—passed out.

"And the angel spoke to the two women and told them they had nothing to fear from him and that their Lord had already risen. You hear me? Already risen! Hallelujah!"

"Hallelujah!"

"Risen and gone on to Heaven to the bosom of his Father. Risen and gone on to Heaven, I say, to the bosom of his Father. Ha! You're already too late. He's quicker than the eye. Ha!"

"Hallelujah!"

"The angel tells Mary of Magdala and the other Mary that they can go now into the city of Galilee. Ha! There they will see their Lord. You see, he came to the tomb understanding their faith with instructions from God.

"We need male messengers of good will such as that expressed by the angel from God to help support the faith of women, in private and in public—indeed, in political places! This is what we need most from the men who rule our society: support for women of faith, women who show faith in themselves, hope and courage. But where can it come from? It can come from the faith we are all capable of, faith in the teachings of Jesus. Do unto others as you would have others do unto you. Faith!

"Now, you remember, the two Marys hurried off toward Galilee but didn't get far before they ran into Jesus himself. He was on the path just in front of them, probably so unearthly looking He was afraid He might scare them out of their wits. After reassuring them, He urged them to go forth with their mission, to go on into Galilee and pass the news of His Resurrection on to His disciples.

"And He also told them to tell His disciples to meet Him in Galilee. Are we to live with the spirit of this, see Him meeting with the believers in a symbolic place or a real place called Galilee? I think both!"

"Yet, while the two women hurried on as instructed, there was no way they could stop the unfolding of events. And you know the results. Jews believed he had not risen, the soldiers were paid to lie, Christians believed the words of the disciples, who, on a hillside near Galilee, listened to the Lord's last words spoken in human presence. He said to them, 'I represent all power both on

Earth and in my Father's Heaven. You, my followers, must now
go into all nations and baptize all the people, spread the word in
my name, teach the peoples everywhere the Word, save them in
the name of my Father, Myself, and the Holy Ghost.' " Jeremiah
stopped here and hung his head a moment, as if in deep thought.
Then he said, "I shall be at your side, giving you support, till the
sun burns out and the world ends."

"Hallelujah! Amen!"

Jeremiah's sermon went on and on, child. You know how my
son can talk! He talked about Atlanta politics and God like they
was on speaking terms. They might be but I ain't never seen God
speaking with no politicians let lone whole cities! It just ain't the
nature of God. Not the God I think I know.

As much as I love the boy, I was tired of listening to him and all
this nonsense bout women's rights as a excuse to just get the
congregation to vote for Renee. You know, his talking bout it like
he did embarrassed me a bit. I say womens got all the rights they
deserve already. We mess up the rights we already got. And that's
the truth!

They sent the kids round to take up collection and the choir
singed some more songs and that was bout the end of the service.
My arthritis was acting up and I was ready to go home. Looking
at the pained look on Juneboy's face, my guess was he was too.

Jeremiah was at the door shaking everybody's hands as they
left. He knowed not to shake mine. I went on out but then
Juneboy, who was behind me, said to Jeremiah, "Jer, you built
your church on a solid foundation. I don't feel the floor shaking
when I walk. Somebody must be blessing you. Who knows," he
said, with that little laugh of his, "it just might be old Scoop
himself."

You shoulda seed them two boys laughing like they knowed
something nobody else on God's earth knowed bout.

As we left, I had a troubled mind. I knowed that Renee was
playing with fire now. There was no way she was going to do any
good for herself without the family support. And her own family
and the powers in Atlanta was for Senator Cooper to represent
this district.

Fore me and Juneboy turned in I ast him what was going on between him and Jeremiah and he just looked at me a long time like he didn't know what the devil I was talking bout. We was in the back at the table and the TV was low. Juneboy said, "Aunt Annie Eliza, how much do you know about Jeremiah's relation to my father?"

The minute he said this I knowed I didn't want to know no more. I membered more than I wanted to. I had put a lot of that stuff outta my mind for years. Jeremiah had had his early bad years as a teenager but he had got hisself on the right track and went on to college. I knowed about his fascination with no-count Scoop. And maybe more.

"I know some things," I said.

"You know he ran numbers for Scoop?"

I knowed it but had forgot it as best I could. I didn't say nothing.

"Did you know Jeremiah put himself through college with—"

"Oh, no! I worked my fingers to the bone to put that boy—"

"But it apparently wasn't enough, Aunt Annie Eliza." He was giving me the sweetest, sympathy-cuddled look you ever wants to see. "Numbers money got him through and, not only that, numbers money Scoop left in banks all over the South helped build Jeremiah's church."

"How you know that?"

"I did some checking, starting two years ago when I got interested in tracing my father's tracks."

"It ain't the truth, Juneboy. Somebody done lied to you."

"I wish it weren't. Ask your son."

"Did he tell you he built his church with Scoop's money?"

"He didn't deny it."

Child, it was some old ugly gossip. I tasted it at the back of my tongue. It made me wants to vomit. Why was Juneboy bringing this mess up now? Had he come here to make trouble?

Long after Juneboy had tucked in I sat numbed on the couch just looking off into space like a crazy person. I thought back over the day, the trip to Lexington, Jeremiah's sermon.

I tried to watch a late movie but I couldn't keep my mind on it. Jeremiah's sermon kept bothering me. I really disliked the way he had used it to promote his own wife. That was pretty cheap. I'm sho he didn't mean it that way but it just came out like that and looked pretty bad. But what made it worse was pretending he was talking bout women's rights. And he wont!

It got me to thinking bout what he shoulda said in his sermon. The way I see it, he shoulda give examples of strong womens the peoples could think on, shoulda talked about they deeds that made them strong, liberated womens. Marys in the Bible was fine but they wont good enough for me as strong women, except as he said, in they faith. Faith is great but peoples need more than faith to get they rights.

I thought of my own momma. Jeremiah course never knowed her well enough to use her as a example, but she was a strong lady who didn't take no stuff off nobody. Now, if that had a been me up there speaking on women's rights I woulda used Momma as a example of a woman who took her own rights and made everybody respect them. You know, when my momma—Eva Mae Obscure—was a girl, she worked in the house of a white family in Monroe and this family gave her so much respect you would have thought she was a member of the family. Why? Cause she carried herself in such a way folks had to respect her. She didn't think little of herself. She believed in herself. Now, where she got all that belief from, I can't say. She told them what to eat and even when to go to bed and when to get up and how to act. I mean, she was only a teenage girl but she was in charge of that family. You see, the woman had female trouble and was always in pain and kinda drunk and not able to take good care of herself let lone the children—there was three of them. And the husband was a farmer always gone out on business or working hard with his hired hands out in the cotton. My momma was in charge. She was the lady of the house. Momma had a lot to put up with, I tell you. She knowed that one of the house servants, a real handsome boy named Billy, was messing round with Miss Lady a lot. He was always sneaking into her room and stuff. The farmer man was away so much he never knowed a thing. This was for

Momma a burden, to have to keep this hanky-panky stuff to herself. She never liked being un-honest, you see. But she got ahold of the colored boy and told him he playing with fire, that if he valued his life he better try to find a way to break it off with Miss Lady. You see, Momma saw the boy as being without a mind of his own in this matter. He was like a tool in the hands of Miss Lady. She was always drunk and sick so she too was outta control. There was nobody to blame. He was just a boy and poor Miss Lady was so sad and helpless. But Momma was afeared the whole thing was gon turn into a nightmare. And it almost did.

Well, nothing bad happened. Nobody ever found out, cept Momma. And it was while working for this family that Momma met Poppa — the great Cherokee, Olaudah Equiano Sommer.

Well, I couldn't concentrate on the late movie and I was just a thinking bout Momma and trying to member other strong womens but I kept coming back to Momma, as she was when I knowed her, growing up under her.

When I finally did get to sleep Momma was in there with me, in my dreaming. I don't often dream bout her. Sometimes in dreams I knows she there but I can't see her. She can be back in the kitchen or out in the yard hanging up clothes or out in the tomatoes picking tomatoes, and that way she be in the dream I be dreaming but I don't see her face and her big strong black arms and her simple cotton dresses with the headrag tied round her head to keep the nappy edges back and the sweat from running down into her eyes and into the corners of her mouth. I see Poppa much more often in my dreaming. But this time, this Sunday night, or Monday morning I guess you would say, I could see her face clear as the day she laughed at me finding a Easter egg under the front porch plank when none of the other childrens had been able to find that last one.

There she was, gathering firewood in a clearing in the forest. She gathered it on the eastly side of the clearing, then took six or seven armloads of it to the westly side and put it down. Then she gathered up another five or six loads and dropped them at the northward side and then gathered up a lot more firewood and piled it to the south of the clearing. Then she started all over again, moving the piles at the east to the west and the piles at the south to the north and on and on. She kept switching the piles round until the piles got all mixed up and I don't think she could tell which piles she was moving where. But she kept doing it and watching her doing it gave me a powerful headache. I had this headache right up through the dream, just watching Momma in her agitation. I could tell she was agitated cause of the expression on her face. She had that old hard, suffering look she used to gets when she was angry and determined to do something somebody didn't wants her to do.

But she gave up on the firewood by sunrise. I woke up a little bit but went back to sleep. Momma was there again, still moving things round. At one point, she was moving the furniture round. She took all the dining room furniture in the living room. She moved the living room things in the kitchen. She took the stove and the kitchen table and the chopping block and the well buckets into the bedroom. She put the bed in the kitchen and poured water on it. I watched it run off the side and watched it just drip from the spread for a few minutes. I tried to say something to Momma bout what she was doing but she couldn't hear me. As I watched her change things from they places, I slowly came aware my headache had gone.

8

First thing Monday morning when I turned on the television there was Renee and Dale on "Good Morning Atlanta," that show with the host who got bad teeths. I forget his name. Don't worry, it'll come to me in a minute. It's one of them shows where peoples can talk up a storm for as long as they want. We got shows like that here in Atlanta. But child, let me tell you, that television did a number on Renee.

Renee looked fatter than she was. Besides, she was stuffed into a silly looking evening gown. I swear, I'll never understand that girl. Imagine going on a morning talk show wearing a dumb evening gown! She was just sitting there with them big fat thighs crossed like her self-confidence was holding the whole world together. I wont too partickler bout seeing her like that first thing in the morning.

Bill Hatton. That's his name, Bill Hatton.

My eyes was acting up that morning so the screen looked a little blurry. I thought my cataracts was coming back.

I started to wake Juneboy to tell him to come see but I didn't cause by the time he woulda got out there they probably woulda ended the interview. Maybe I couldn't see them all that good but there sho wont nothing wrong with my ears.

I had my cup of coffee in my hand and I pulled up a chair and sat right in front of the screen.

This Hatton fellow says to Renee, "Just for openers, tell me in your own words, Mrs. Hicks, why you think you might want to run for the Georgia state senate."

"Because I think our district, the district I live in, is in bad need of some honest, up front representation. We've gone without integrity far too long."

77

Cooper started to interrupt but Hatton hushed him up and let Renee finish saying what she was saying.

Renee said, "I think I can gain public support if I'm given half a chance. I might not have all the money necessary to run a smart campaign but I'm sure going to try it anyway."

"Why do you think the public wants you?"

"When they hear my aims, the public will support me."

"What are those aims? Aside from bringing integrity to the state senate. What are they?"

"Well, I'd like to try to help do something about job conditions and to do something about this messy situation of unemployment. I mean, black kids out there on the streets with nothing to do. Somebody's got to try to help them find work. Maybe more jobs can be created. That sort of thing needs to be checked out. In East Point the situation is unbelievable. You hear businessmen talking about stimulating business in the district but they don't seem to ever get around to it. Where are the positive civic leaders? Huh? And crime. We have more than our share of street crime and break-ins. People who say I don't have enough experience forget that I grew up in this city and I know what's going on here. I think I know how to help."

Dale tried to interrupt again but Renee wouldn't let him get a word in edgewise.

"Equally disastrous is pregnancy among teenage girls. I want to find more funds for sex education in the schools and encourage parents to support programs of sex education and even provide these programs with contraceptive information and devices and even pills so that we can sensibly approach the problems these kids are facing. All they want when they go out and get a baby is love, they just want something, somebody to love. We need to provide families with therapy. When a girl gets pregnant, nine times out of ten she's unhappy at home. We got to get to the root of that unhappiness and provide therapy not only for the girl but for the family of the girl before she gets pregnant, so that she won't want to get pregnant, won't need to go out and have a baby. If such families can't be helped we need to try to take these girls from these families and find happy, loving families for them.

"Also there's the problem of rape in the district. We need tougher laws to be able to put the rapist away for longer periods of time. We need better lighted streets. We need programs to help get at the cause of rape. These programs can be set up in prisons or in rehabilitation centers. We need crisis programs for rape victims. Right now there is only one voluntary group in the area presently trying to provide this service. It's not nearly enough.

"In my campaign, I would stress the need for help for alcoholics too. I see drunks on the streets in East Point and it makes me sad because this is such a great city and everybody in despair should be given a chance to get beyond that despair. The hospitals should have more funds to form programs to rehabilitate people who are victims of alcoholism. The same effort should be made to get people off other addictive drugs. In the high schools and even in the elementary schools we have kids hooked on dope, kids snorting coke and smoking joints and taking acid. This is disgraceful. Something has to be done about it and right now. With better representation in the senate, I believe many of these ills can be corrected."

"Okay," said Hatton, "thank you, Mrs. Hicks. Let us now turn to Senator Cooper for a response and for his views on the existing situation. Senator you've just heard Mrs. Hicks' accusations and her expressed goals in running for the senate. What's your response?"

"She talks horse —. In my opinion, the district I represent is in good health. We have a hospital that provides the best medical care in the whole city of Atlanta. The people who voted for me can tell you I have done a fine job in the senate. We've successfully reduced crime in the streets. There hasn't been a rape case reported in six months. Homosexuality is down. Hospital care up. Police corruption doesn't exist in my district. The last time we had a case of police corruption was before I was elected."

"The senator refers, I'm sure," said Renee, "to reported cases of rape, to reported cases of police corruption. And what's wrong with homosexuality, anyway?"

"I didn't say anything was wrong with it. I didn't interrupt you. Now, I would appreciate it if you let me talk."

"Talk!"

"I'm only trying to set the record straight. Mrs. Hicks doesn't seem to understand that the people in the district I represent voted for me—and will vote for me again in November—because they like my program. I deliver. What does she have to give them that she can prove is worth their time?"

"As I said before, integrity and all that it implies!"

"You can't be a resurrectionist without having been a witness to the first condition. You have no ground to stand on."

"I do too!"

"You do not!"

"Okay, okay, you two. Let's get serious! Mrs. Hicks. Question. Tell me, your brother-in-law is a cop: if you were state senator and if he was involved in corruption in your district, what would you do?"

"First, my brother-in-law, Officer DeSoto Hicks, doesn't work the district I would represent, but I'll answer your question anyway. It's easy. I'd turn him in. I would support an investigation into the alleged corruption. But let me say the example is not a good one. My brother-in-law would never be involved in exploiting anybody."

Dale said, "I resent the blatant innuendo by Mrs. Hicks that I am less than honest. She is a lying . . . uh . . . she's not fair, is all I have to say."

"Senator Cooper," said Renee, "kiss off!"

The screen blinked. I reckoned Renee had messed up her chances when she said them words, cause the screen blinked. I never heard "kiss off" before but by the way she spoke the words I knowed they was bad words and meant to be a insult. So stupid of her. She seemed to be making more sense than the senator all along. Then at the end she lost everything, if you ast me. How could she expect public trust using language like that?

I heard Juneboy going into the bathroom just as the host was thanking Renee and the senator for appearing on his show. I swear he was trying to keep from laughing in they faces. I was glad he didn't. His teeths so bad I wouldn't a been able to eat breakfast that morning.

Round noon Renee came busting in through the front. The girl looked like a madwoman! She was babbling something bout somebody beat her up. I sat her down and told her to talk slowly. Juneboy helped me get her calm. He brung her a glass of water and she took it and took a sip. That seemed to get her calmed down some. We was back in the back room and the television was still on since morning. I turned it off so I could hear Renee better.

"After the debate," she said, "I was on my way out of the studio and Senator Cooper was walking behind me. He stuck his leg in front of mine and tripped me." The girl started sobbing and just a wiping snot and tears away from her face.

Juneboy wanted to know if she'd been home yet, if Jeremiah knew what had happened.

She shook her head no, he didn't know yet. She had been home but nobody was there. The kids was in school. The sitter was gon pick them up there and take them to the zoo this afternoon.

What else happened at the studio? Did she hurt herself falling?

"I hurt my knee. Look at that." She pulled her evening gown up and showed us her hurt knee. She got them big pink fat knees and sho nuff the skin was rubbed off the left one.

I ast her if she was sure the senator did it on purpose.

"Momma, there's no way that man accidentally got his leg between mine and tripped me like that. I felt him stick his leg in front of mine real hard. It was as intentional as day following night."

"Well, what you gon do?"

"I'm going to sue him, that's what."

I told her a lawsuit like that would hurt her chances to get his seat but she said she thought just the opposite. Once people heard how rotten he was, tripping a lady, the voter turnout would be for her in the state primaries.

Juneboy didn't say nothing.

"Well," I said, "did he help you up?"

"Momma! Where is your mind? Are you kidding. He stepped right over me like I wasn't there. You hear me? Stepped over me!"

I started to tell her what she shoulda done while he was stepping over her but my mouth was too clean for the words.

"Wasn't anybody else around?" ast Juneboy.

She said she didn't see nobody.

"He probably wouldn't have done it if there had been a witness," Juneboy told her.

"I think you're right. Just think about it! A state senator tripping a woman."

"You wont just any woman. You gave him a hard time on that show. I watched it. Juneboy was still sleeping."

"He deserved the hard time I gave him."

"I know he did. He musta been plenty mad at you."

"Momma, I'm so angry—"

"Here," I said, "I'm gon get some alcohol and clean your knee and put a bandage on it."

I went to the bathroom and Renee followed me and in there I fixed up her knee for her and told her she would be wasting time and money trying to sue Cooper cause her knee wont hurt that much—just a scratch, so small I covered it with one regular-sized Band-aid.

She said maybe I was right.

Then she told me that this morning she found out that the reason Cherokee Jimmy was late coming to the dinner table Friday night was cause he was out at a public phone down the street calling Cooper to tell him bout her plans to nounce her candidacy that night with Mayor Jones and all the others present.

I ast her how she found this out but she said she couldn't tell me cause she had promised not to. I felt a little hurt but I tried not to show it.

I ast her how he had found out fore she made her nouncement.

"Jeremiah told him."

"Jeremiah told you that?"

"Yes he did."

I was sitting on the edge of the bathtub, looking up at her where she stood by the facebowl.

I said, "Renee, honey, I just don't honestly think it's a good idea for you to get yourself out there into public life. It's a dog-eat-dog world out there. You think you know enough politics?"

"Momma, I know as much as any of those jerks. I may be younger and less experienced but I think I'm in a better position than somebody like Dale Cooper to know what's going on in the district. Everybody's putting me down and I don't like it. But I'm not going to let it stop me. I mean, it was disgraceful the way everybody reacted at the dinner party. Cooper talks about blacks on welfare with the same negative warp you hear these white politicians going around doing — as if the majority of people on welfare weren't poor whites."

"Still, Renee — "

"Momma, I feel strongly about this thing. I am going to run for the senate. Nothing can stop me. I might lose but I'm going to try. I may not be perfect but I'm not any worse than those guys. And there is Uncle Mitch. I feel like I kind of owe it to him to make something of myself."

I didn't know what to say. I thought about Curtis, Jane and Jo. I membered what Mayor Jones told her. But then I figured she wont gon listen to me nohow.

We went back out and she ast Juneboy if he wanted to go grocery shopping with her. The gal sounded real strange, said she had some research to do. You know the first thing that crossed my mind, don't you? Yes, indeed. I've knowed that gal has had her some boyfriends on the side and I didn't put it past her to try to get her hands on Juneboy. What difference did it make to her that he was her husband's first cousin?

I told her Juneboy was maybe tired and needed to rest. But he said, "No, I'm not tired. Sure, Renee. I'd like to go. It should be an inspiration to run around with a cousin like you."

I didn't know what he meant by that and I didn't think I wanted to know.

Juneboy got hisself ready and Renee was blabbing way bout wishing there was time to take Juneboy one night to Dante's

Down the Hatch to hear the Paul Mitchell Trio and I thought, "That gal always thinking sinful things to do."

Then they was ready. I walked up to the front with them. At the door, Juneboy said to me, "It isn't every day a guy gets to go out shopping with a pretty lady who is also the upcoming state senator!"

I just gave him a look.

"You're an inspiration to me, too, Adam," Renee said. "Being a bigshot doctor. I like success. It makes me happy."

Juneboy laughed that old laugh of his.

I said, "Y'all be careful. They a lot of fools out there in them streets driving cars."

9

Right after they left I called the mayor's office to see if I could see
him. I didn't have much hope that he had time to see me. The
secretary took my name and phone number. She wanted to know
what I wanted to see him about. I told her to say I wanted to talk
with him bout my daughter-in-law Renee Hicks. She said she
would give Mayor Jones my message.

I took the dirty clothes downstairs to the basement and put
them in the washer, turned on the machine, then went back up
and set up the ironing board in front of the television set in the
back room. I got the rough dry stuff — my dresses, bathrobe, the
bedsheets, dish towels, bath towels, my underthings — and
started ironing them. "General Hospital" was on. The only time
I can stand to iron these days is while watching my soap operas.
Maybe I ironed too many years for other peoples to do it any
other way. I guess I was also just waiting to see if Mayor Jones was
going to call me back. Then fore I knowed it I wasn't even
thinking bout old George. Luke was in trouble again and this
time he knowed he was in love with Laura. Course lot of peoples
forgot that years ago he raped her. Then Dr. Hardy was trying to
comfort his wife Audrey. She was mighty upset bout something
that happened in a episode I guess I missed. And for the first
time I started figuring that Scorpio wont just a policeman, that
he was some kinda goverment agent. I like his accent. Poor
Jimmy Lee was still trying to prove to the Quartermaines he was
just as good as them though born out of wedlock, fathered by old
man Quartermaine who didn't want no part of him. Leslie and
Rick was happy for the time being. Looked like to me Grant was
going to pretty soon marry this fast woman who was just now
getting untangled with Jimmy Lee. The phone ringed. I think it

ringed two or three times before I heard it, cause Jimmy Lee was bout to kiss this gal who was thinking she was in love with Grant and now didn't much want to be kissed by Jimmy Lee. The phone was over on the table by the couch so I answered it without stopping my watching.

It was Mayor Jones' voice speaking to me. He said, "Annie Eliza, what's up?"

"Mr. Mayor —"

"Now, Annie Eliza, you know you always called me George. Why, since I become mayor, you become so formal with me?"

I can't tell you how my heart was warmed up by that expression of friendship. Tears came to my eyes and I covered the mouthpiece so he couldn't hear me sniffing like some old mushy fool. Knowing he was a busy man, whether he was Mr. Mayor or just plain George, I got to my point: "I need to talk with you bout Renee. It's about her plan to run for the senate."

"Okay, Annie Eliza. When can you get down here?"

"When you have the time, George."

"That's the spirit. How about three this afternoon?"

"All right, three o'clock."

"See you then, Annie Eliza."

★　★　★

The mayor's receptionist was named Victoria Price. She was a white gal with blond hair and lots of makeup. Some folks say she looks just like Marilyn Monroe but I swear fore God I can't see it. She did something to her switchboard and Mrs. Ruby Bates, the mayor's executive secretary, came out to greet me. I stood my ground. She was a tough looking older white woman — not as old as me, but older than Miss Price. You could tell she dyed her mousy brown hair sort of red-like to make herself look younger. She didn't smile. I knowed all these people's names cause I see they pictures in the *Constitution* and the other papers and you know the kids talk bout everybody working down there in city hall so it feels like I knows them all anyways even fore I see them.

I followed Mrs. Bates into her office and she told me to have a seat and said the mayor would be with me in a minute. She pointed to a table by the couch and said, "There're some magazines there, picture magazines, Mrs. Hicks."

So I sat myself down and took up one of them magazines, sinful as they is. On the cover was this half-naked woman looking up from the paper with this sleazy half-smile like she done got something stuck in her throat she shouldn't been eating in the first place. But this was a colored magazine trying to look like one of them white magazines. And this gal course on the cover was a colored gal but she looked light as the day is long. The caption underneath her said her name was Hollace and that in the summer when she was not in college she worked for the Civil Liberties Union and that she was very interested in civil rights. Inside the first page was a ad for a big Atlanta insurance company. The picture in the ad showed a elderly couple, bout my age, looking like they didn't have a worry in this life. The words under the picture, in big letters, said: WE CAN NOW RELAX AND ENJOY LIFE. What a laugh, I thought. The insurance Bibb left me over the years hadn't covered half the problems me and the boys had when they was growing up. We was just lucky none of us came down deathly sick and in need of a long stay in the hospital. It wont Bibb's fault though. Back in them days Negroes couldn't get good insurance even if they had the money to pay for it. Beneath the writing in the ad they had the name of the insurance agent you was spose to call to get as relaxed and happy as the man and woman in the picture. His name was Clarence Norris. They had a little inch high, inch wide picture of this Clarence fellow. He was grinning like he knowed something nobody else knowed.

I turned the pages, not looking too closely at what was on them after that ad. A big fat man relaxing in a armchair in front of a television. Then they had all the stores listed where you could buy that chair. It was made by Heywood Patterson and Company of Julesburg, Florida, the same company Bibb and I got our first bedroom set from. The chair the fat man was so happy to be sitting in didn't look like it was made as carefully as the stuff

Bibb and me got back in 1931. Month of May, I think it was. I sorta read a few paragraphs of the main story, bout young pregnant girls in Atlanta and what should be done bout them but I got tired of the subject. You see it on the television all the time. My momma woulda told them like she told us. Keep your dress down. That's all you need to do. Keep your dress down and your bloomers up. So after that I just looked at the ads. One struck me specially, this one you see for the Lenox Shopping Center. Lots of the stores out there had sales on just bout everything you can think of. One of them was selling clothes dryers for half price cause they was going outta business. And for years I needed a new one. So often I have to take the stuff outta the dryer and hang it up in the basement or, if the weather is nice, out in the backyard to dry. But I just looked cause I knowed that even at half price I couldn't afford one and I sho wont bout to ast Jeremiah for no money though he had plenty to spare. I just didn't want to get into another scrap with them. Every time Jeremiah give me something Renee get a tight lip that last for weeks, even if it's a birthday or Christmas present. But some of the ads was just nice to look at. There was this big old orange cow in one and he was called Ozie the Cow and it was a ad for children's clothes. A whole bunch of little babies and tots was sitting or standing round him all dressed up in they new Ozie the Cow outfits. Made me think of the company that was almost closed down a couple of years ago cause they was making children's pajamas that caught fire real easy.

I heard Mrs. Bates' buzzer. When I looked up from the magazine she had her phone to her face and was saying, "Yes, Mr. Mayor. Sure thing." (And I just thought, "My! How times have changed!") Then she hung up her little pretty phone and looked over at me and told me I could go on in now.

Mayor Jones, in a different suit—a brown one—from the one he wore to Renee's shindig, met me half way. He had a smile that kinda said I'm-happy-to-see-you-but-don't-take-up-too-much-of-my-time-please.

He led me to a big expensive chair that looked like it had been handed down from some royal family courtroom way back fore my great-grandmomma was born, one of them velvet red and gold ones. There was bout four or five others like it scattered round his big old expensive-looking desk. I sat down carefully. It was a good chair. I could tell. I eased my back gainst it and it helped the tiredness there. (Driving always gives me a backache. I still felt it from the drive up there.)

I thought George was going to go and sit in his big old black leather chair behind his desk but he didn't. He sat in a chair just like the one I was in, right close to me and leaned forward with his elbows on his knees. He rubbed his fat hands together. I guess I never noticed before how short his fingers was, but he had the soft hands of a preacher, not the hands of a man who done worked a long lifetime.

While he was rubbing his hands and smiling at me with his head cocked a little bit to the side, I noticed a family picture of him, Roddy, his wife, the boys, Louis and Jerome, when they was real little, and the three girls, Rosa, Ruby, and Lena, when they too was younger. It was one of them studio pictures where everybody look like they smile is frozen and made of plastic and there ain't a spot nowhere or a wrinkle in a sleeve or a button unbuttoned. They all looked perfected by something or other, I can't say what.

On the wall behind the desk was a row of pictures of faces. Some of them I knowed but most of them I didn't. I recognized the last three mayors so I figured the others was mayors I never paid no tention to or forgot or never knowed. There was also a picture of the Reverend Martin Luther King, Jr., standing in front of Ebenezer Baptist Church with a crowd of young folks. Next to it was the official picture of Mitch Wright when he was in Congress.

"Annie Eliza," Mayor Jones said, "what do you want to tell me about Renee?"

"Mr. Mayor —"

"George."

"George. George — yes. I come to ast your help." I had so much on my mind all at once I couldn't get my words out. I said,

"Did you see Renee on the 'Good Morning Atlanta' show this morning?"

"Not yet. But it was taped automatically and I'll see it later. What'd she say?"

"She came on mighty powerful bout running for the senate —"

He cut me off, "Do you want her to run or not?"

"At first I didn't but now I think I do and I've come here to ast you to support the child. She needs your dorsement. She'll do a better job than that old Cooper we got now. After hearing her talk this morning and hearing him talk back at her, I made up my mind. Renee might not be the smartest child in the world and she sho is a lot spoiled and ain't never learned how to preciate how lucky she is to be born to the family she was born to, still she is a whole lot smarter than Dale Cooper and got more credit-it-ability, like she said. So, yes sir, I come to ast you to help her . . ."

He was just a grinning at me. He wont saying anything yet and sat like that, leaning forward, not speaking, just looking at me like I was a piece of candy in a candy store window and he was a little boy without so much as a dime.

"You're right about one thing, Annie Eliza. Renee is no Shirley Chisholm! But listen to me, let me tell you a story. When I was a little boy, my momma gave me the last money we had in the house — about twenty-five cents — and told me to go to town and buy some fatback. This was long, long before the Depression. You and I both were grown by then. Well, I took off, barefoot — because I didn't own any shoes. I had two younger sisters and a younger brother. You know my brother. We were all hungry, had been eating turnip greens and mush for over a month. Momma had earned that quarter by washing clothes for white folks in the surrounding area and it took her a long time to earn it. So I held on tightly to it. We lived way in the sticks and I had about fifteen miles to walk to get to the nearest town.

"I walked and I walked. My feet burned on the hot clay road. I walked in the grass on the side to cool them but it was easier to walk fast in the road and difficult to do it in the grass. So as soon as my feet cooled a bit I got back into the road and walked on till I couldn't stand the burning. But I kept walking one way or the other.

"I passed a tree where just a week before a Negro named Andy and one called Roy had been hung by the neck till they were dead then burned right there near the tree till their bodies were nothing but ashes on the ground. Everybody knew about it and it wasn't the first time it had happened in our backwoods. I kept on walking right by that place although I looked at it as I passed and I looked back over my shoulders as I moved on up the road.

"I passed old Charlie Weems in his pasture plowing with his old broken-down mule. I wanted to stop and chat with Charlie but I kept steadfast on my mission, my sisters, my brothers, and my mother were hungry and waiting for me.

"At the edge of town a pack of white boys jumped me and took the quarter and ran off before I could get myself up from the ground. I knew it would have been foolish to give chase because I couldn't have beat them all had I caught them. Plus it would have brought the white men out of the barbershop and out of the general store and very likely I would have ended up skinned alive like little Olin, a second cousin of mine. They said he whistled at some broken-down old white woman right out front of Old Man Johnson's plantation.

"When I finished crying till I couldn't cry anymore, I got up from the rock I was sitting on and went on to the grocery store where I was supposed to buy the fatback with Momma's quarter. I told Mr. DeKalb, the butcher, what had happened and asked him if there wasn't some work I could do to earn a quarter so I could buy the fatback I came to buy. He thought about it a long time and said no. He couldn't think of anything for me to do. But he said I might go on up the road to the blacksmith shop and see if Victor had a quarter's worth of work for a strong boy to do. He also told me it might take a few days to earn that much doing work for Victor. I went up there and Mr. Victor had no work for me but he sent me to Mr. Belvedere, the lawyer. Mr. Belvedere said I could sweep his driveway for a penny. So I did. Then he sent me on to Mr. McPhearson, the gas station attendant. I raked leaves for him for two hours. He gave me three cents. Mr.

McPhearson sent me to see Old Lady Johnson. I cleaned out her basement and she gave me a nickel. By this time it was nearly dark. I asked Eugene Williams, a Negro who worked for a white family named Darrow, to stop off at my momma's place on his way home in his wagon, and tell her I'd be a day or two late getting back with the fatback. I told him about the boys taking my quarter and asked him to pass the story on to my family so they would understand. He said he would and meanwhile I found a patch of tall grass just outside of town and there I spent the night looking up at the stars most of the night. I slept a bit but by daybreak I was up and wandering through town looking for work.

"Well, to make a long story short, I did odd jobs all day that day and all day the next day before I had earned enough to buy the fatback my momma sent me for.

"When I got back everybody was happy to see me and Momma put on a big pot and we cooked some turnips and greens with the fatback. Now, Annie Eliza, the funny thing about that experience was this: I didn't even know I was being courageous but I was.

"When Renee understands that little boy that I was, when she has some sense of how he and his family survived, send her to me and I will not only recommend her for the state senate, I'll actively campaign to send her to the White House!"

He stood up to show me my time was up.

Landsakes! I didn't know what to think!

He walked me to the door, being just as friendly as you please. I musta been in a state of shock or something cause I couldn't even say good-bye but I was leaving sure as chitlins smell bad.

10

You know I had a good mind to walk down cause I half the time don't trust elevators. I should have walked down. I left Mayor Jones' office feeling real strange. Like I lost something but couldn't figure what it was. I stood there waiting for the elevator, feeling like I was gon cry.

When the elevator door opened, guess who was standing there looking me dead in the eye? Three mens. And I knowed them right away. The tallest one was old Cherokee Jimmy. In the middle was Ellsworth Wright. Just behind Ellsworth was, you guessed it, Dale Cooper. Had I paid tention to my first mind I never would have run into these mens. Feeling awful like I was feeling made it worse than you can imagine, girl.

"Well, well, imagine seeing you here, Annie Eliza," said Dale.

I greeted him like a polite person spose to do. But just as I was bout to give him a piece of my mind, the elevator door started closing. That old playboy Ellsworth grabbed it and pushed it back. I got on. I thought they was getting off but I guess the door closed again fore they could get off. Cherokee Jimmy pressed the "open" button but nothing happened. The door stayed shut and the elevator started moving up.

"These things happen in this modern technological world, Annie Eliza," said Cherokee Jimmy. "What brings you uptown?"

"I had to see the mayor on business."

"On business?" Cherokee Jimmy said, ribbing Dale. At the same time Cherokee Jimmy pressed the button for the floor the mayor's office was on but the elevator kept right on going up like it was the express to heaven.

"What kind of business?" ast Senator Cooper.

"My business, Senator." There was snap in my voice. I didn't give a hoot if he was a bigshot, he had no right treating me like I was some child.

"Annie Eliza," said Cherokee Jimmy, "I always did admire your spunk and your sharp tongue."

I looked at his big head and his pig eyes and that big wrinkled forehead and those bloated whiskey cheeks and that nose spread out all across his face and them big rubber lips and that fine suit he was wearing with the silk necktie and I thought, I just thought, "What a ugly, ugly big old chunk of nigger. Musta been born a water-head baby. And when he talks at you he kinda leans over toward you so you can smell his bad breath." Lord, child, I knowed right then and there why I had never felt comfortable in the same room with this man Cherokee Jimmy.

"I sho wish I could return the compliment, Mr. Barnswell."

"Where you get this Mr. Barnswell business from? You always have called me Cherokee. Everybody—"

Ellsworth laughed but I hadn't heard anything funny. I looked at the boy. "What's so funny, Ellsworth?"

"Nothing, Annie Eliza. I was just thinking—"

"With what?" I ast him. He was like somebody who had never been a friend.

Dale said, "You better tell that daughter-in-law of yours she had better not cross my path again or—" He stopped.

"Go on, say it, Dale." I dared him. Years ago Dale and me was pretty good friends but, child, today you wouldn't a knowed it on sight.

"Hey, Dale," said Cherokee Jimmy, "that's no way to talk to Annie Eliza. She's one of our respected matriarchs!" By the way he was smirking I could tell he wont saying anything he wanted the senator to take seriously.

Ellsworth said, "What's this all about?"

The elevator stopped. We all stopped talking. Cherokee Jimmy pressed the fifth floor where the mayor's office was. The elevator didn't move and the door didn't open. I got scared. This had happened to me once before when I was a young woman coming uptown here to scrub floors in a office building. My body membered every scarifying minute of that long stay till the firemen got the doors opened and let me and the other girls out.

Then, the elevator started moving again. Somebody down below musta called it. All I wanted was to get to the ground floor.

As the elevator was going down, again Ellsworth said, "Jimmy, what's Dale talking this rough talk to Annie Eliza for? What's going on?"

"Didn't you see the debate this morning on 'Good Morning Atlanta'?"

"I haven't been up that early in ten years," said Ellsworth, laughing at what he thought was his own smart tongue.

Dale was looking at me real mean-like but not saying anything. He was acting like I hadn't knowed him for the better part of twenty years. I said, "Dale, you're a mighty brave man to talk to a old woman so tough. I now understand why you tripped my daughter-in-law and made her fall on her face."

He turned purple as a beet. He bristled like some big old bear in the woods. His hanging jowls shook. His old muddy eyes got just as tight and mean as a snake's. He was breathing so hard I thought he was gon have heart failure. "You're a lying old woman, and your daughter-in-law is a *slut!* We don't need sluts in the Georgia state government. You tell her that for me. And tell her—"

"Wait a minute, Dale—" said Cherokee Jimmy.

I don't know what possessed me to say it but I blurted out, "She's gon sue you, you know. You can't go round tripping up peoples and think you can get away with it!"

"Let her go right ahead, Annie Eliza. It will be the end of her little silly idea of running—"

Then suddenly the elevator stopped and we got quiet again but the door still didn't open. Ellsworth come just a getting real crazy. He banged and kicked the door. He called out to the top of his voice like some old cotton picker out in the field calling supper time. Over the intercom there was this soft-like music, Duke Ellington, I think.

The elevator just sat there. I was scared, sho, but not as scared as I would have been alone in there with nobody to die with me.

The mens was talking mongst theyselves and I wasn't paying no tention to them anymore. I was just waiting and hoping.

I thought about that time I was lost in the woods when I was a little girl. It was getting close to dark and I couldn't find my way back to the place where Ballard, Rutherford, and Kathy was playing. I knowed it was in a cave, a big one, and we had just found it that day. They was playing house in there and telling each other stories bout the boogeyman and the devil when I went off by myself, tired of letting them scare me. I had in my mind that I would go for a walk and pick some pretty wildflowers and come back in a little while. When I knowed I had lost my way and every way I turned was the wrong way, at first, I didn't get all worked up, I just kept right on trying new ways to walk, pushing my way through brush and lifting limbs and going on, but it didn't do any good. I was lost, very lost. I called out pretty soon, called Ballard's name. But I was too far away for him or them to hear me. I found out later they had gone off looking for me and they was calling out to me too but I couldn't hear them. They went off in the wrong direction and I was still going in the other wrong direction. So we was getting farther away from each other. It got dark quick and I heard all kinds of animals in the under-brushes and I started crying. My legs was bleeding and itching from walking through the brushes and the weeds. I was thirsty and I knowed I was gon die, and if I wont gon die Momma was gonna kill me anyways. I was very lost. Then—it musta been bout three or four hours after I left the cave, but it seemed like months—I heard all these voices echoing through the woods, calling my name. They was Momma's and Poppa's and Ballard's and Ruth's and some other peoples' who had come with them to help find me and I called back to them and we kept calling to each other till they found me and they found me crying and disable to speak. Poppa carried me home in his arms and I didn't even get a beating that night. That was unusual but I was happy bout not getting a whipping for doing something wrong. Well, I felt just as lost there in the stuck elevator as I did that time many years ago.

Cherokee Jimmy took hold of Ellsworth and held him. "Calm down Elly, just calm down."

Then suddenly the elevator door slid open and it was like the gates of Heaven opening!

* * *

When I got back home Juneboy was there by hisself. He was lying down on the couch but the television wont on and he wont reading nothing. I thought he might not be feeling well. I went over and ast him if he was all right, if I could make him a cup of tea or get him a glass of buttermilk or some ice cream. It musta been five or five-thirty. It was too early for dinner.

His eyes was open but he didn't look like he was seeing nothing. Then he sat up and smiled just as sweet as you pleased. It was like he was coming back from far off thinking.

I didn't want him to start speechifying to me but I wanted to know how his time with Renee had gone. So I ast. While I made us some tea, he come just a telling me how much fun Renee was. He thought she was pretty smart too. I ast bout the Farmer's Market. They drove out there and bought tomatoes but it started raining hard so they ended up going round the city to a whole bunch of supermarkets and neighborhood grocery stores.

I put the tea on the table and he came over and sat with me. I ast why they went to so many stores. Juneboy said he wont tirely sure but it looked like to him Renee was fixing to do some research on tomatoes in connection with this conspiracy thing she mentioned at the dinner party. Looked like to Juneboy she was checking crate labels and packages of tomatoes in the clear wrappers. He said she bought one or two from a whole lot of different crates of loose tomatoes and she bought the wrapped ones too. And she snuck and tore off the labels from the crates when she could get them off. Some, he said, was marked Georgia, others Florida or Mississippi. By hook or by crook, she was gon get what information she was out to get, it looked like. I was personally scared for the child. As I listened to Juneboy it seemed like to me Renee was getting herself in some very foreign water.

Me and Juneboy sipped our tea and sat there quiet-like. I didn't know if I ought to express my fears to him or not. So I decided to change the subject. I ast just how was Renee so much fun? He laughed, then said she was full of jokes. Had a sense of humor bout things. When she was pulling off the labels and picking out the tomatoes she kept talking bout getting arrested as a thief, you know. Even though she was planning to pay for them, you see, she musta felt kinda guilty, for some reason.

11

All of us was gathered round the television set in the den at Jeremiah's cause Senator Cooper was gon appear on that talk show called "Good Night Atlanta." It was ten-thirty and the host of the show, Harry Burke, had just come out trying to act like Johnny Carson with the music and all behind him. He was standing there telling some kinda joke I didn't get, then he nounced his guest for the night. The joke was about Ethel Waters and the Mills Brothers and had something to do with ills brothers and ethyl gas. It wont funny, I could tell that much. Then he did some kinda little skit from *Green Pastures,* acting like he had wings and went flapping all over the stage. He was one silly man.

It was still Monday, and everybody had been trying to comfort Renee all afternoon and all evening. Juneboy and I went over to Jeremiah's round nine, right after supper. DeSoto and Whitney was already there. Jeremiah and Renee had put the children to bed and was sitting in front of the television looking real gloomy. Jeremiah, I understood later, had been swearing all afternoon that he was gon let the Lord deal severely with Senator Cooper for tripping his wife. Jeremiah said the Lord already had a plan for taking care of Senator Cooper.

I was feeling kinda strange that night and it was probably cause the moon was still sorta full. It looked full to me even if it wont. I had a headache and my arthritis was acting up, this time real bad in the bend of my left arm. Usually I gets it in my fingers.

So, this fool Harry Burke was still clowning round and jiving while we waited for Senator Cooper. I told Jeremiah how Cooper and Cherokee Jimmy ganged up on me in that elevator and he said he was working on their cases and the Lord would take care of them too. Nobody messed with his momma and got away with it. I told Jeremiah that Ellsworth was what they call a innocent bystander. He didn't mean no harm.

Burke was now doing his dumb imitation of Bill Bojangles Robinson, which was all right until he stopped and come just a trying to do little Shirley Temple. The man was such a jackass!

Then Burke went and sat hisself down, thank the Lord, and his sidekick, Fechitt Tucker, sitting two seats away, ast him something bout his trip to the interior. You knowed it was a way of getting him started on another one of his corny jokes. I didn't pay no tention to what they was saying.

Jeremiah noticed I wont interested in the jokes and he said, "Momma, come in the dining room a minute . . ."

I got my old self up and followed him. He put his arm round my shoulder and put his head real close to mine. Jeremiah said, "Keep this to yourself. I have just had a revelation. Dale Cooper is going to commit suicide tomorrow. And it won't have anything to do with politics."

I gave Jeremiah a look. Did he think he was the messenger of God?

"Momma, I tell you this because you are the only person on earth I can trust. I trust you with all my soul. The Lord God just revealed this news to me and I share it with you because he wants me to. All power to the Lord! Now, let's go back and watch the show."

I believed in my son. I wanted to always believe in him.

We went back to the den. There was forty-leven things on my mind and I couldn't get one straight.

While Burke was jiving round with his first two or three guests I talked with Whitney bout her work for the lawyers. She said they was keeping her real busy. She had that very day typed up ten briefs and made a lot of calls for the three mens she works for the most. There was a woman lawyer in the office too. Whitney said she was looking for another job. There was no way she could advance on this partickler job.

Then somebody said, "Here comes the Devil!" and sho nuff it was Dale. Burke and Dale sat down after shaking hands. One sat on a little white couch and the other one sat on a leather armchair and there was this coffee table with a vase of flowers on it between them.

Burke thanked the senator for coming on his show and then he went on bout how this was the first big exclusive interview somebody had had a chance to do with Dale since Dale debated his Republican opponent, the past Senator Kidd McCarthy who, everybody knowed, was a close friend of the Ku Klux Klan bigshots in Georgia.

A commercial about floor wax came on and after this blond woman stopped looking at her face in the floor and the big voice in the sky outside her kitchen window shut up, the television went back to Cooper's face.

Burke said, "Tell us, Senator Cooper, how you got started in politics, how you became a public servant, what inspired you to devote your time and energy to helping humanity."

"Harry, it all stems from an early incident in my childhood. I was born in the small, small town of Epworth, up near the Tennessee border. We were a poor family. The first school I ever attended was one held in the Negro church. We colored children used to gather there every morning for three hours to learn reading, writing, and arithmetic. The afternoons we spent picking cotton for the white folks. It was not until I was ten years old that the Negro community was able to gather together enough money to build a little one room schoolhouse for us children. The preacher's wife, a Mrs. Ida Mae Phillips, taught all the various grades. She was a tireless, dedicated soul."

"Is she the source of your inspiration?"

"No. Her death is."

"Her death?"

"Yes, Harry. You see, all the people—black and white—respected Mrs. Ida Mae. We all knew she had a hard row to hoe. Not only was she in charge of the education of all of us children—and there must have been fifty, maybe sixty of us at that time, back in the thirties—she also had to go home and mind her own young ones and a husband and a sick mother in a wheelchair. Her husband worked at the sawmill. He had no time to help with the children. He worked from sunup till sundown.

"We'd see her up bright and early feeding the chickens and the hogs and getting her husband off to work; we'd see her getting her own children ready for school — and they minded her in class just like everybody else did. Back in those times, Mrs. Ida Mae looked very old and very tired to me, a little boy. But, in retrospect, I'm sure she was not much older than twenty-five or thirty. I thought she was a hundred and sixty!

"Well, she went on like this for a number of years. Somewhere along the way the Phillipses managed to buy a used Packard, so, as soon as Mrs. Ida Mae learned to drive it, she would drive her husband to the sawmill, then drive herself and her children to the schoolhouse. Before that, they had walked like the rest of us.

"Well, one day, a Saturday, she told her family she was going into town to do some shopping. She took the car and she drove into Epworth, bought flour, lard, canning jars, and a bunch of other supplies. On the way back she struck a tree. Now the tree was about fifty feet from the road. The sheriff said she had to have meant to do it because the tree was so far off the road. Others said she lost control of the car and the car just found the tree on its own and smashed right into it. The tree was on the edge of a little cliff. The car catapulted and ended up upside-down below the cliff in a ditch.

"Now it just happened that my brother, Vincent, and I were out hunting rabbit that afternoon when we saw smoke. We followed the smoke and found the Packard. Mrs. Ida Mae, who, as I told you, had always struck me as old, had crawled from the wreckage. Her dress was torn off and she was lying there naked except for her underclothes. There was no sign of blood. She was not dead when we found her. Her eyes were opened but she could not talk. She even lifted a finger toward us, beckoning, obviously asking for help. It was the first time I had seen a woman's body. It surprised me. My brother and I were scared too, at the same time, but we couldn't take our eyes off her. I said to Vincent, 'We must get help!' I told Vincent I'd stay with her while he went up on the road to stop the next car to ask for help.

While he was up there trying to stop somebody — and, by the way, about five cars went by in an hour — I waited with her. Her eyes were still open. I could see she was still breathing. Something about the youth of her body — the body of a girl — transformed something in me. I felt it very deeply. I tried talking to Mrs. Ida Mae, hoping that by talking with her, I could keep her living.

"By the time Vincent returned with a white man, I think Mrs. Ida Mae was dead. In any case, by the time the white man got into Epworth and told the sheriff, and the sheriff and the coroner got out there, she was dead for sure.

"It was this incident, Harry, that inspired me to want to serve humanity. You see, sitting there waiting for help, I myself felt so helpless, I cursed that condition and swore that, as soon as I was able, I would gain strength — with God's help — to prevent this sort of needless death from happening."

Harry Burke said, "But it was nobody's fault. It was an accident, Senator. No amount of power on earth could have saved her. The situation was beyond your control."

"Don't you see, Harry? Vincent couldn't get anybody to stop for a whole hour!"

DeSoto laughed.

Jeremiah was mumbling to hisself.

Whitney rested her head against my knee. She was sitting on the floor right in front of me. It was the way me and my sisters used to sit for each other when we would braid each other's hair or straighten each other's hair. Whitney was like a daughter to me. She reminded me of myself when I was young.

Harry Burke was asting Senator Cooper some other question bout the early part of his career.

"The man is chicken," said Renee. "Did you hear that story he just told?"

"He's a coward," said DeSoto.

"A coward and a snake," said Whitney.

"Mark my word," said Jeremiah. "The Lord has plans for this man. He tries to come on like a great humanitarian but the Lord can see through phonies such as Senator Cooper."

The show went on and the children listened to it but I was
tired so I got up and told them I was going on back to the house
and lie down. It had been a long day for me. Juneboy knowed
how to get back by hisself.

The minute I let myself into my house, the telephone in the
hall come just a ringing. It was my sister Esther. She wanted to
know if everything was going all right with her son being here
and all.

"Child, it's a delight to have him here with me. He's a real
gentle boy and it's been so many years—"

"Yes, it has, Annie."

I told her bout DeSoto's plans to take Juneboy to the big
annual policeman's ball tomorrow night.

"That's very nice of DeSoto. Is Jeremiah going?"

"Oh, yes, he wouldn't miss it for the world. You know Renee
is running for the state senate?"

"No, hush your mouth!"

"I declare!"

"Well, is she got any chance?"

"It's hard to tell. The man she's running gainst is a real animal.
He tripped her this morning in a television studio. The kids is
over there now at Jeremiah's watching him on a talk show. The
man's just trying to make hisself look like a lamb of Jesus."

"Well, bless Renee's heart. I hope she wins."

"Yeah. She might win and then regret she's winned. Girl, I tell
you, these politicians can be dangerous as a bear surprised in the
woods."

"I know what you mean."

"Well, don't worry bout Juneboy. He's having hisself a good
time down here—a much better time than he thought he was
going to have, hating the South like he did all these years since he
was a little old bitty thing."

★ ★ ★

I turned on a comedy and got settled on the couch to watch it. I
think it was the one bout the white family with the little adopted

colored boy. They is two or
concentrate on what was going
told bout finding his schooltea
bothered me. At first I didn't kn
mind, worrying me so. I kept goin
him little and seeing his little broth
the woman on the ground and I
yellow, you know, pretty like I use to
thirty. Mens used to whistle at me ev

I guess I fell to sleep and come jus _____ _____ bout me and
Esther when we was little. We was ru.....ng out through a sugar
cane field. The sugar cane was high, much taller than us. I was
chasing her and I guess we was playing tag. We was almost out of
breath when we came on a Negro man lying there deep in the
sugar cane, wounded, blood all dirty and gritty all over his face
and hands and the front of his torn shirt. He reached out to us,
just like I imagined Dale's teacher done to him and his brother.
The man in the sugar cane sort of frowned at us as we stood there
staring at him. Esther had her finger in her mouth, no, her
thumb. She always sucked her thumb when she couldn't figure
what was going on. I ast the man if he needed help, if somebody
had hurt him. He said he had hurt himself. He said, "I was trying
to fly from the cliff back yonder, and I fell and broke my leg. My
wings broke off over yonder. See?" Sho nuff, there was a set of
broken wings bout fifty feet from the hurt man, laying all tangled
up in the sugar cane. I ast him why he wanted to fly. He said it
was a speriment. If he could fly with his home-made wings, then
everybody round these parts would respect him. He said he had
never gotten no respect. I sent Esther to get help and I stayed
with the man to talk with him so he wouldn't die. Maybe talking
with him, I thought, would save his life. While I waited with him
for Esther to come back with help, with the man who owned the
sugar cane field maybe, I ast the flyer who he was.

He told me his name was Lightning Hartley. He lived about
twenty minutes from here and he said he knowed my father and
mother but didn't see them much since he lived so far away from
us. As Lightning Hartley talked, he turned into Juneboy talking

...re just like he had every right to be there. But, as ...ghtning Hartley's voice didn't change, he kept right ...ng in his deep southern accent like hisself, not like ...eboy with his up North educated talk. Lightning Hartley told me he had been trying for years to fly cause many, many years ago he had died and his soul had gone out into a big old empty space. Because he had died in some unnatural way, he couldn't go up to Heaven and they didn't want him down in Hell either. So he had been floating round out there all by hisself, in pain, feeling no comfort. He had tried from time to time to come in, and the only way he could come in out of the emptiness was by flying in, back to earth. All the times before this time, he had not been able to get his wings to work the right way, or the moon had been full and a lot of bad luck had been in the air, dogs barking, roosters crowing at the wrong time. This was the first time he had got his wings flapping the right way, and he was flying, actually flying for a little while, a long while, he said, cross that stretch out yonder beyond the sugar cane field, on into this sugar cane field. It was a landing all right and at first he thought he had come in from the empty place out there, and he had in a way, but he had fell before he reached his landing strip, he said. I ast him where was his landing strip and he said it was his own home, the place where he felt safe and some comfort. So he had this broken leg now and though he wont out there as far as he had been in the emptiness, he still was not back on earth and live yet. He wanted to know if I understood. I thought I did and I told him I did.

I must have woke up when I heard Juneboy coming in.

12

Tuesday morning was a real pretty morning. In the backyard the birds was singing and jumping all over the yard, pecking at the worms. In the night there had been a sprinkle and all the bushes and plants and vines on the fence out there was real dark green with the raindrops glowing on them in the early morning sunlight. I felt real happy. I don't know why but I did. Maybe cause my arthritis wont acting up so bad.

I went out in the yard and hooked up the hose and screwed on the sprinkler and set it on the grass. The grass was growing much better since Jeremiah and DeSoto growed up. I likes to water in the mornings fore the sun gets too hot.

I checked my flower bed to see if any buds was out yet, if anything was blooming yet. The sweet peas was just bout ready to pop they little heads out and become flowers. The tulips I planted last fall was bout seven inches high already. This year some pretty little old wildflowers — pink and purple and blue — was growing along the edge of the flower bed. They was so cute I didn't have the heart to pull them up even though I knowed that later on I was gon regret not pulling them. I think they was paintbrushes and bluebonnets. It was the first time they come to visit my yard.

I went back in the house and made coffee. It musta been going on eight. I turned on the television while the coffee was brewing. I got the eight o'clock news. The weather forecast was good, with sunny skies and temperature in the seventies. This was normal for April.

I sat at the table there in the back room and looked at the screen while the news was being reported. I hadn't heard a sound from Juneboy upstairs. A little boy had been struck down by a car. He was delivering newspapers in his own neighborhood. In critical condition at Grady. There was now another hotline for rape victims and they gave the number. There was a hotline for depressed peoples too. They could call and talk to somebody. There was a hotline for alcoholics and one for mothers going crazy taking care of they little childrens. Everybody got a hotline it looked like. Then there was a man who had wrote a book. He was some professor or somebody. He looked like my Dr. Limerick — grizzly and with them real thick eyebrows and fat hands. His book was called *Georgia Rediscovered* and it was all about the early years of Georgia as one of the original thirteen states, he said. He talked about the Cherokee Nation and I got real interested in that cause, you know, Cherokees was amongst my ancestors. Anyways this man said he researched what had happened before 1788, the year Georgia became a state. If I heard him right, when the white folks came over from England or wherever, they found the Cherokee Nation already here and doing just fine. But the white mens got busy trying to conquer the Cherokee Nation. He said that in 1715 there was a war called the Yamasee war. In that war the white mens got a whole bunch of black mens to help them invade the Cherokees but the black mens stayed on even after the invasion and become part of the Cherokee Nation. They settled down and married Cherokee womens. And when the Cherokee come just a fighting the Creeks, the black mens fought right along with the Cherokee mens. The white mens couldn't understand why the black mens had stayed; so pretty soon the white mens stopped taking slaves to fight the Indians. I thought all of that was pretty interesting stuff.

Then suddenly there was a special news bulletin right there on the news show itself. The newsman talking to me said he was switching us to another newsman. This one was a woman. I had seed her before. She was tall and had a strong face. I liked her cause she had a deep voice. She was standing in front of a big white house in a rich neighborhood. You could tell by the look of the house and the trees and the grass out front, just behind her. Her name was Rita Mae Grant. She was wearing a light blue blouse and a dark blue skirt. She looked respectable, not like some of these womens you see all the time on television. She looked like she wont trying to pick up nobody.

Miss Rita Mae Grant said, "Good morning viewers. I'm standing in front of Senator Dale Bean Cooper Jr.'s home. I was summoned here only minutes ago. We got a live one on the wire while in the van. Not much is clear. One thing I can tell you, though, is that the senator has been taken away on a stretcher. All we know at this point is that Senator Dale Cooper has been taken to the hospital. Neighbors said they heard a gunshot in his house in the wee hours of the morning but as of now there is no firm evidence that the senator has been shot. He is on his way in an ambulance to Grady Hospital. Hopefully, later, at Grady, we will have more news. Now, back to the studio and—"

I got myself as fast as I could into my bedroom where Juneboy was sleeping. But there was only the empty bed.

The minute I saw the bed empty I heard the water running in the shower. He was taking a shower.

I couldn't wait to tell him. I knocked on the bathroom door. When I heard him call out I opened the door.

I shouted, "Juneboy, Senator Cooper been rushed to the hospital!"

Well, you see, at this point I hadn't membered Jeremiah's prediction. I was just too plain excited. I didn't know what I was doing.

It took Juneboy a minute or two to understand me. I stood outside the bathroom door and he turned off the shower and wrapped one of my big towels round hisself and come out.

I told him again.

He said, "You're kidding."

I told him I wont kidding.

He said, "Holy smoke."

I said, "I better call Renee."

The phone was right there—just a step away, in the hallway— and I picked it up and dialed Jeremiah's number.

I could tell by Jeremiah's sleepy voice they wont up yet. I apologized for calling so early but that it was important. I told him bout Cooper being taken with a wound to Grady.

He ast me if I was sho. I told him I was. I told him to turn on the television, turn on the radio.

I hung up.

I went back to the back room and poured Juneboy a cup of coffee and myself another one.

When Juneboy was dressed he came back and just took his cup up without me telling him it was his. He knowed.

So, I figured the rest of the morning was gon be real busy for everybody. Dale wont dead. Nobody said he was dead — not yet. All we knowed was he was at the hospital.

I turned the station and got another newsman. He said he was reporting from Grady. He had no new news on Cooper's condition but he was talking with one of the policemen who helped bring Senator Cooper to the hospital. Behind the policeman being interviewed I could see my son DeSoto just standing there listening. I couldn't tell if he had helped too or not. The policeman said, "A neighbor of Senator Cooper's heard a shot in the early morning hours. His guess was three or three-thirty. Investigating officers, including myself, knocked at the door of the senator's home and got no response. Not in possession of a search warrant, we did not enter. With the special permission of the chief of police, we were able to force entry. The senator's house was not in disarray. There was no sign of previous forced entry. We found the senator in his bedroom in bed. He was not wearing clothes. There was a large, rosy, bloody wound in his right side. We immediately called for the emergency unit and, once they arrived, he was rushed to the emergency room at Grady Memorial Hospital." The newsman said "Thank you" to the intelligent policeman and the policeman and DeSoto left the screen. Then a commercial for spaghetti came on with a man who was spose to be Italian, talking in a Italian accent, kissing his fingers and blowing the kiss out at me. He looked pretty silly to me. Then there was one for some chain restaurant showing fried fish, spose to be crispy and packed with a whole lot of flavor and stuff. Probably more stuff than flavor.

Juneboy stood there beside me watching the screen. He was drinking his coffee.

Maybe a hour or so later, Jeremiah called back and said, "I talked with George just now, Momma. He says that it appears that Dale's condition is stable but the funny thing about the wound is it does not seem to have been inflicted by either a knife or a bullet. The doctors at Grady can't figure it out. Remember what I told you last night?"

"I sho do."

"The Lord is at work here, I tell you, Momma."

"The Lord or somebody."

"It's the work of God Almighty, Momma."

"I don't know. I'm gon keep the television on to see if I can hear any more. What's Renee gon do now?"

"What do you mean?"

"I mean is she gon still run?"

"She ain't said nothing about not running. Harry Burke just called her, by the way. He wants her on tonight. So she will be late getting to the ball."

"I'll stay home and watch her. I never liked going to them kinda things nohow. I'm too old for such foolishness."

"No you won't. You chickened out last year and you know it hurt DeSoto's feelings. You promised you'd go this year, so you're going—if I have to drag you there. Me and DeSoto together will hogtie you and carry you." Jeremiah was laughing like he said something real funny. If he had, I hadn't heard it. My hearing ain't as fine as it used to be, you know.

While I was talking with Jeremiah I was watching the screen and Juneboy was now sitting at the table with his coffee cup on the table and he too was watching the television. A coffee commercial showing the coffee pouring from the pot into a cup was on and the voice was saying something bout this big, busting flavor that explodes in your mouth and how dark and rich this coffee was to the last drop.

Me and Jeremiah hung up and I guess me and Juneboy waited bout another hour fore we knowed that nothing new was going to come on bout poor Dale. The morning soap operas was on all the stations now cept the educational station.

I took Juneboy out in the backyard and showed him my
flowers beginning to bloom. He looked like he was real interested cause he was looking carefully and listening to me. I could
tell.

At noon Rita Mae Grant came back on the "Midday Report."
After the national news you could see her standing beside
Republican State Senator Tommy Blackmore, a white man. This
man was running gainst Dale Cooper and had been telling
everybody in the newspapers and on radio and television he was
gon take Senator Cooper's seat in November. Rita Mae Grant ast
Senator Blackmore if he thought the political picture was gon be
different now that Senator Cooper might be out of the race.

Blackmore said, "I don't think anything has changed; besides
it's too soon to tell."

What about Senator Kidd McCarthy? Was he worried that
McCarthy might challenge him for the Republican spot?

He said, "Cooper defeated McCarthy for a set of good reasons
and McCarthy has done nothing to improve on his previous
performance in the Senate."

I switched the channel. That other newsman — I forget his
name — we saw earlier was interviewing Councilwoman Sandra
Valerie Wright. She had too much makeup on. Sandra need to
get somebody to tell her how to do herself. You could tell the
newsman was sort of lapping her boots cause of her late husband,
our great man, Congressman Mitchell Wright. The interviewer
ast her if she was now gon support Renee Hicks for the Democratic slot. She said, "No, I don't think so. It would be foolish to
speculate this early. Senator Cooper, you know, is still very much
alive. I supported his candidacy four years ago. I haven't changed
my position."

"What position does Mayor Jones take on Mrs. Hicks'
candidacy?"

"You'll have to ask the mayor himself, I'm afraid. I can't read
his mind."

"Mrs. Wright, you know they are saying that Senator Cooper's
wound appears not to have been inflicted by any known weapon
or instrument. What do you make of this?"

"I make nothing of it. All the evidence isn't in yet. We must wait and see what the final reports say."

He told her thank you and that his time was up.

After a quick commercial for "no salt" rice cakes and one for Snickers candy bars, another man came on talking bout—in his own words—"the current crisis in defense spending."

I changed the channel. A pretty woman was spreading lipstick across her lips. She winked her eye at me. No, maybe she was winking at Juneboy. I looked at Juneboy. He was lying on the couch reading a book. *Huckleberry Finn,* I think. Now that's a book I ought to read one of these days. It's been in the house since the boys was little but I just never gets round to reading books the way I used to read books to them when they was little.

I changed the channel again.

"Juneboy is this thing bothering you? I know I leave it on too long. I should just turn it off when ain't nothing worth watching is on."

"It's no bother to me, Aunt Annie Eliza. I can just tune it out, you know. I don't even hear it." He put the book down. "Are you going to the ball tonight?"

I turned up my nose at the idea. "I sho don't want to but the boys they trying to make me go so I guess I'll go but I'm sho I'll be the only old person there. They just don't understand."

"You might enjoy it, Aunt Annie Eliza."

"I might at that."

"I promise to dance with you."

"That's sweet of you, Juneboy. I'll make you keep your promise."

* * *

Still in uniform, DeSoto stopped by round three and I fixed him a cup of hot chocolate. He likes his hot chocolate, always have liked it since I used to make it for him when he was little and just starting to go to school.

He wanted to make sho Juneboy had a dark suit. Juneboy told him he had a dark blue suit. DeSoto, you know, gets so worked up over this policeman's ball every year. He offered to let Juneboy use his extra tux. I didn't even know the boy had a extra tux. I knowed he owned one tux but not two!

I told DeSoto I saw him on television.

He said, "It's not the first time, Momma." Then he turned to Juneboy, sitting at the table with us, and said, "Every time she sees me on television she thinks I'm a moving star."

"Well," I said, "you are a movie star—in my heart."

He kissed my cheek.

Juneboy ast DeSoto if anything new had turned up concerning Senator Cooper.

DeSoto sipped his hot chocolate before he spoke. Then he blinked them big old pretty eyes at both of us and said, "There sure has."

"What?"

"At the station a little while ago the special investigators questioned Cherokee Jimmy, because apparently he was the last person seen by neighbors leaving Dale's house late last night. Some of the neighbors heard a gunshot and the next door neighbor even reported he heard a scuffle around midnight, probably just before Cherokee Jimmy left.

"Dale himself isn't talking to us about the wound or sore or disease or whatever it is in his side and he's also tight-lipped about the gunshot.

"Cherokee Jimmy did say he had an argument with his friend Dale but he wouldn't say what they were fighting about. But this next door neighbor of Dale's said it sounded to him like a lovers' quarrel. Don't look at me! I know only what I'm told! Anyway, the neighbor said Cherokee Jimmy was accusing Dale of being unfaithful. Apparently, Dale had just come back from visiting somebody. He said it was a boy, a sick boy, a relative. Cherokee Jimmy didn't believe him, didn't believe this boy was a relative. He insisted that Dale had visited a secret lover. The fighting went on and on, said this neighbor. It kept the neighbor awake.

"Then there was the gunshot. Some of the other neighbors say it was a little after midnight, others say it was way after midnight. What we don't know is who shot at who—Cherokee Jimmy or

Dale. But the special guys dug a bullet out of the couch, so apparently only the couch was shot. Cherokee Jimmy isn't talking, Dale isn't talking. But Ballistics is trying to see what it can come up with."

I just looked at DeSoto. All growed up and talking like he knowed what he was talking bout. I couldn't help but see him as a little boy trying to be a big man.

He stood up all ready to go.

I was ready for him to go.

I made up my mind right then and there to find out what happened to Dale, what this sickness was and who was that boy he visited in the night. I'm nosy like that. It all sounded pretty fishy to me. I had a good mind to go right up to Grady and ast Dale hisself but I thought better of it cause he was sick. You see, I got this real hankering to know what's behind things. I get to thinking on a thing and it won't let me have no peace till I get to the bottom of it. And it don't have to be nothing in the line of my own business, you know.

Well, I was gon find out one way or another.

13

After DeSoto left, Ballard came by. It musta been four-thirty. I thought something was wrong cause he hardly ever come over here, specially during his work hours. He looked real depressed. Juneboy was in my room taking a nap.

I said, "Ballard what brings you here this time of day?"

He followed me back to the back room fore he answered. I warmed the coffee and poured me and him some.

"I had to go to Buckle's job today and bring him home. He was blind drunk on the job. Didn't know what end of the broom he was spose to be pushing. He was like a babbling fool. They was real nice — his bosses, I mean. They didn't even fire him, not yet anyways. I took him by the hand and took him to the janitors' dressing room. He kept giving me a hard time, talking nonsense. You know I can't stand drunks nohow. Well, I had the damnest time trying to dress him. Never even dressed my own kids when they was growing up. Imagine me dressing a grown man! I just ain't got the patience Donna Mae got with this fool husband of hers. Somehow, I got him dressed and got him outta there into the street and he tried to run away. I had to drag him back and force him across the street by twisting his arm.

"Somehow I got him into the parking lot and again he tried to get away. By God, he was a mess! I could have killed him he made me so mad. Peoples was staring at us. You know I ain't never had no time for this kind of foolishness, Annie. What am I gon do with that fool? I have a good mind to move out. I would if it wont for Donna Mae. And my share of the house payments. I'd just as soon be by myself in one room."

"You got him in your car, I guess, huh?"

"I stuffed that nigger in my car! Feets first!"

116

I couldn't help laughing, seeing little Buckle being stuffed by old big tall skinny Ballard into Ballard's old Lincoln.

"At one stoplight he tried to jump out. Said I was taking him to the jailhouse. I said, 'Buckle who am I?' He said he didn't know but he knowed I was not his friend. I was taking him to the jailhouse and he hadn't done nothing wrong."

"You think maybe he went off his head?"

"That nigger been off his head since he was born."

"Then it was just the liquor?"

"It's done rotted his brains out."

"Guess Donna Mae wont home when you got him there."

"Naw, she wont. She don't get in till bout eight. This is that new shift she on. Member?"

I had forgotten. "Yes, I do. Did you make him eat something to sober up?"

"Peoples across the street was looking out from behind they curtains and, I swear, I was bout ready to leave him in the car rather than embarrass myself in front of my neighbors dragging that drunk nigger up the front steps."

"Why didn't you take him through the garage?"

"I did but it didn't do no good. Everybody saw anyway."

"But, Ballard, everybody round there knows Buckle is a drunk. They seed him like that before, I bet you."

"Anyhow, I just stopped by here to blow off steam. I'm on my way back to the shop. Got a big delivery to get ready this evening. You know, some niggers too lazy to come to the cleaners to pick up they clothes, they rather pay extra for delivery than walk two blocks. Our peoples is a mess, I tell you."

We laughed together. "Leave me outta that. They your peoples, not mine!"

He slapped my knee and grinned. I hadn't seed Ballard laugh or grin in years. Or it seemed so.

★ ★ ★

All the while Ballard was there the television was on low. When he left I went and turned it up. On right then was a game show I

don't usually watch. Some married couples trying to guess what
the other partner like and dislike and stuff like that. Real foolish
peoples giggling and insulting each other. I sat there sort of half
watching it as I finished my coffee. But I was really remembering
me and Ballard when we was little. He was my big brother and I
looked up to him. All of us younger ones, cept Prudence, the
oldest one, did. In some way Ballard and Prudence was our
poppa and momma, at least part-time.

I guess the time I respected Ballad most, the time that got me
forever in his debt was the time I was feeling so low after being
betrayed by Poppa. I still sometimes cry bout it, all these years
later. Maybe it was cause Poppa was Cherokee, I don't know. You
know, strange and distant. I never understood him.

This one time I had been playing with a little girl down the
road Momma had told me not to play with. I used to sneak
through the garden fence so she couldn't see me going off down
the road to play with that bad little girl. Momma said she was
bad. I never was sure what she did to get so bad but I liked her
cause she played fair. We played rope and sang "Lil Liza Jane." We
played jacks. We played with her dolls and she never got mad at
me and pulled my hair or nothing like that.

So one day when Momma was out in the field and Poppa was
in the house getting hisself a drink of water, he saw me coming
back through the fence and when I got in the house he ast me
where I been. I told him I was just out walking in the weeds out
there on the other side of the garden. He gave me a look and said
I didn't have to lie to him, that I could trust him always and that I
should tell him everything and never keep anything back.

Well, I looked up at my father. I loved him very much. And I
trusted him. When he told me something I believed him. So I
told him I was down there playing with that little girl Momma
didn't want me to play with. He ast me why I liked the little girl
and I told him all the reasons I just now told you. He just smiled
like he understood and I ast him to promise not to tell Momma.
He swore to me he would not tell Momma. It was a secret
between the two of us. And do you know what? The minute
Momma came in the house that evening, he went blabbing to

her bout me sneaking off playing with the bad girl. At first Momma said it was Poppa's imagination, that I was a nice girl and that I wouldn't go behind her back and do something she didn't want me to do. Well, by supper time Momma was changing her tune and I knowed by bedtime I was in for a beating for sho.

I never forgave Poppa for that. It taught me not to trust grown peoples and I guess even today I try to be careful who I share a secret with. Peoples can let you down something terrible. Anyways, it was the next day that Ballard gave me a talking-to, telling me I had to learn to accept Momma's and Poppa's faults, that they wont perfect, that they made mistakes like everybody else. He was wise for his age. And I think from then on Ballard was more poppa to me than Poppa was.

★　★　★

By the time the six o'clock news was coming on, I could hear Juneboy back in there doing something. I was anxious to see what they might say bout Senator Cooper. First thing they showed was Cherokee Jimmy's face in the highlights. Then a commercial bout Noxema and the tragedy of teenage pimples or something. I waited. They was going to interview Cherokee Jimmy. It looked like the police had let him go cause you could see he was standing outside the police station with this reporter who was gon talk to him later on in the news. I had to wait halfway through the show, watching a whole bunch of dumb commercials bout liquid makeup and a credit card that could change your life. Then they flashed back to in-front-of-the-police-station and the reporter there put the microphone in front of Cherokee Jimmy's mouth after asting him what happened.

Cherokee Jimmy said, "A very close friend of mine, Senator Cooper, is gravely ill at Grady Hospital with a sickness the doctors don't seem to understand. The police, in keeping with their usual lack of tact, dragged me here for questioning — no, for a humiliating interrogation."

"Councilman Barnswell, can you tell us in your own words, what you saw when you found your friend Senator Cooper afflicted?"

"Sure. When I was unable to get him by telephone I went to his home, fearing some problem. He has a heart condition, you know. To make a long story short, I found him cleaning his gun. Contrary to the stupid reports he was not shot. He just accidentally fired his own gun while cleaning it."

Then this commercial for fingernail polish remover came on showing these big pink fingers sparkling like fresh washed dinner glasses made of crystal, the kind Momma left me and Esther. Momma said Kathy didn't need no good glasses cause she had married a common man, Donald Benge. Momma never had no use for poor Don, even if he was — back then — a part-time preacher. In Momma's mind Donald wont nothing but a common laborer.

I heard the phone ringing and Juneboy musta picked it up and it musta been for him cause he was on the line bout a half hour. Then he came back and told me it was Internal Medicine at Emory and they wanted him to give a talk on his sickle cell anemia research. He ast me if it was all right for him to stay till Friday morning and I told him to hush his mouth, he didn't have to ast no such silly question — he could stay a year and it would be fine with me. Family is family. But better than that, so far he was easy to be in the same house with. The peoples at Emory musta heard bout Juneboy's lecture at Spelman College.

Then he went and telephoned the airline peoples and changed his reservation to leave Friday morning. Then he took a shower.

When Juneboy was outta the bathroom I went in there and took my shower. A old woman, you know, has to do certain things in the bathroom, things she don't need to tell other peoples about. I wont feeling too comfortable. My hands was aching and my shoulders too. I felt some real "discomfort" (Dr. Limerick's word) in my belly. While I was getting myself ready for the ball, I could faintly hear the television through the wall. I guess Juneboy was watching the national news. I kept being real quiet so I could hear some of it, what was going on in the world.

You know it's real important to know what's going on in the world.

I kept thinking bout Ballard coming over here like he did. It was so unusual. My mind was just full of stuff: Dale Cooper, Renee, Ballard, Juneboy, this stupid ball. I felt like I was gon come down with some sort of nervous attack, the kind Esther gets. They say we gets these attacks cause of our white blood, not cause of our Indian or Negro blood. Lord! That's the line-of-goods Jeremiah tries to sell me.

I don't sit down in the tub much no more. You know. It's too hard for a old woman like me to get up outta that tub — without help. So I took myself a shower and fixed my face and my hands and fingernails. While I was working at myself, to be "present-able," as Miss Lena Horne say when she on television, I come just a thinking bout Ballard again and when we was little. Not long after he give me that talking-to that saved me from hating Momma and Poppa for the rest of my life, he and me went for a walk, and Ballard told me there was a restless force in me, a kinda hunger. He said I was like the leaves in the fall wind. I was kinda all over the place, moving and unsure of myself. I trusted Ballard so I listened to him. He said young girls start feeling this restless wind in they blood at about my age and they sometimes don't even know what it means. I sho knowed I felt restless but I don't think I woulda called it a wind. That's why my older brother impressed us so, he was always being like a poet. As I think back, he musta been doing it with them country gals around there. Even with that girl Momma didn't want me to play with.

14

We was all at the same table. The ball was being held this year in a big ballroom at the Hilton. There was others — mostly friends of DeSoto's — at our table too. They was so far down the table I couldn't talk to them if I had wanted to. Our table was right close to the dance floor. I liked my seat cause I could see the dancers going and coming. The music wont that loud stuff that makes your ears ache: it was dance music the way I always thought dance music was spose to be fore the rock and roll and this rock music you see on television, if you watch that kinda show. The mens in the band was older mens and they played numbers by Cole Porter and Gershwin and W. C. Handy. I could see the dancers dancing and some of them danced real well, but not like the dancers in my time, when womens wore long dresses to dances and men wore bow ties and there wont many fights over women. Leastways I don't member going to dances where there was fighting between roughnecks. It was dark in there cept for the little lights along the ceiling, kinda dim. Couples kept getting up from the tables and going onto the dance floor, dancing slowly and hugging close. I thought of Bibb and how he never learned to dance well but he always tried and most often he stepped on my toes every step of the way.

I was the oldest person at the table. There were no doubt about that. I sat between DeSoto and Whitney. DeSoto was at the head of the table, sort of half turned away from us, watching the dance floor when he wont out there strutting hisself round with Whitney or Ted's wife, Janice, or Joe's wife, Betty, or Richard's wife, Sadie. These real close friends of DeSoto's was down at the other end, like I said. Donna Mae was just the other side of Whitney, and Buckle (who shouldn't a been there in the first place) was next to Donna Mae. Buckle had put his own bottle on the table and Donna Mae took it and put it in her purse. It was, like DeSoto said, a cash bar. The peoples running the bar coulda got real upset. I don't know who the couple at the far end was. Across on the other side was Jeremiah, looking so unhappy. He always hates to have to come to places like this. Jeremiah is too serious bout God, you know. He don't have no time for clowning and dancing and peoples drinking, although Jeremiah can drink as much as anybody I ever knowed — and do! But that's between me and you! And he wont shy bout drinking his scotch tonight. Maybe he was drinking his blues away. Renee was, probably at that there moment, speaking on television bout her campaign. Maybe poor Jeremiah was feeling guilty bout not being with her, or at least seeing her on the television screen. I noticed he wont talking a bit to Billy next to him. I'm talking bout Donna Mae and Buckle's Billy! And poor Juneboy was sandwiched between Billy Buckle and another man and then that wife of Richard's, Sadie, then Richard hisself. And the couple whose name I never got. And coming up the other side was Joe's wife, Betty. Then Joe. Then Janice, Ted's wife. And then Ted, just the other side of Buckle hisself. Buckle was already falling asleep and the party was just starting. Whitney, smart child, ordered some snacks when the waitress came round. Of all the peoples in our family, married or natural, Whitney got more feeling and concern for folks feelings and she takes sympathy on poor Buckle. You don't come by too many folks with as much patience as Whitney got. She's a good girl. I wish I had birthed her myself.

I was sitting there eating the snacky stuff and drinking my orange drink (I don't drink alcohol) when, outta nowhere, Juneboy got up. You see, the minute he got up everybody thought he was gon ast one of the womens to dance — there was Whitney, Donna Mae, Janice, Sadie, Betty, and that other woman down there at the end. Well, it was the first time in the whole first hour or more that Juneboy had stood up when a new dance thing started. All the other mens had been swapping and dancing all over the place. I'm sho DeSoto was thinking poor Juneboy wont having a good time. But he stood up just as the music was getting going for this new dance, like he was bout to ast a woman to dance. So everybody—forgive me, I'm a little embarrassed: I thought so too, that he stood up to ast a young woman to dance with him. But he ast me. Me. Me. Not even my own sons had ast me to dance yet. Well, Jeremiah would not ast such a thing. He had a image, as he say, to maintain. But even so, he could dance with his mother and what's wrong with dancing with his wife? Course she wont there. DeSoto never thought to ast me to dance! No reason why he should have. So when Juneboy pushed his chair back and got up, everybody was interested.

Then, you see, they all saw Juneboy come round the table, passing that couple at the end I don't know, and all the way up to my side where I was, and in very gentlemanly fashion ast me if he could have this dance. Not even Bibb Hicks ever done anything so romantic in all his born days. I was so swept off my feets I couldn't think of a way to say no. He'd kept his word!

I can't tell you what we looked like out there on the floor but it sho felt good, being danced around, led, by such a beautiful dancer, my nephew, sweeped away sort of, you know. It was the highlight of the evening for me. Juneboy held me round the waist and led me like he knowed everything bout dancing since the beginning of dancing. All I had to do was follow him, God bless him. For the first time in many a years, I felt young and happy—though I felt a little embarrassed with my sons watching me, and I was trying to think what they thought. But Juneboy was they first cousin and, well, they had no accounting for jealousy. They had they chance and they didn't take it!

Since you know the highlight of the evening for me you might get to thanking nothing much interesting happened—but you wrong.

My own son DeSoto—he musta been drunk—got hisself up and made a nouncement. I could see poor Whitney being embarrassed. DeSoto said (and this was not that far into the night), "I want to propose a toast, a toast to politics and to religion. To politics first because it is through political power that we will, as a people, make progress, from the shackles of disease, poverty, and ignorance. And to religion because we need to keep close to our bosoms the heritage of the church—the single institution wherein we have been able to survive and grow strong in America!"

Drunk or no everybody stood up and clapped for him and I felt proud of DeSoto.

One of them dingbats down at the far end of my side said something like, "Power to the preachers! Power to the politicians!" And like ignorant folks, them round her broke out laughing like she said something real cute.

Let me tell you, though, while Juneboy was dancing with me he told me bout him and his girlfriend. Course I ast him first. He said she was the nicest woman he had ever met, she was intelligent and had integrity. You know Juneboy uses big words. (I knowed he had called her collect two times already on my phone. That by itself told me she was white cause you don't call no black gal two times collect and get away with it.) I ast him what kinda name this Kirsten of his had. He said Steinkoenig was German and it came down on her father's side but her mother had peoples from Scotland and Wales. I ast him if he had a picture of his girlfriend. He took out his wallet while we was dancing and showed her to me. She was real pretty with a face I could trust.

When we got back to the table everybody started teasing Juneboy bout trying to court me. He so shy all he did was blush and say something bout me being the best looking woman at the table and he couldn't resist—which embarrassed me cause, you know, everybody knowed it was out of charity that he danced with me. Or maybe it wont, but everybody thought it was. Specially when there was Whitney and them other gals—Janice, Sadie, Betty, and even his cousin Donna Mae.

Then he danced with Whitney next, anyway. I watched them. They sho was talking a lot. Juneboy didn't hold her close or nothing like that but they seemed to be dancing just for the purpose of talking. I couldn't help wondering what they was talking bout. They kept it up right through two numbers. Shucks, they probably was just talking bout the things on all our

minds: poor Renee, Senator Cooper, Cherokee Jimmy. The
whole mess. Yet I couldn't help wondering.

Whitney and Joe danced the next dance. He was just like his
name. The top of his head came to bout the bottom of her nose.
They was fun to watch.

It was while they was dancing that the big nouncement came.
Nobody believed a word of it. Not at first. The second time it
came over the loudspeakers there wont no mistake. They said
somebody done shot President Muskdeer! There was a lot of
fussing about and moaning and sighing and eyes stretching and
carrying on, but after bout ten minutes the band started up again
and peoples went to the dance floor. In my lifetime alone so
many presidents been shot and shot at and public figures killed
or wounded I guess everybody felt kinda like I felt: helpless.
There wont nothing you could do bout it so why have a heart
attack over it?

DeSoto ast me to dance. I told him I was still worn out from
dancing with Juneboy. Maybe on the next round.

I thought, if Momma could see me now she'd think: "Annie
Eliza done lost her mind, dancing and staying up all hours at her
age!" But then Momma—after a whole life spent in the
church—started drinking beer when she was almost seventy!
Poppa was long dead by that time. Esther gets herself a can of
beer just about every day. Her doctor tells her it better than
taking pills for her nerves, and cheaper too.

DeSoto kept after me till I got out there with him and that boy
was just too fast for me so I stopped fore the music stopped and
told that boy that his poor, tired old momma just couldn't keep
up with all that fast stepping. So DeSoto took me back to my seat
and Whitney leaned over and whispered in my ear, "You got to
watch DeSoto. He's crazy! He'll dance you all night if you let
him!"

And I said, "Ain't it the truth!"

Jeremiah let me and Juneboy off in my driveway. It musta been
bout leven or leven-thirty.

I used the bathroom first, got ready for bed, soaked my teeth,
and put on my face cream and nightgown. I went back to the

back room and turned the television real low. I can't go to sleep without watching something. I got a late movie, in black and white and stretched out under my comforter, with my glasses on my nose. These glasses I don't wear if somebody's around—they so ugly—but they all right for the dark and alone like this. I got a real pretty ones I wears when I goes out, like tonight. I wore them when I went to see Mayor Jones the day before.

The minute I was settled down the phone ringed. It was right there beside me on the table so I picked it up and I guess Juneboy picked up in my bedroom at the same time. He probably thought I was already sleep but it was for him anyways. I felt real guilty for not hanging up but I heard the white girl's voice, and I was just a little curious. So I did something I ast the Lord to forgive me for. I listened to Juneboy and his girl friend, Kirsten Steinkoenig, talking. I won't stoop so low as to tell you what they said. You want me to tell you? Oh, girl, you is a mess! You as bad as I am!

Well, Kirsten said something like, "Hi. Hope I'm not calling you too late," and he said, "No, my aunt is asleep," and he said if he sounded like he was whispering it was cause he didn't want to wake up his aunt. Then she said she missed him a whole bunch—a whole bunch is what she said—and that she was cold, in bed alone, and that this whole year, so far, had been real, real hard for her, up there in New Haven, with him down in D.C. and he said he knowed what she meant cause he felt the same way. Then she said she loved him, loved him very much and was miserable waiting for him to return and he said he loved her, too, very, very much and was just as miserable, waiting for him to come back to her. Child, I thought I was listening to one of my soaps. It was so lovely, so romantic. Then she told him that the pregnancy test was negative and you could hear him sigh a sigh of relief. She said, though, that she wasn't so happy bout not being pregnant with his baby. He told her they had time, later on, to have a baby. Juneboy told her he wanted to marry her just as soon as his research in D.C. ended, the minute he got back to teaching at Yale. Child, listening to my nephew talking to his girlfriend, I went all Jello inside. They was two peoples who loved each other and wont gon let the world and its ways stop them. I admired my nephew and was glad for him, glad he had for hisself a girl to make him happy. She sounded like a nice, real intelligent girl. They talked on. When she laughed I knowed she was a trustworthy girl. There was honesty and music in her laugh. She was just telling him bout something funny that happened in one of her classes. I got the impression she was the teacher and one of her students gave her a real dumb answer. Juneboy understood the joke and he laughed. I didn't get the joke but I warmed up to the good feelings I felt going on between them. Then he ast her bout the project. And she gave out this big sigh like she was real tired of whatever it was and wished he hadn't brought up something not happy. She told him she was finished with it and that — in her own words — "it failed." He tried to cheer her up but she cut him off and told him that there was more important things in life. She said that after "much trial and error the damned things started coming up" and grew for at least three days, then something happened. But the most "brilliant moment" — Kirsten said — was when "the little guys bloomed so beautifully at three in the morning. The curse was nobody was there to see my success. You weren't there. Not my mom, not my dad, nobody! I was all alone. My hour of glory and I was all alone!" Then she went on to say that the "little guys died by morning." She sounded so sad it was like she was talking bout a pet cat or a dog. Juneboy — I could tell — knowed what she was talking bout. I kinda figured this speriment had something to do with this class she was teaching and maybe her research let her down.

She ast him bout his daddy, if he seen the grave yet. Juneboy's voice got real tight-like. Then he told her bout the parking lot. I thought he was gon start crying but he didn't. Then he went on, child, to say he was discovering his father and hisself, anyway, through us, all of us and a lot of things he forgot was coming back. I had the feeling he meant he was coming down off his high horse. He said his past and we didn't scare him anymore. He said one of his biggest fears was that he might get down here and feel out of place, like he didn't belong. And he said at first it was a little bit hard but that his Aunt Annie Eliza was so easy to be with that he was shamed of his own worry. I knowed what he meant cause I sensed how ill at ease the boy was at first. Then he told Kirsten bout Renee, bout her running for office, said he really liked the child. He went on and told his girlfriend bout seeing DeSoto and how good that was, how much he liked DeSoto, but the boy never mentioned one word bout Jeremiah.

Well, fore they hanged up they went through that whole "I love you and miss you so much" thing again. She wanted to know if he was still leaving for D.C. in the morning. Then he told her bout Emory University wanting him to give a lecture on his research Thursday morning. He told her he had rescheduled his leaving time for Friday morning and that he would call her the minute he got into D.C. She said she wanted to come down to see him right away, maybe Friday afternoon and spend the weekend. She told him they could see the new show at the National Gallery.

I eased the phone back after they finished and I laid there looking at the black and white movie and thought Juneboy musta heard the television in the background whiles he was talking but maybe he thought it was all the way in New Haven.

Then they flashed a bulletin bout the president's condition. The bullet had been removed and the president was in stable condition. They said the would-be assassin had been captured almost right off and was in custody. They didn't say where the bullet had struck. (I found that out the next day. The president was hit, you member, in the upper left thigh, real close to the you-know-what.)

That night I dreamed a dream I hadn't dreamed in a long, long time. I have had this dream, in different shapes and forms, since the kids was little. There I am, in the dream, getting up onto the Peachtree bus, going uptown—and this was in the days fore the super-expressways running through the city. I gets up onto the bus. The two boys are old enough to be walking by the time of this dream. I'm holding they hands. We steps up onto the bus. And, you see, this was after Martin Luther King, Jr., and Rosa Parks, mind you. I still feels, when I steps up onto the bus, I gots to go to the back of the bus, with my children. But in the dream I says, "Hell, I ain't going to the back of the bus. Me and my children, we gon sit in the first seats we can sit in." And there we sit. We sit and nobody bothers us. I got Jeremiah on one side of me and DeSoto on the other.

And I members Bibb's momma. She looked like a white lady. There was so many like her. Just goes to show you white mens been busy with the black womens from the start of all this. Bibb's momma use to walk right up on any bus going through Atlanta and sit anywheres she wanted to. That was how white she looked. You see, if sha felt like sitting in the back with her own peoples, if there was a seat, she sat, and if there wont no seat she sat in the first seat she found. Just amongst ourselves we use to laugh at the stupid way everything was run.

Later in that night I had a real bad dream. I think listening to Juneboy talking to Kirsten made me feel so bad about myself I got trapped in this bad dream. It comes only when I done done something real bad to my own self-respect. It was a dream bout Juneboy and Lauren. Everybody thought Lauren was the oldest cause she was the biggest. This was after Scoop and Esther broke up and Juneboy and Lauren was staying down with Momma and Poppa. Even though I dreamed this it really happened too. Momma was sending them to me for a week cause she had to go somewhere, a revival meeting or something. I got the date of they coming mixed up. They came from her to me and God knows I thought it was gon be the next day. Them two children sat in the bus station for twelve hours waiting for me to pick them up. They was too little to know to call me. Didn't even have my phone number. There was a holy woman, a nice lady, who had come in on the same bus with Juneboy and Lauren to see her folks and she saw these two little children still sitting there in the bus station when she was going back to where she came from — twelve hours later.

15

Wednesday morning fore anybody had any right to be up, me and Renee was in the back having coffee and talking real low so as not to wake Juneboy. She had done real fine, she said, on the talk show last night—and I believed her. One thing she can do, I got to give her credit, is run off at the mouth real well. She might not always knows what she's talking bout but she talks it to a real fine finish. She'd just run out from her house and come up here while the kids was still in they room watching the early morning cartoons and fore Jeremiah was up and about. She do this sometimes. She'll come over and have her coffee with me.

Then she said, "Momma, this is what I couldn't tell you Monday afternoon. I am about to help blow the lid off a racket. At the Farmer's Market, Juneboy and I saw with our own eyes what was going on. And it's not just tomatoes. It's turning out to be the whole fruit and vegetable industry in the state. And a lot of bigshots in this city are involved. The mayor's office is beginning to take us seriously. Jeremiah still says I'm barking up the wrong tree. He wants me to stop my investigation. He thinks I'm going to get in trouble, maybe shot or something. We've been fighting about it. But I can't let him stop me. Clarence Toussaint L'Ouverture Butler and I are going on TV in the morning to talk about this thing."

"Honey, ain't you just a little bit scared of sticking your neck out so far? You know necks can get chopped off."

"Sure, Momma. I thought about it. But I'm not going to let these people scare me off. Who does Cooper think he is, anyway?"

"Have you heard anything more—?"

"Nothing. He has this mysterious disease in his side. Nobody knows what it is. He's still at Grady. It's probably just cancer or something like that."

"Well, Renee, honey, you like my daughter," I told her, feeling a little false in saying so, "just like my own flesh and blood, and I don't want to see you in over your head. You know, I went to see Mayor Jones, trying to get him to—"

"I know, Momma. And I appreciate it, but—"

"How did you find out?"

"Clarence told me. I don't know how he found out. He said you made an eloquent plea on my behalf. But Momma, don't you see, the mayor is irrelevant. He is an old-fashioned country guy, full of corny stories about his own excesses. What's wrong with me—a woman—having a chance in this city? I won't bite my tongue about anything truly important.

"Momma, I'm sorry to be talking at you like you were some audience. It's just that I've been doing this every day now for over three months, at clubs, PTA meetings, civic groups, church groups. But you know, you are the only one I can talk to with complete openness. Jeremiah is supportive, sure, but he has his own concerns. You *listen* to me. Jeremiah just pats me on the shoulder and tells me how much he loves me."

"He loves you very much."

"Sometimes I wonder, Momma."

"Don't wonder. He loves you very much."

"I guess so. I hope so. God knows I hope so."

"I know he do."

* * *

Renee was gone at least a hour and a half by the time Juneboy got up. I heard him in the toilet. By then I had the television on. There was a commercial about menstrual pain, I mean these tablets you can take for it so you can go out playing tennis or jumping over fences or swimming, if you like. I ain't had to worry bout no menstrual pain in many a year, so the girl in the commercial was bout as far from me and my concerns as a airplane is from a snake. I thought back to my first period and how scared I was seeing blood coming outta me down there. Momma said, "Put a rag on, girl, and go back out there and help them other children pick that cotton." There was a lot of cotton that summer.

That was the summer Momma made me start doing everything and I hated her all summer. Ballard and Rutherford didn't have to wash clothes and cook and iron clothes and help Momma make lye soap and dumb stuff like them things. Ballard and Ruth got to help wring chickens' necks and chop wood and we girls got to cook the grits in the morning and warm the fatback grease to pour on the grits and wash the dishes. I always knowed we was doing more work than Ballard and Ruth but for a long time I thought that was the way the world was. Mens wont spose to do as much work as womens.

Then they showed a bright commercial about body scenting mist. And, child, I thought to myself, "Body scenting mist. Now, who in the world need to spray they body with body scenting mist?" The commercial told me I can spray it not just behind my ears or on my hands or arms and places like we spect but I can spray it in them secret places too. It said this stuff makes your confidence real powerful.

Juneboy finished in the bathroom and came out for his coffee, which I had already made for him. I felt guilty bout listening to his conversation and couldn't look him straight in the eyes at first but then I told myself, "Annie Eliza, you a old woman and what you does is accepted, so don't feel guilty. You only looking out for these young folks who still have they life fore them."

Juneboy ast, "Did I hear Renee talking this morning or was I dreaming?"

I laughed. "I'm sorry. Me and Renee got early coffee. We does that sometime. Hope we didn't wake you up, Juneboy."

He was moving round the table, holding his coffee cup, like he was trying to get some of its warmness into his hands.

"What'd she say about her show last night?"

I told him. And I told him bout the tomatoes — and bout how scared I was for her.

He sat down, looking at the television like he was still sleepy, kinda dazed-like, and said, "Aunt Annie Eliza, I wouldn't worry about Renee as much as you do, if I were you."

I told him I dreamed a dream bout the Farmer's Market. And I did! Cept in the dream I was a little girl tee-teeing on the outskirts of where they was having a old-fashioned marriage, maybe the marriage of my oldest sister, but that didn't make sense. It musta been a marriage of old folks, cause there was Momma and Poppa and they old friends and everybody celebrating like at a big homecoming back to our town of Monroe. I can see it just as clear as I see you. This couple, kinda old—second or third marriage—jumping over the broom to seal they marriage, just like in the olden days of slavery. I was tee-teeing like that cause that's the way we little childrens—and grownups, too—had to tee-tee when we was drinking a whole lot of punch at them big weddings and church gatherings.

And just as Juneboy was talking and I was thinking, the phone ringed and I ast him to answer it, since I was already getting ready to scramble him some eggs and fry him some bacon. I didn't want to talk to nobody nohow.

Child, it was Donna Mae. She was crying, out of her mind.

I said, "Donna Mae, calm down, talk to me. Tell me what you trying to say."

She said something bout Buckle. Child, the minute she said Buckle I knowed what her troubles was. That man, I tells you, shoulda been put outta his misery years ago, by hisself, I mean, cause you see that's what he's been trying to do all this time, is kill hisself.

". . . and Aunt Annie Eliza I went down there and caught him on his hands and knees and it seemed like to me he was licking the screen. But he claim he was adjusting the picture. Anyhow, I just went crazy—"

"Donna Mae, calm down. What you say Buckle did?"

"I think he was licking the television screen, Aunt Annie Eliza."

"Licking the television screen?"

"Yes, yes, yes, licking the screen. And there was these nasty peoples on the screen doing you-know-what, lots of them — and using their mouths and every other kinda opening they had. I tell you — "

"Donna Mae, Donna Mae. Oh, my Lord — the man's done lost his mind. Where is he now?"

"He down there in that basement. He won't come up."

"What you doing home this time a day?"

"My shift changed. He didn't spect me home, you see. I didn't spect him to be home either. He was spose to be at work. But he claims he came back home cause he wont feeling good. Says he got a fever and a sore throat."

"Child," I told her, "You just go down there and take that VCR off the set and lock it up somewhere where he can't get to it. The man sounds to me like he plumb sick to his soul."

"I guess I could do that. I hadn't thought about taking it from him. It's sorta like taking his bottle. He might die or something."

"You hang up now, girl, and go and take the VCR from that man for the good of his own soul. Hear me?"

"Yes, Aunt Annie Eliza."

"And you call me back if he gives you any trouble."

"All right."

I hung up and said, "Lord have mercy."

Then I told Juneboy. He looked real disgusted like he smelled something rotten. Then he said he felt sorry for Buckle. Poor Buckle.

★   ★   ★

Some mens from Emory came by and took Juneboy away round leven, for lunch they said. Juneboy told me just before he left with them that he had to discuss his lecture for Thursday morning. I didn't like the look of any of them mens that came for him. They was polite, sho, but they didn't seem to have no feeling for nothing else.

But you know, child, I was already getting tired of Juneboy being around. My life was so scattered cause of him being here, in my bed, and me on the couch — even if it is the place where I sleep most of the time — and everything, I just couldn't figure anything too straight. Just as I was feeling all of this and feeling sorry for myself and guilty at the same time for feeling it, Juneboy came back and I made us some tea. It musta been bout three.

I don't know what got into me, but I ast him bout his divorce and what his ex-wife was like and he looked like he didn't want to talk on it so I told him not to, and said I was sorry, but he said it was all right and he would talk on it.

"I was trying to work my way through college when I met Margaret," he said. "I had come back from the service and was ripe for falling in love, ripe for self-deception. Margaret had been going to some very private place before I met her. At this private place she was in communion with what she called spirits, the ancient spirits of all the women who had ever died, I think. She was strange but fascinating. Her father was a man in grief. He had accidentally killed a playmate when he was a child and now he went around like a man carrying a huge wooden cross everywhere he went. When people asked him why he carried the weight of this accident with him everywhere, he told them he had no choice. This was the man who raised her. You can imagine the influence. And her mother! Her mother had no sense of reality. Her whole life was one long struggle to keep herself poised correctly in the imagination of Margaret's dreary father. The mother was carried across streams. She was washed and rubbed and spared any unpleasantness. This sad man kept his wife totally removed from the real world. He thought this was what she wanted and she, too, assumed this was the life she had been born to live.

"Now, when I met Margaret the first thing she told me was this: 'You have come just in time. I thought you would never get here. I've been waiting all my life for your arrival.' Then she told me she had been walking on a long, long road but no matter how many steps she took, no matter how untiring her effort, she never made any progress, never advanced.

"When I met Margaret, she was a secretary in the History Department at Yale. I liked her intelligence. She read a lot. I even liked her sadness, at first. It was sort of like my own.

"She had been married before. The wedding was huge and quite plush. She had been handed over to her husband in the manner of the old days when families arranged marriages. Handed over to him for two reasons: his family had more money than hers and she was already pregnant with his child. At least she told everyone that her prospective husband was the father. She also felt that this husband was evil enough to deserve being deceived. She would marry him and literally put him through hell.

"For their honeymoon, they flew to a tiny island in the Pacific. While walking on the beach they came upon a dying dog. Margaret's husband wanted to put the dog out of its misery, but Margaret felt such sympathy for the dying dog that they got into a fight over what to do. Margaret won the fight. She sent her husband back to the hotel to fetch the hotel doctor. The husband returned minus the doctor — who refused to come — and Margaret pitched a fit! She accused her husband of being heartless and threatened to leave him if he did not bring the doctor. The poor guy returned to the hotel and again failed to convince the doctor that he should come to the beach to attend to a dying dog. When he returned to Margaret with the bad news, she sent him to town for the town doctor, but the town doctor also refused and the husband went to the doctor outside of town, on the edge of town, and this doctor, busy eating his lunch, also declined to return to the beach with the husband.

"Well, as you might have guessed by now, the dog, meanwhile, had died. Margaret never forgave her husband for the dog's death. She refused to have sex with him for three months. After the honeymoon, for days she made him play housekeeper in exchange for one kiss a day. He was grateful for even one kiss per day. When the wind of her lust blew through the house he tried to catch a sniff of it. In autumn, in summer, in spring, she kept him at arm's length. Through their first long, hard winter, she slept alone in the big bed and made him sleep on the couch. She bought a cake once in a cakeshop and had them write an insulting message to him on the cake. She had it wrapped and gave it to him. He unwrapped it, read the message, and broke into tears. While he was at work, she had her lovers in her arms in the bridal bed denied him. One Halloween night she played a trick on him so mean I cannot tell you, Aunt Annie Eliza. Well, my whole point is this: I should have known from these events that she was not going to be a good wife to me."

I ast Juneboy what happened to the child of her first marriage.

"She lost it in her second month."

"Her first marriage ended because she managed to get her husband entangled in a fight with one of her lovers. The lover killed her husband and did only five years for the murder."

I ast him didn't he know any of this before he got involved with this woman?

"Yes but I didn't want to know what any of it meant. I loved her, remember. I wanted to be happy. Our first child was born a year after the marriage. We gave a party for the baby. Margaret got into a fight with one of the other mothers. They threw things at each other. All the mothers there either took sides or snatched their babies and left. I came home right in the middle of it and almost lost an eye. A fishbowl was thrown at my head. I handed the lady who threw it a rose, just to try to comfort her. She tore it apart. The rose had been intended for Margaret, who wasn't anywhere in sight. Husbands came over and got into the brawl. One woman ended up naked out on the lawn and a boy delivering the evening news ran into a car backing out of a driveway because he was so struck by the furious naked woman. The boy's neck was broken and one hand was crushed underneath a tire.

"Our second child was born a year later. Margaret didn't like this one. She used to keep him in a dark room so she didn't have to see him. She fed him in the dark, changed his diapers in the dark, and raised hell when I brought the kid out into the light. She immediately took the boy back into the dark. The only daylight the kid ever saw was the daylight I exposed him to, when I was home. He became a creature of darkness, developed darkness habits, behaved like a night animal. His eyes eventually could not adjust to light.

"I knew I was unhappy with this woman but the habit of being with her, and even the habit of being with her sickness, had gotten into my system. Trying to leave her was like trying to stop smoking or drinking or having caffeine. I became comfortable with the habit of unhappiness, comfortable with the habit of Margaret.

"We had babysitters. Our sons were always happy to have babysitters. They loved them and wanted to marry them and go away with them to strange countries. Even when they were as young as three and four, they had these cravings. They also loved having the babysitters bathe them and tuck them in. Except when I tucked them in, these were the only times they were properly tucked in. Margaret had no patience for tucking in children about to drift into the deep pit of sleep. When children are about to go to sleep, they are terrifed that they will never return from the bottomless pit we call sleep. They need to be reassured that we will be here, waiting for them, and that if anything happens to them while they are down there, grazing and stumbling, we will be here standing guard, ready to save them from the mouth of the biggest monster of all — death. You know what I mean, Aunt Annie Eliza?"

"Sho, Juneboy. I sleeps myself every night."

"Yes."

He got real silent now. Just sat there looking down at the floor.

"So what broke up the marriage?"

"Huh?"

"What broke up — ?"

"Oh, Aunt Annie Eliza, if you haven't understood by now, I guess I can't find a way to explain!"

16

On the midday news the mayor was quoted as having said that womens with childrens shouldn't seek political offices.

Dale's sickness hadn't changed.

Jeremiah called me from his office and told me he had had a confrontation with Cherokee Jimmy. Jeremiah told Cherokee Jimmy that if he ever insulted me again he, Jeremiah, would personally kick his you-know-what for God Almighty.

This day was the anniversary of the day Mitch Wright was stricken down with a heart attack while talking to them civil rights children. The television man said flowers from the Urban League was being placed on his grave. They showed a picture of some peoples doing this. I had forgot this was the day he was kilt. There is so much to remember. No one person can handle it all.

Renee called just fore she went shopping to say that French John had clawed his way into one of the pillows on the couch. What was in there he needed, nobody knows.

I took my wig to my beauty shop lady. She washes it and presses it and makes it look real nice. I do this bout once every month.

I called Whitney at her law office up on Piedmont and ast her if she and DeSoto wanted to come over for dinner with me and Juneboy tonight. She said they already had a invitation.

Juneboy went out for a walk.

I read in the newspaper that some man had accused Senator Cooper of having approached him in a public toilet. They did not give the man's name.

There was nothing bout Renee's Greenhouse Tomato Conspiracy.

I member thinking: "I sho hope that gal know what she is doing."

I thought of Betsy down in the crazy house and wondered what she thought bout all day. It was clear she was losing her mind. I member Bob trying to protect her. He would lead her round like you see these retarded peoples being led round by folks who got good sense. At one point Bob and the rest of the family thought they would just keep her at home and not let her go outside, you know, keep her in her room and just feed her like that. That way, the family didn't have to be embarrassed. Then Mitch got into it and had a plan to have her sent out to the West Coast, to California, I think, where she was spose to get good care, but that plan never saw the light of day. Maybe Mitch had a fight with Bob or maybe there was too much money needed for the plan to work; so poor Betsy ended up being sent down to Milledgeville. She had something, though, when she was not crazy. She was a smart woman, a woman with lots of courage, child. She was what Momma called a go-getter and she didn't take no stuff off of nobody. Renee like that herself. That's where she gets her stubbornness from, I guess.

I membered when Renee served on the city council. First thing she did was go out and bought herself a whole new wardrobe. I thought, "Is that gal crazy?" Jeremiah never complained one bit. She started going to the council meetings like somebody going out on stage at some fashion show. Renee always had her way, long as I can remember. Some mens would have knocked her in her big head and made her be more practical.

Well, by the middle of the afternoon, while I was watching the soap operas, and wondering if Juneboy had walked somewhere where he got hisself into some kinda trouble with street thugs, the telephone ringed. It was Ballard calling from Spic and Span. He told me he was moving out. Donna Mae didn't want him to but he said he couldn't take it no more. Buckle was too much.

I ast him if he had a place.

No. That was why he was calling. He wanted to know if I knowed anybody with a room for rent, over my way. He wanted just a room, like in a family house, and use of the kitchen.

I thought on it, but while he was on the telephone I couldn't think of nobody with no room for rent round here. So, I told Ballard I would think on it till I came up with something.

Then I ast him bout his commitment to the house note and he said he was gon still pay it cause he had part ownership of the house and it was partly in his name too.

He ast me bout my arthritis and I told him it was pretty good today but that I thought maybe my cataracts was growing back cause when I watched the television I saw this haziness.

Then Ballard had to go back to work and I went back to my soap operas. A commercial for tennis shoes was on. They had this redheaded gal running after a tennis ball on a tennis court. You could see her shoes while the big voice in the sky called out that these shoes was the "ultimate" shoes.

Then a lady came on reminding everybody bout the voting dates. She told the date for the precinct caucus, August 12 was the date of the primary election and the general election was on November 4. The city elections, she said, was on November 3. May 7 was the school district elections. That was less than three weeks away. She gave the addresses of the polling places but I didn't pay no mind cause I knowed where mine was. It was always at Harriet Beecher Stowe High, just four blocks down from here.

While I was watching the television, I got to thinking bout Renee running for office and wondered if the public would accept her if they knowed bout Betsy. Now, somebody trying to keep her outta office might just start using that gainst the girl. I hoped she wouldn't have to run into that kind of embarrassment. But she was making herself more and more respectable every day. Why, that very morning I read in the newspaper she was asting for campaign support from wealthy business folks. The article went on to say that she was "articulate and dedicated." Dedicated to what? They listed her degree and all the clubs she was a member in. They even mentioned that she had been out to Los Angeles to study at the Urban Affairs Institute. She was a member in a lotta organizations I never even heard tell of:

National Conference of Christians and Jews, the Georgia Commission of Children and Their Families. On and on!

★ ★ ★

Later, I drove to the supermarket to get some things I needed. I had made out myself a list but walked right outta the house and left it on the kitchen table. I tell you, my mind just deserts me sometimes. But I didn't turn back cause I figured I could member most of the things on it anyhow. On the way, I had the car radio on and who do you think was talking on the colored station? Right! Renee. This was one of them interview shows. Renee musta been ast a question bout her opinion of Negroes in politics cause she was just talking up a storm, showing off how much she knowed and giving her opinion on everybody she could think of. She was talking bout everybody's right to vote. She went back through Atlanta history and gave her opinions on peoples like Benjamin Davis. Now, I member him. He was the editor of the *Atlanta Independent*. That man Davis was a good man. He stood for the rights of the poor peoples.

What I couldn't figure was how Renee learned all this history. Was they teaching these peoples in high schools and colleges now? Musta been.

I got to the parking lot of the supermarket and just turned off the motor and sat there with the radio on listening to the girl talking on and on bout her views, hoping my battery wont gon die on me. The man was asting her some of everything he could think of. Bout the Civil Rights Commission, bout the difference between the North and the South. She told bout a whole black nation set up in north Florida. I member Poppa telling bout that nation one time. But Georgia was a little bit different from the other slave states, Renee told the man. Georgia, she said, didn't care that much bout so-called uprisings. Georgia was more interested in using the slaves. Georgia even enlisted them in the — what was her word? — militia.

She talked bout us being the Deep South, like folks up North say. My daughter-in-law sho was something smart on the radio. I was beginning to think I would vote for her. Maybe I had had some bad ideas bout her cause of her love for clothes and material goods, you know, and the way she treats them kids and Jeremiah. But maybe she wont so bad, not as bad as I thought. And she do act like she cares bout me.

She talked bout these times too. All that trouble we had in the sixties. We wont as bad as the rest of the slave states. We was trying to follow the Supreme Court order here in Georgia. In 1964 we had the only desegregation system in the whole South right here in Atlanta. I member them days, I member them well. They was hard days. Very hard. We compared well to the other states round us. Renee reminded me of things I plumb forgot for a long time.

He ast her if she got her inspiration from the great black leaders of the past and she said yeah, part of it, she reckoned, but she got a lot of it from peoples out there nowadays, young peoples who ain't giving up hope, from peoples like her cousin Dr. Adam North doing research on sickle cell anemia at Howard University. She even told the man Juneboy was down here visiting and how inspiring it was to see him and know he was so committed to serious work to help humanity.

Then the man ast her bout these mens she's running gainst — Democrats and Republicans in the primary. In the quiet between his question and her talking, I heard her smiling, could see her. I turned the radio off.

I got myself outta the car and started cross the lot and just as I was waiting for a car to pass fore me, I looked up and seen the man driving the car and I swear fore God he looked just like Poppa when he was younger. He musta been Cherokee, full blood. It was so strange seeing somebody looking that much like Poppa all these many years after his death.

I guess I missed Poppa more than I ever let on. There was things bout him I didn't like sho, but I still missed him just as much as I missed Momma. I got a cart and pushed it into the supermarket and started down the first aisle. Poppa went a lotta places, specially fore he married Momma, but I don't think he ever saw anything like a supermarket — didn't live long enough.

He was in the First World War, the war to end all wars. I member stories he told bout being in France and the French womens. Momma would slap him playfully when he talked bout French womens with that silly grin on his face. He use to say he and the other soldiers had to fight the womens off there was so many of them after the American guys. He helped this one French girl a lot and even gave lots of canned goods to her mother and father. The white American soldiers didn't much care for the colored boys and Poppa messing with the French womens. I guess they was jealous. So there was a lotta fights between the colored and white Americans over the French womens. Course Poppa was Cherokee but he always passed for colored anyways cause that's the way he thought of hisself. On top of having to fight the white boys, Poppa had the bad luck of having a commander who was a redneck cracker from the sticks of Mississippi. And this cracker use to do all kinds of mean things to his colored boys. His whole company course was colored. That's the way the army was in them days — segregated by race.

But Poppa never let nothing depress him for too long. The cracker commander would say, "Olay, here's a mop. Mop the floor."

Poppa would say, "The floor was just mopped."

And the cracker would say, "So what? Mop it again." Things like that.

And Poppa would take the mop and whistle hisself a happy tune and mop the floor again. You see, he was just putting in his time. Poppa had a pretty good disposition most times.

Momma tended to be sullen a lot. She was one of them moody types. Course she could sing while she worked and in her own quiet way she could be happy too, but mostly she was not big on talking and she was usually in one of her moods. Peoples looked at her like she was somebody from somewhere else. See, she didn't exactly belong in Monroe. Some folks thought she was a hoodoo woman and they stayed way from her. But it was just her quietness that scared them off. Momma didn't know the first thing bout no witchcraft. Maybe it was her name, Eva Mae, that kinda scared peoples too. Evil Mae they called her.

None of us ever learned a whole lot bout Momma's background. All any of us knowed was that she had two or three sisters and no brothers and that she was raised mostly without a father. Some stories have it that she came from Alabama, others say her folks was riginally from Oklahoma or Texas. Maybe Momma never knowed for sure where she was born. I member once she talked on her father, said he was a soldier in the Civil War, and I think I even member seeing a picture of him — or somebody related to her — in a uniform. He was a handsome man with a broad face, wide cheeks and eyes like ice water, and this big handlebar mustache. Momma said they was all scared of him all the time. Everybody jumped when he came round. Even her momma got outta his way. He musta been a pretty grizzly fellow. Even after he died Momma and her sisters and they momma use to keep right on acting scared of him like he was still living. They was scared to touch his things, scared to go in his room and look through his drawers or in his closet. They kept his room locked up for a whole year after he died cause they thought maybe he might come back and if anything was touched he would get them all and turn them every which way but loose. They couldn't help feeling scared even though they all had seed him put down into the ground and the dirt throwed on the coffin.

Well, I done my shopping and while I tried to member my list by heart, I was thinking these thoughts bout Poppa and Momma and wondering how times flies and how little we ever get to know bout anybody, even our parents. It makes you wonder why anybody was born and live through a long life and then die. You wonder sometimes what it's all for, then you stop wondering and you member that life ain't so bad most of the time though you never know what's gon hit you next. Like poor Dale Cooper ending up with that strange wound in his side. If it ain't you, it's somebody else.

By the time I got to the checkout counter I had a carton of buttermilk, eggs, pork chops, a package of bacon, neckbones, a whole chicken, tomatoes, grapes, Cream of Wheat, sugar, Lipton tea, cake mix, a roll of paper towels, a box of wax paper, a box of aluminum foil, four rolls of toilet paper, a can of olives, a box of cornmeal, three cans of hominy, a box of grits, a bottle of vegetable oil, a bottle of aspirin — for my arthritis — and three bars of Camay face soap.

17

I was up two hours fore "Good Morning Atlanta" was to come on. I took me a shower. I knowed Juneboy wont gon be up fore seven, the time he ast me to wake him up. Them professors from Emory was gon pick him up at eight cause his lecture was to be at nine. It was still dark outside. The hot water made my arthritis go way, somewhat. Dr. Limerick try all the time to get me to take baths but, you know, they so much trouble compared to just standing there taking myself a shower. I just put my shower cap on and stand under the water five minutes, cleaning myself, and I'm done. After my shower I finished up in the toilet and went out to the kitchen and made some coffee.

I turned on the television and turned the channels until I got the early news. This Oriental lady from New York gives the early news. I likes her. She talks with a lotta intelligence and she got personality. Then there was a commercial for a Clairol product that "washes away the gray." The lady in it was spose to be my age but she looked like somebody twenty-five years old, ready to go out and rope a bull.

The president, the Oriental lady said, was recovering just fine. He would take a vacation at his other home after they let him outta the hospital there in Washington, D.C.

My coffee was ready. I took my first sip while watching a airline commercial showing a pretty island somewhere where there was a half naked dark woman swaying her hips on a beach with the moonlight behind her.

Then the Oriental lady told about a airplane crash. None of the peoples survived. I think she said over a hundred died in the crash. A very wealthy socialite was on the airplane. She said the lady's name like I was spose to know it, but I didn't. This socialite, said the Oriental lady, "cultivated a Europeanized personality" but she was just a American, you see, without them ancestors and great, long customs and traditions they have over there in Europe. The Oriental lady said the socialite was a "tragic figure" cause she was a dope addict, drank all the time, and I thought of peoples on "Dynasty" and peoples on "Dallas." That whole world of these peoples seem to me to be so far, far away. I never been farther away than Chicago.

Then they had the breakfast cereal, the typewriter, the girdle, the candy-coated almond, the dog food, the Chap Stick commercials on, and I watched them all while my coffee was cooling. I had nothing better to do.

I woke Juneboy at seven, then went back real quick to the back room to see "Good Morning Atlanta" coming on. They had the camera on Bill Hatton first, just like they always do. He told all what was gon happen this morning on his show, then they moved the camera to his co-host, Mimi Seucks, and she smiled her big old smile and nounced the special news, that is, that they was gon have special guests, Mrs. Renee Hicks, niece of the late Mitchell Wright, and Representative Clarence Toussaint L'Ouverture Butler, on to talk bout what they thought "is a serious breach of the public's confidence."

Meanwhile, the newsman gave the national news. Then in the local news he said, "Political fights for offices at the state and city levels are intensifying daily. Undisclosed sources have informed us that Congressman Fredrick Wright and the widow of Congressman Mitchell Wright, Councilwoman Sandra Valerie Wright, are in bitter disagreement over Mrs. Renee Hicks' bid for a state senate seat. Latest word is that Councilwoman Wright has come out in favor of her niece."

Child, that was news, if I ever heard news!

I could hear Juneboy closing the bathroom door, going in or coming out, I don't know which.

They showed Fred talking to a reporter. He said he was still going to vote for Senator Cooper. The reporter ast him what if Senator Cooper was too sick to take office? Fred said there was

no evidence that Senator Cooper wont gon recover from his
illness.

Then they showed Sandra. This same reporter was talking to
her, but at a different place, a street corner. I recognized it. It was
right in front of her office building. She said to the reporter that
she thought it was time for a change of representation in East
Point. Her decision, she said, didn't have nothing to do with
Senator Cooper's misfortune or with the rumors bout his sex
life. She spoke up for Renee, saying, "She did a fine job when she
was on the city council and I think she will bring integrity and
good will to the senate. I plan to vote for her."

Well, child, I tell you. I clapped my hands. For the first time I
think I liked Sandra, seeing her speak up like that.

Juneboy finished in the bathroom and came out and got
hisself some coffee and joined me in front of the television just
in time to see Mimi Seucks asting Renee and Butler the first
question. This was the first time I had seed Butler. He was one of
them slicked-down looking Negroes — you know, lots of grease
on the hair, and a gold tooth right in front. His eyes was red, too.
But he spoke with intelligence.

Miss Seucks ast Renee what she meant by "The Greenhouse
Tomato Conspiracy" and Renee come just a talking bout she and
this Butler fellow had evidence that some of the wholesale
houses was jacking up the prices on tomatoes they getting from
outta state and in the supermarkets and places the storekeepers
was selling these things at prices higher than they was spose to
sell them at. I couldn't figure who was making the profit but I
guess Renee knowed what she was talking bout. She sounded
like it anyways.

Mimi Seucks cut Renee off, saying, "What you're implying is
that state government is involved in interstate price fixing?"

"We're raising questions about evidence that points to that. All
the evidence is not in yet," Renee said.

Seucks said, "How much covert money are we talking about?"

Renee said she didn't know but she guessed it was thousands
and thousands.

Seucks said, "People are eating a lot of greenhouse vegetables and fruits."

Butler said, "It's the trend. Everybody wants to stay slim, so everybody's eating salads."

"Is this problem purely local? Tri-state?"

"At this point," said Butler, "it seems so."

"Yet it might be national—international," said Renee.

"Let's hope not," said Mimi Seucks.

Then the so-called press conference was interrupted by a commercial, this one was for eye shadow.

Butler and Renee was thanked and they was gone and then a commercial for fingernail polish came on.

Right after the show the telephone ringed and I said, "hello," and this mysterious voice said, "Annie Eliza Hicks?" and I said, "Yes" and he said, "You don't know me but I'm calling to tell you your son the preacher is mixed up in this Greenhouse Tomato Conspiracy. You might want to warn him that he's playing a dangerous game to say nothing of being on the wrong side of God."

Then the man hung up fore I could ast him who he was and what the devil he was talking bout, accusing Jeremiah of some nonsense like this tomato scandal. I didn't believe the caller for a minute. So many peoples is just plain jealous of Jeremiah. Every important man got his enemies.

But a little bit later I started wondering if it wont true. You know once a idea is put into your head you can't help but give it some mind. Besides, I don't know even half the things Jeremiah is involved in like his investments and things like that. But I do know he be all the time busy with them, even got the church investing in things. I know that much. I try to stay outta my boys business. They grown now and what they do they do on they own. They spose to know how to take care theyselves by now. That's what I was thinking. But this was one time I just couldn't sit back and do nothing. I decided to do my own investigating.

Who could I turn to, to find out? I could go straight to Jeremiah hisself and ast him, but he wont likely to tell me the truth if he was really mixed up in this mess. If he was, one thing for sho, Renee didn't know nothing bout it. If he was, God help us all.

I thought of calling that man Clarence Toussaint L'Ouverture Butler and trying to see if he knowed more than he was saying.

In the meantime I didn't say a word bout it to Juneboy. He was a outsider anyways and would be gone in no time.

★ ★ ★

Juneboy's professors came for him. One was out there in the car and the one that came up on the porch was one of the ones I think I saw before. Juneboy was all dressed up in a suit and a necktie and he looked real respectable.

These peoples make me feel like I'm just a pickaninny. You know my joke bout the pickaninny? You don't? Well, I'll tell you sometimes. I once told it to a lady I worked for. I use to wash and iron for that lady, did it for many, many years. She was good to me during hard times. She was the only white folks I felt comfortable enough with to joke, like. I use to go to her house on Monday morning and wash her clothes. Monday was the wash-day, you know. I washed her clothes, and I would go on to some other woman's house and wash her clothes too, and then on to another woman's house, wash her clothes, clean her house, sweep her yard or basement, whatever. I always had a objective in my mind, you see. I knowed what I wanted outta all of this. I had to survive. Bibb was dead. I had the boys. I wanted the boys to grow up to be important peoples. That was my objective: to give them a chance, a life.

So I washed clothes for a lot of womens who didn't want to or have to wash them for theyselves. Sometimes I would go in early and wash and then go back later in the afternoon and fold and put away the clothes. I ironed britches and dresses and even diapers. I ironed for ladies who was not too happy theyselves. They was just there in the house and had children they had to deal with all day. I helped them for years. I tell you, I never envied any of them. They was a sad, miserable bunch of peoples.

* * *

I called Mr. Butler right after Juneboy left. But there was only his answering machine. I left my number and ast him to call me. Bout a hour later he called and I told him who I was and told him I wanted to talk prudentially with him and made him promise not to tell nobody bout our conversation. When he knowed what I wanted to talk bout he said he would come over now.

He got hisself here, child, in no time flat. You shoulda seed that man coming in all outta breath. I poured the poor man a cup of tea and we sat at the table and I told him bout the telephone call and what the voice said bout Jeremiah. He smiled and said it mighta just been a crank call and that he hadn't heard nothing bout Reverend Hicks being involved in this situation. He did know, he said, that a company called Georgia Fruit and Vegetable Company was one of the leading outfits laundrying money. I didn't know what laundrying money meant but I let him go right on talking.

Then he gave me this sharp, squinty-eyed look and said that since I swore him to secrecy he kinda felt like he had the right to ast me to keep a secret too.

I told him sho.

He said Senator Blackmore had some evidence that Senator Cooper was up to his neck in tomatoes. I gave Butler a look. The way I figured it, Blackmore had many reasons for wanting to dig up some dirt on Cooper. But then Butler told me that Cooper had money invested in this Georgia Fruit and Vegetable Company. He said it was the biggest fruit and vegetable wholesaler in the state.

After Mr. Butler left, I thought for a long while bout calling Senator Blackmore and I even thought of calling that Georgia Fruit and Vegetable Company. But what would I say? Would they tell me anything?

I had the whole morning ahead of me but the only thing I had to look forward to was my soaps. This Thursday morning there was a story on one I don't mostly watch, a story that reminded me of the time we had a house guest that stayed too long. Poppa always said, "Fresh fish and house guests should be throwed out after three days." These peoples in the story on the television was having a time trying to get along with the mean old son-of-a-gun, her father — a widower — come to spend some time (how much he ain't said yet) with her and her husband. At first, the first day or two, everything was fair as a middling and spick as a ham. Then long come the third day, and wooooh.

Our visitor was Momma's favorite preacher. And, child, you know how preachers can overstay they time and overeat they share! That man near bout put us outta house and home! Poppa kept trying to get Momma to stop killing and cooking all the chickens in the yard. He said even a preacher ain't spose to eat chicken like every day in the week was Sunday.

Well, this preacher was the first fella who ever tried to get into my panties. I tell you this cause I know you won't tell nobody. That man was a hog, child. The minute my poppa turned his back and the minute my momma left the room, he was all under my dress. I was too young to know anything bout the real thing. I had ideas. I saw the roosters get the hens. I saw the pigs do it. And I knowed bout male and female, generally speaking, you understand.

He got his finger in.

I kinda pushed him away, you see. Knowing he was Momma's hero, I didn't much want to pitch a fit. Momma might have got her switch on me, and I already had scars from the last beating I got — for letting a boy tote my books home for me.

But pushing him away didn't stop that man. He had got his finger in and he wanted more. Every chance he had, whenever Momma and Poppa and the rest of the family was not watching, he had his hand up my dress.

He begged me to let him just stick the tip in and he swore up and down that just sticking the tip in wont gon do no harm. A gal couldn't get pregnant from just having the tip stuck in.

I kinda halfway believed him. Sticking the tip in didn't seem like so much to worry bout.

But I thank the Lord today, he never got his chance — though I was, after the third day of his pushing on me, curious enough to let him try it.

* * *

I finally got up the nerve to call Senator Blackmore but his secretary told me he was not available. I left a message saying I had information bout the Greenhouse Tomato Conspiracy. And wouldn't you know it, Senator Blackmore hisself called me right back in five minutes. He wanted to know what I knowed. I told the man bout the call accusing my son and I could hear him freeze on the other end and I regretted it the minute I said it cause I thought to myself, "Maybe if Jeremiah was innocent this man might get him in trouble anyhow," but it was too late. I cared more bout the truth than I did bout Jeremiah's innocence. I'm a woman of God. Like Jeremiah spose to be a man of God. I could hear the senator start breathing again. I told him I was only interested in finding the truth. I told him I knowed bout his investigation. I told him I thought the call was a crank call. I wanted to know, I said, how much he knowed bout this scandal. He said he knowed nothing bout Reverend Hicks being involved and that he thought the call might be cousins to the fact that some woman, he knowed for sho, who was a member of Hicks' church, was definitely involved. Child, this was news to me. I wondered who she could be and I ast him, but he said he couldn't tell me her name cause of his investigation.

He ast me if the man who called sounded colored or white. I told him I didn't know. And I didn't. Nowadays you can't always tell the way you could twenty years ago.

The senator told me to call him if the man called again. In the meantime, he said he was gon try to find out what he could to make sho my son wont mixed up in this thing. I thanked him and hanged up. Then I started crying cause I was so scared and I knowed I had just done the wrong thing by talking to this man.

But I kinda got over it in a hour or two.

★ ★ ★

I was all wrapped up in my soaps and worrying bout Jeremiah when the telephone ringed and all I had to do was reach over my head and lift off the receiver. It was DeSoto. Now, child, brace yourself. I had to brace myself. DeSoto said, "Momma, Jeremiah's been shot."

I leaped up from the couch like I was sixteen.

"Shot? Jeremiah shot?"

"Yes, Momma."

"Why? Where? Where is he?"

"He's at Grady. I just took him."

"DeSoto, DeSoto! Is he gonna die?"

"No, Momma. I don't think so. He was shot through the ear. You see, he was shot only through the left ear. They got to — "

"Shot through the ear? DeSoto, what do you mean?"

"Listen, Momma. I got to hang up. I'm at the hospital. There isn't any need for you to come up here. Jeremiah will be released in the next hour or two."

Oh, you can imagine how upset I was! Jeremiah — shot? And, silly game, shot through one ear? Jeremiah? A highly respected member of the community, a leader, a man of God? A man of God do not get shot through the ear.

I waited for them. I knowed they both was gon come. They wouldn't a been my boys had they not come, in a time of troubles. They had to come to me — or bring me to them. When everything else broke down, we was all we needed. We was alone, otherwise.

Sho nuff. DeSoto and Jeremiah came up on the front porch two hours later. It musta been bout one. I never saw DeSoto looking so pleased to be leading his older brother, the big man of the family. DeSoto sorta had this smarky grin on his face. You could tell he sho had some plans.

DeSoto said, "Momma, don't ask any questions."

I helped him take Jeremiah to the back room.

We put him down on the couch.

The television was still going.

I was very upset and at the same time happy to see Jeremiah and being able to tell that he wont gon die from the bullet wound.

First thing I ast Jeremiah, once he was lying in my spot, the spot where I lie to watch television, was "Who shot you, my son?"

And he said, "Momma, a villain shot me."

DeSoto was standing right there by me. I didn't know if I trusted either one of them to tell me the truth. I wanted the whole truth. Jeremiah wont looking me in the eye and I knowed what that meant.

I gave him a look. "What you mean, a villain, Jeremy?"

"An ungodly person, Momma."

DeSoto come just a throwing his arms bout like he was having a fit. "Momma, I told you not to ask him questions. Can't you see he's still in shock?"

"In shock?"

"Yeah, in shock, Momma. Don't ask—"

"De, Momma can ask me any question she wants. I've got nothing to hide."

I was standing right there in front him, looking down at the boy, waiting. "Well, I'm waiting."

It was just like when they use to come in after school sometimes and had been fighting with other boys on the way home and I had to demand the whole story and they would beat round the bush. One time they came in like that, both with bloody noses. I ast what happened. They said they was trying to help a boy named Pip get away from the police. The police was gon kill him if they got they hands on this Pip. What had the boy done wrong? They said he hadn't done nothing wrong, all he done was defend hisself gainst some white boys who jumped him first, he accidentally killed one of them. But you see, they said, Pip had been minding his own business when these white boys came on him in White Park.

I told them, "Even so, nobody was spose to go round killing nobody."

They said, "But it was a accident."

"Still," I said, "the law was the law." And I told them they could get in trouble helping Pip escape. And they said they didn't care, they would go to the lectric chair with Pip. But, as I recall, some of Pip's relatives helped him get outta town and he was sent up North somewhere and nobody ever heard from him again.

There was another time when Jeremiah almost got hisself sealed up in a cellar. Again, they was playing with bad boys. DeSoto came in crying out of his mind and he led me to the place where Jeremiah was in the cellar of this old bandoned house. The boy couldn't get out. As it turned out, some boys— colored boys, this time—had lured Jeremiah into the cellar by telling him there was something down there real good waiting for him. But he had to go down to get it. I later figured out it was that old nasty gal Pattie round here giving herself to all the boys and mens in the neighborhood. Well, they just told Jeremiah Pattie was down there and Jeremiah being a virgin and knowing so many of the other boys had been with her—cause they bragged on the playground bout it—he was anxious to get his little thang in her too. Mannish boy! I don't think DeSoto was there at first. One of the boys told him bout it later and he went to the cellar but couldn't get Jeremiah out. You see, they only told Jeremiah this Pattie was down there waiting for him but she wont. Well, child, I took me a axe to that door till I got Jeremiah outta there. Them boys had nailed it tight. They was some mean little devils.

Now I was waiting for Jeremiah to talk to me like I use to wait back then and he was stalling now just like he had something real bad to tell me and knowed he was gon get a punishment for what he done.

I was looking at the big bandage on his left ear. It looked like that picture of that crazy artist who cut off his ear. You know the one I mean.

"Well, Momma, I was only trying to help this woman, you see. She came into my church just a little over a year ago."

"Who is she, Jeremy?"

"I don't need to tell you that, Momma. Just let me finish. She already had two children, a boy and girl, out of wedlock. She was divorced, or so she told me. But she wasn't divorced at the time she told me she was. She didn't file for divorce till just a month ago. She was separated."

"Get to the point, Jeremy," I told him. Right then and there when he was talking I made up my mind to find out who this woman was.

"I am, I am, Momma."

"You see, she couldn't work because she has this mysterious nerve disorder. She has to lie down suddenly sometimes. She might just fall out in the street somewhere or on a bus. She has to be careful about driving a car because the attack can come on her without warning. She's living with her mother out in Power Springs but she used to live in the city when she was married. Her mother helps her with the children. As her minister, I used to—"

"Jeremiah Bluford Hicks, stop beating round the bush!"

DeSoto was still twitching but less so. He was listening too, as best he could while twitching like some old junkie.

"Momma, what I did was no different from what I do for all my congregation. I stop by to visit many members of my church. The first time I went out to Power Springs to pay this sister a visit she was lying on the couch, helpless, unable to even get herself a glass of water."

"Where was her mother?"

"Her mother was out shopping and the children were in school. I opened the screen door and let myself in, because I could see her lying there on the couch through the screen door. I figured she was having one of her attacks. I did what I could for her. I sat there beside her and held her hands and prayed to the good Lord for her speedy recovery. And when I finished praying she told me a story that charmed my heart. She said when she was a younger woman, before she was married, she had been very lonely, and had tried to cure that loneliness by always seeking out large gatherings of people—crowds. She spent all of her time on buses and at busy intersections and in busy coffee shops and in department stores and she went to every parade she knew about. She had this pain deep inside where she couldn't stop hurting. I felt very sympathetic toward her, especially since I could see that pain she spoke of right there in her sad, sad eyes. Well, that was the first time I ever visited her home.

"The next time, about a month later, no, maybe two weeks later, she was well, and her mother was home. Her mother seemed a little suspicious of me. The mother was not a member of my church. She was Catholic. I tried to be friendly toward her mother but the old woman just wouldn't let me. I had already met the boy and the girl in church because they always came with their mother.

"Sometimes when I went out there she and I would go for walks in Wild Horse Creek Park. Our talk was purely spiritual. I had only her interest at heart. I was not trying to go to bed with this woman, Momma. I know what you're thinking."

"You don't know what I'm thinking, Jeremiah. I'm thinking I'm gon shoot off your other ear if you don't get to the point."

He gave me his sorry look. "The point was I was kind to her and she turned villain on me. I never meant her any harm. I even taught her to sing spirituals. I taught her 'Every Time I Feel the Spirit' and I taught her 'Give Me That Old Time Religion.' She thought she knew how to sing these songs but I taught her the right way. Then she turned on me today."

"She just up and shot your ear off?"

"We drove out into the country. Took twenty out. We were walking in the woods. I was reciting some verses from Luke and just walking along beside her, feeling quite happy. I just put my arm around her in a friendly manner. Just being friends. And suddenly she snatched this little pistol out of her purse and shot me. I pushed her just in time, otherwise she would have got me straight through the head, between the eyes. I swear, Momma, she was aiming for my forehead."

I looked at him a long time. I looked at DeSoto looking at Jeremiah. I could tell by the look on DeSoto's face that he already knowed this much and more. I smelled a rat. I can always tell when my boys is lying to me.

"Jeremiah, till you get ready to tell me the whole truth, go on home and let your wife tend to you, son."

He just lay there looking down at his hands, resting on his thighs.

Then DeSoto helped him up.

When DeSoto got Jeremiah in the car I went out and grabbed DeSoto by the back of his shirt, child, and marched that boy right back up the steps and into the house just like I use to do when he was a little old mannish boy. I pushed him gainst that wall right over there and I said, "Listen here, young man, you gon tell me right now who that woman was who shot off Jeremiah's ear. You ain't walking outta here till you do!"

He come just a grinning and looking foolish.

I shook him. "Don't forget I can still take you cross my knee and teach you a lesson."

He was looking so surprised I almost laughed and messed up the whole act.

Then I softened up a little bit on him. I couldn't help it. I said, "Tell me, DeSoto. I won't breathe a word of it to Jeremiah."

He wanted to know why I wanted to know.

"Cause I feels insulted," I told him, "when you and Jeremiah treat me like a child. It makes me real mad."

"Ah, okay. Her name is Marianne Plains."

"And her address?"

"Momma, I don't know her address. You're not going over there are you?"

"Course not." I turned him loose. "You better not be lying to me, DeSoto. I'll come and get you. You know that."

"I'm not lying; that's her name. Don't you know her from church?"

I couldn't place that name on no face that came to mind.

"Okay," I said. "Not a word of this to Jeremy. You hear?"

"Course not. He'd kill me if he knew I told you."

"He won't find out. You run on and take him home."

"Yeah. Renee's going to kill him anyway."

"She should."

* * *

I looked up Marianne Plains in the phone book and called her.
The minute she spoke through the phone, I saw her face in my
mind. I knowed the voice. I didn't know her cept on sight. Had
not done more than say hello in passing. The younger womens
in Jeremiah's church don't have much to do with us older gals. I
member somebody saying she had a good paying government
job of some kind. She was real pretty too. And educated. She
could speak well when you heard her talking. That's what I
membered when I heard her speak.

I told her I was Jeremiah's mother. She told me to call her
lawyer, that she had nothing to say to me.

I said, "Young woman, I am not calling you to complain.
Maybe you had a right to do what you did. I don't know. I'm
calling you bout tomatoes."

She got real quiet then. Then she wanted to know what bout
tomatoes. I told her I wanted to meet with her and talk bout the
Greenhouse Tomato Conspiracy.

She told me to come to her house.

She gave me her address and I wrote it down on the pad by the
phone. I told her I would try to get there in the late afternoon. I
told her I would call just fore I got started.

She said okay.

* * *

I knowed Renee was gon raise hell. I was just waiting and
wondering how she was gon do it. What kinda story was
Jeremiah gon make up for her this time?

It didn't take long.

Bout two hours later Jeremiah came flying back into my house
saying Renee was trying to kill him. He said she got the butcher
knife at him. He didn't look any more hurt than before so I was
not too worried. They'd fought before.

Two minutes after he came in, here come Renee herself—all red in the face but she wont carrying no butcher knife.

Jeremiah was in the back on the couch and scrunched up like he use to do when he was a boy and didn't want nobody to touch him.

She come just a talking to me in this hysterical voice and going on bout what a rotten scum Jeremiah was. Said he had lied to her bout his ear. He went home and told her he had been in a slight accident in Deacon Ben Smith's car while Deacon Ben Smith was driving. But what Jeremiah didn't know was that Renee had already heard bout him being treated at Grady for a gunshot wound in the ear. Who told her I didn't know at the time and if I knowed later on I done forgot now. I knowed I was gon have to referee again.

She shot on back there like a bull charging a red cape and standing there in front of him with her hands on her hips she said, "Now, Reverend Hicks, why don't you repeat for your mother what you said to me regarding the trouble with your ear?"

He didn't say nothing.

"Cat's got your tongue, Reverend?"

"Renee," he said, "I'm not going to argue with you. I was simply trying to spare you."

"Spare me?" she shouted. "Spare me *what*, Reverend?"

"The details of—"

"The details of your love life?"

"That woman is a member of my church and that is the extent of my concern with her. I don't have to lie to you about anything. My conscience is clean and the Lord is my witness."

"Leave the Lord out of this, Jeremiah. You're talking to your wife now, not your congregation. Where were you when she shot you?"

"What difference does it make?"

"Okay. Maybe it doesn't matter where. Would you care to tell me *why* she shot you?"

"I'm tired Renee, I'm tired."

Renee looked to me like she was at her rope's end. I felt sorry for her. Even if he was my son, I didn't like him very much as I stood there just behind Renee looking at him.

"I'm tired, Renee, I'm tired," she said imitating his voice. "Too tired to be honest with your own wife, huh?"

He didn't say nothing.

I said, "Jeremiah, it ain't none of my business, but I don't see how you can have the Lord as your witness and at the same time treat your wife the way you doing here right now. Least thing you owe her is the truth, no matter what it is."

"Momma, I'm telling Renee the truth, she just never believes me. She's always looking for lies. I've had nothing to do with that woman and none of the women in my church."

Me and Renee just looked at him. We both knowed that was a lie and it looked like maybe the lie itself was his truth and if he believed it there was no way she or me could change the way he saw things in his own self-interest.

Renee just started crying, sobbing big tears. Her shoulders shook, and I took her in my arms and patted her back. She cried gainst my shoulder for a long time, telling me through her crying bout all the times in the past when she knowed he was involved with various womens in his church. I let her go on and tell me bout the times even though I already knowed bout them.

Well, she cried herself sick and I ended up walking her back to her house leaving Jeremiah at my place.

★   ★   ★

After they was gone I got on the phone and called this gal Marianne Plains and told her I was on my way. While driving out there I was listening to the radio news like I usually do. The newsman said that Dale Cooper had made arrangements to go to Boston to see a doctor who was gon test him for this disease called coreyox. I smiled to myself and prayed a silent prayer for the man from the bottom of my heart.

The house was nice and in a nice block near Wild Horse Creek

Park. Marianne Plains was the woman I thought she was, the one I membered from church. Real pretty, like I say. The government girl. She was one of the few single young womens in Jeremiah's church. I membered hearing a lot of the menfolks was after her skirt.

She ast me to come in. She led me into her living room. My fingers was hurting and I almost had a mind to ast her for a glass of water so I could take my medicine. But I didn't.

She ast me to sit down. I did. I sat on the couch and put my purse on the floor by my leg.

She sat down across from me giving me this stiff look like she thought I was gon slap her.

I just looked at her. I was gon bluff. I said, "You and Jeremiah is up to your necks in trouble with this tomato business, young woman. You may as well tell me everything. I might be able to help you and my son. The mayor is a personal friend of mine."

She got stiffer. "I have no idea what you are talking about, Mrs. Hicks."

I told her she knew very well what I was talking bout. I told her Senator Blackmore was bout to go to the police with what he done found out bout laundrying and I told her it looked like a lot more than tomatoes was involved. I said maybe the whole fruit and vegetable market in Georgia was involved.

I could see her giving this some thought. Then she said, "Jeremiah is the only one I know then who's in trouble, Mrs. Hicks. I'm in no way involved."

"You shot Jeremiah today cause he double-crossed you, didn't you?"

She got all excited and her voice got real high and squeaky. "No," she said. "I shot him because he attacked me." She gave me a soft look and her voice came down some. "I know this is hard for you, being his mother. But Jeremiah is no angel." She took one of them deep breaths, you know. Then she said, "My former husband used to beat me. After I got away from him, I promised myself that if another man ever tried to beat me I was not going to take it lying down."

Gainst my own will, I believed her. But child, you know, I didn't want to. She looked so little and helpless sitting there fore me!

What would happen to the family and the church if this vegetable mess was connected to Jeremiah? I almost decided right there to get up and leave. I didn't want to hear no more. But you know I couldn't do that.

I said, "I know Jeremiah ain't perfect but he is a good preacher and maybe the only reason he ain't pressing no charges gainst you is cause he has the power to forgive."

"I'm sorry, Mrs. Hicks, but you are wrong. Jeremiah wouldn't get anywhere by pressing charges against me. And he knows it. I was only defending myself."

"But you tried to kill him."

"I was only trying to stop him from hitting me."

She got up and came over to me and got down on her knees and lowered her head.

"Feel this spot," she said. She led my hand with her own to a big lump on the top of her head. Then she said, "He hit me with a bottle right there after he had punched and kicked me for twenty minutes. That's when I got away from him and got my gun."

I felt ashamed for Jeremiah. Lord, child, I didn't know what to do. I was so ashamed, I almost cried. And yet I still didn't want to let myself believe her.

She stood up and went back to her seat. "No, Mrs. Hicks. I am the one who should press charges. But don't worry. I won't."

I looked at her as straight as I could. "Why do you say my son is in trouble with this vegetable business?"

"Because he is a leading stockholder in the Georgia Fruit and Vegetable Company. So is Senator Cooper. Mrs. Hicks, your son has been buying tomatoes and other fruits and vegetables from Mississippi and Florida farmers at very low prices and selling them on the market as though they were grown in Georgia. He's laundered the profit and has stashed it away in accounts in foreign countries. I know of one in Switzerland because I saw the bankbook."

"Why should I believe you?"

"Don't. Ask Senator Blackmore. You said you're in touch with him."

"He said my son wont mixed up in this thing."

"You asked me to tell you about it and that's all I did. I can't make you believe me and, frankly, I don't give a damn if you don't. I sort of hope they fry his behind."

I grabbed my purse and stood up.

She stood herself up too. She looked like a young racehorse, child.

"I don't have to listen to you talk that way, Miss Plains. You tried to kill my son. Now you, you — "

"Actually, Mrs. Hicks, I don't really wish your son any harm. I once loved him. I also once trusted him and believed him. A year ago he started telling me he was going to divorce his wife and marry me. I gave up on that dream slowly but surely. He was lying from the beginning. And now he's just not that important to me anymore. But, you see, I won't take physical abuse from any man."

I left in a fit of anger. I tell you I coulda chewed nails — and digested them too — I was so mad! Mad at Jeremiah. Mad and shocked. He had no skuse to be mixed up in this crooked mess. And I just knowed he was, felt it deep in my bones. My whole body was in pain just like my mind. I spoke out loud right there in the car to my son, said, "Wheresonever you may be, you lucky to be there cause right now if'n you was here I'd strangle you myself."

I was driving so crazy-like I almost had a accident cause I ran a stoplight. You know they take your license if you as old as me and you have accidents.

Anyways, I got myself home safely but I was still mad. Fuming! I didn't spect Juneboy to be back from his scientific peoples yet and he wont. The minute I walked in DeSoto called. He said, "Guess what, Momma?"

"What?"

"I found out who that boy was."

"What boy you talking bout?"

"Cooper's sick boy. Remember?"

"Yeah. Well, who is he?"

"His nephew. Cooper's brother's youngest child. He died the night Cooper visited him. Police medical report says the death may have been caused by something called coreyox. The special guys got a lot of the story wrong. Cherokee suspected something else — remember? It was nothing like that. Cooper was visiting his brother, Vincent, and his family that night. I saw the death certificate an hour ago. I thought you'd like to know."

Yeah, I wanted to know all right but there was still a heck of a lot of unanswered questions. Would Dale die too from this strange disease? Was Jeremiah going to go to prison? What would happen when Renee found out — if there was something to find out?

I started thinking real hard bout going to see Dale Cooper. I just needed to get my nerves up to do it. And I didn't want to catch nothing.

But first I had to talk with Jeremiah hisself. It took all my energy to control myself and try to stop shaking. I was talking to myself like I ain't done in years. I was telling myself what I was gon do to that rascal.

I called him at home and told him I had to talk with him. I told him to get over here right away. He understood my tone of voice.

Jeremiah was here in ten minutes. The minute I saw the rat my heart just pulled it old self to a stop and I membered him little. Part of me still wanted to sock him for the stupid thing he done. But running over here like he done impressed me. That's good for him to have to hop for somebody cause he don't never have to do it.

"What is it, Momma?"

"Sit down, son." Real sudden-like, I felt myself real calm. We was in the back. We sat at the table. "Are you doing illegal things, Jeremiah?" I felt calm but I guess I wont. Maybe I was trying to keep from going crazy.

"What are you talking about, Momma? Of course I'm not."
He jumped up and rammed his hands in his pockets and started
pacing like he do, you know. He stopped and frowned at me.

"Tomatoes. Georgia Fruit and Vegetable Company. Laundrying. Lying bout cost. Jacking up prices. Thems the things I'm
talking bout, son."

"Ah, Momma, you been listening to some nonsense! Who've
you been talking to?"

I know my boy. I ain't watched him lie since he was a tot for
nothing. I knowed he was lying now. At that point, child, my
heart broke completely. I didn't even want to ast him no more
nothing! I tell you I was so heartsick I coulda died right there in
that chair.

18

Juneboy came back from his scientific peoples at Emory. I ast him how his lecture went, if he was happy with hisself and the peoples listening to him talk. He come just a giving me some of his old crazy talk, saying, "I can't blame it on the configuration of the stars. I simply don't know why there is such a gap between me and the audience. These were science students, people who are going to be internists, dentists, psychologists."

I said, "Juneboy, maybe you don't explain yourself so as peoples can understand what you mean."

"Maybe you're right."

He and me sat at the table in the back room. It was still too early for dinner. He said that maybe I was right bout him. The television was still on, but low. I could halfway hear what was going on on it while Juneboy and me talked. He said: "Yeah, maybe you're right," a third time. Then he went on to say, "Aunt Annie Eliza, when I was in grad school I thought I was going to set the world on fire. My plan was to become the greatest researcher in the area of sickle cell known to nations." He held his hands out like he was holding the globe in them. "I was too cynical though," he said. "I started out too cynical. I meant a kind of concern for people but I now think that there was something a bit too fatalistic in my personality. I was reckless. If I'd become a surgeon I probably would have found myself making moral judgments in the operation room. This guy can live because he's a good guy, in my opinion; this other guy must die, because he is a bad guy. Sometimes I think it's the way teachers graded papers when I was in school. If they liked you, you made it. If not, you didn't."

While Juneboy talked I was thinking how strange a fellow he was and how unlike the boys, my boys, he was. It couldn't have been the difference growing up in the North made, now, could it? Sometimes I thought Juneboy lived in some kinda dream world. And it wont so much what he said that made you think this. It was more *how* he said things, in that far-off voice of his.

Well, I was glad he would be gone by tomorrow morning. Not that I hadn't enjoyed having him here with me. It was a pleasant change for me, even with all the trouble that started coming the minute he got here, and kept right on, from that Thursday through to the second Friday.

*   *   *

While I was making us dinner Renee called and said, "Momma, I got great news! Mayor Jones just called me. He's changed his mind about supporting Cooper. He's going to go public in my support tonight on the late news. Isn't that *wonderful?* And I owe it to you. Your going to him, I'm sure, helped —"

"Well, well, bless my soul," was all I could think to say. "Well, now I thinks the peoples will support you."

"And that's not all. Senator Cooper's been released from Grady. He was released today at noon. That's what I've heard. He has to remain in bed. Some doctor in Boston is supposed to know about his disease. He's hired a private nurse to tend to his needs."

"What's happened to his friend Cherokee Jimmy?"

"I have no idea. Jeremiah and Cherokee had a fight —"

"I know —"

"Now, the only turkey I have to worry about is Tommy Blackmore."

"But what about that other Republican, Senator Kidd McCarthy?"

"He hasn't got a chance, not with his past record!"

"Well, Renee, looks to me like you on your way."

". . . And I appreciate your support, Momma."

Hearing her say that, I felt guilty cause at least at first I hadn't thought she would make a good leader. And I wont telling her all I knowed. And I wont letting on how scared I was for her and the whole family but specially Jeremiah. I just didn't know what to do at that point. I was just holding my breath, child, and hoping for the best, praying to the Lord for help.

★   ★   ★

During dinner Juneboy ast me what it was like when Esther and me was growing up down in Monroe.

"What you mean?"

"I mean, were times hard? Did you have to work all the time? Were you able to play?"

"We played and we worked. Probably we worked more than we played. Why?"

"I asked because at times I think Mother is so unhappy and it seems to me that she has always been a tormented person. And you know personality traits are established in the earliest years. I just wondered if she was mistreated as a child."

"Heavens no, Juneboy! Momma and Poppa was good to all of us. They might not have had the time to pay a whole lot of tention to each one of us every minute of the day but they sho took care of us and we never went hungry. Sometimes a bunch of us had to sleep in the same bed—and get peed on by the little ones and that kinda thing—but we was a happy family. Your momma was a happy child and she wont overworked. She never worked any more than the rest of us. We all had our chores, you know."

He didn't look like he was put at his ease with my saying what I said bout me and his momma and the rest of us.

"Mother once told me she was sent out in the middle of the night to the outhouse rather than being allowed to use the slopjar. She didn't say why. Just that Grandmomma ordered her out into the night. She was terrified of the dark. She stood on the back porch shivering in her little nightgown. She was scared to go down the steps and cross the yard and down the path to the outhouse. There were night sounds of animals and monsters in the bushes at the edges of the yard and beyond she could hear the churning, coughing, and belching of hell itself. She stood on the back porch holding her need to pee till she couldn't hold it any longer. She peed on herself finally. Then, trying to get back into the house, she discovered that the back door had accidentally locked on her. She knocked and knocked and cried out for help but everybody in the house was asleep. She knocked and cried till she was exhausted. She sat on the porch, leaning against the door till she fell asleep like that. Grandpoppa, she said, found her like that, asleep on the porch at sunrise when he was going out to feed the farm animals.

"Mother still has bad dreams that obviously stem from that experience. In these dreams she gets trapped outside of doors, always. In one of them, she is simply stepping outside the apartment door to fetch the newspaper where the boy has thrown it. She is wearing only her nightgown. A strong wind blows the door shut and she is locked outside of her apartment. In another one, she is locked between a screen door and a main door, locks on both doors. Sometimes it's windows; windows won't open and she's trying to get into the house. Always she is trying to get in, not out. She gets locked out a lot. She loses her keys in the dreams."

"Esther never told me nothing bout that night or bout her bad dreams."

I watched Juneboy cut into his pork chop and wondered why he was telling me these things bout his momma. Funny bout the things you member. They don't never seem to be the things somebody else member. I member all kinda things bout Esther and me and the others but when I talk to them bout the things I member they come just a remembering a whole lotta other things I don't have no mind to member at all.

Me and Ballard for years have had conflict over a incident I think he ought to member but he don't and nothing I can say seem to be able to make him. It was the summer of the mosquitoes, when they was so bad. That summer Poppa had got it into his head that he was gonna strike it rich by building right in our backyard a machine that would chop wood and even stack it. We had in them days a wood burning stove in the kitchen and course there was the fireplaces in all the rooms. So Poppa had chopped a lot of wood in his day and he was fed up. He got so busy with this machine, getting scrap iron, junk parts of cars and tractors and boats, and he even taught hisself to weld that summer. He was so busy out there in the backyard, he forgot most of the time to do his usual chores, such as feeding the pigs and the cows and tending to the farm in general. Momma got real mad at him and at supper time she would fuss at him bout his laziness and he kept promising her that his invention was gon make us rich, once he got it working properly. Momma put up with his screwball effort for the better part of the summer. She suffered the embarrassment she felt when the neighbors come just a peeking into the backyard to see what was going on back there. One man, Mr. Love — he was a white man who did all his own work hisself — stuck his neck back there, trying to figure out what Poppa was up to. Poppa took Mr. Love on back there and showed him this contraption he said was gon be a wood chopping and stacking machine and Mister Love come to getting real interested in what Poppa was up to. Poppa talked Mr. Love into investing some of his savings into the machine, telling him he needed additional motors, things like that, you see, to get it working in the proper way. Mr. Love invested, oh, I don't know, maybe as much as a hundred dollars in Poppa's scheme, and Poppa took off for Atlanta once he had the money, and bought hisself a new motor up here in Atlanta. He tinkered round with that no good wood chopper all summer and Momma had to work double to keep the farm going. Us children helped her, course. Maybe that's why Ballard don't member that hot, muggy summer, the summer when the mosquitoes came fore dark every afternoon.

Anyways, Poppa's machine never did learn to chop wood and he ended up in the fall chopping his own wood and paying Mr. Love back his hundred dollars or how-ever-much it was.

But if you ast Ballad anything bout that summer it would be like specting a stone wall to answer you back. Maybe he can't member nothing bout it cause Poppa was so hard on him that summer, as I member — suddenly, just now — making him do the work that Poppa was spose to be doing. I don't know. Ballard just claims he has no recollection of no wood-chopping machine. Esther was too young to member and I don't think Kathy had any interest that summer in nothing but stockings. Rutherford was, as I recollect, more interested in frogs that summer than in human beings.

★   ★   ★

While I was putting the dishes into the sink, the phone ringed and Juneboy got it and talked — kinda awkwardly, I thought — for a few minutes, then called me to the phone. It was Ballard. I sat down on the chair by the phone there in the hall. Naturally, I was specting bad news, knowing what Ballard was going through.

"Annie, I changed my mind. Me and Buckle had a long talk and Donna Mae and me had a long talk. We gon try to work it out. Give it another chance."

I told Ballard I thought he was making the right decision. I reminded him of his age. He wont no spring chicken and Donna Mae loved him better than anybody in the whole world. She was gon always be there for him. Ballard's other daughter, Frances, had gone off in her own way, up North, and hadn't showed much interest in staying in touch with Ballard after Corky's death. That girl, Frances, the second one, was one of them real angry ones. You see them in families. Nobody can do nothing bout them.

Then Ballard told me he had had second thoughts — not cause of his health and age — but cause Buckle seemed like he was gon try to reform hisself.

★   ★   ★

This was the last night Juneboy was gon spend in my house. In the morning he would be gone.

When I finished the dishes I went to the back room where he was sitting on the couch watching television. It was the six

o'clock news from New York. A big old airplane with two
hundred and thirty-two peoples on it blowed up that morning in
midair. The big United States was threatening war on some little
country I never heard tell of. There was a big fight between the
National Rifle Association and some folks who wanted more
gun control. Somebody right here in Atlanta had spoke out
gainst racism, a white politician named Morris Page. Everybody
knowed Page had his eye on the White House. The anchorman
said the president was still recovering nicely. Somebody was
pushing for tax reform. Somebody else wanted the United States
to stay outta other nations' affairs. Somebody else was gainst
nuclear testing. Another man said it was necessary for peace. A
reporter interviewed a man who talked bout how bad the president's foreign policy was. A woman spoke bout acid rain. Some
Cubans in Florida was saying they hate Castro. A nightclub
somewhere in Europe blew up. Five American soldiers died in
the explosion. At a protest rally in Charleston, South Carolina,
there was the Ku Klux Klan peoples in they white robes and
carrying posters.

Then a blueberry muffin commercial came on and a lady with
a nice face was holding this muffin out at us, so close to the
screen that it got big as her head in the background. I guess she
wanted us to see the fine texture, up close, like we might be able
to take a bite out of it.

I got the *TV Guide* to see what was gon be on after the news.
Thursday night was a pretty good night for good shows. I likes to
watch romantic shows with good love stories in them. I don't
like to see the violence — peoples shooting at each other and cars
crashing and mens beating up womens, mens chopping off
womens' heads, or driving off cliffs. I likes comedies too. I don't
mind love and funny things. Whiles the commercials was still on,
I told Juneboy what the choices was starting at seven and going
through ten.

"The only thing that sounds interesting, Aunt Annie Eliza, is
that 'Wild, Wild World of Animals.' But I don't care what we
watch."

His mentioning this show created a real problem for me cause it was opposite one of my favorite shows, "Barney Miller." Anyhow, since he didn't care we ended up watching "Barney Miller." While we was watching it the doorbell ringed. Juneboy said he would get it.

While Juneboy was outta the room, Barney was trying to explain to Wojo how he should try a little harder to put up with Sergeant Luger. Wojo looked like a little boy who just got his allowance withheld for a month. When he look that way, I always laughs something crazy.

It was DeSoto, still in his uniform.

"Hi, Momma. I just stopped by to find out what time I should pick up Adam to take him to the airport."

"I told you I can take a taxi, De."

"I won't stand for it, my man."

They agreed on twelve cause Juneboy's flight time was two thirty.

Then DeSoto said, "Hey, why don't I pick you and Momma up at eleven in the morning, take you out to my house? Whitney wants to be able to say good-bye to you. That way we can all have brunch together. A kind of good-bye party, you understand."

I said, "DeSoto, now, how you know Juneboy got that kinda time when he got a flight to catch?"

Juneboy answered for him. He said, "It sounds wonderful to me."

So I told them it was all right with me too. DeSoto said, "I'll even invite Donna Mae and Buckle. We'll have bloody marys with our eggs."

I gave DeSoto a look. "Now, you know that man don't need no encouragement to drink that early in the morning cause he gon be doing it anyhow."

DeSoto sat down at the table.

The news was ending and the anchorman was telling a funny story, the only happy story he had, which he saved for last. It was bout a family reunion. Everybody was crying they eyeballs red. And hugging.

Then DeSoto ast if we had heard bout the mayor supporting
Renee and bout Dale being outta the hospital and if we had
heard Tommy Blackmore's attack on Renee.

"Attack on Renee?" I lost control of my voice.

"Yeah. He was on a radio program. I heard it while on duty,
driving around. Blackmore started out putting Kidd McCarthy
down. Called him everything but a child of God. Then the host
asked him about Cooper and he sort of went easy on Cooper. He
said Cooper had to be out of the race. No question about that.
Then came the question about Renee. He said Renee was inex-
perienced and arrogant. Those were his very words, inex-
perienced and arrogant. The host wanted to know what he
meant. Blackmore said that she was using her ties with the
Wrights to jockey for power in a city and for a people she had no
empathy with or sympathy for. She was an arrogant woman
speaking a mouthful of feminist slogans to win support. Now, I
guess this interview was taped before the mayor announced his
support of Renee. I don't know. It might have been live. Come to
think of it, Blackmore wouldn't give two hoots about changing
his position on Renee even if he knew the mayor had come out in
support of her."

I ast DeSoto if Blackmore had said anything bout Renee's
mother or bout the Greenhouse Tomato Conspiracy.

"No. But he described a meeting he had with Renee when she
was on the city council. The man was talking with hammers and
nails and swearing by the holy gate. To hear him tell it, he was
walking in the lane with all the people of good will and Renee
had been locked out of the house of the pure in heart. I mean,
this man uses this Bible Belt talk to sucker in support for what he
calls his conservative views, when his real position is purely
reactionary.

"He quoted St. Luke, saying judgment time was at hand. He
went into Revelations. When he was told that Renee also believed
in God and came from a holy family, he talked about Egypt as the
land of slaves, and how the slaves finally came free out of Egypt,
saying he was better equipped to speak for freedom for all than
Renee."

Now, as DeSoto talked I got to thinking, I knowed he had some radical ideas, and they come out once in a while, but this time it was pretty clear to me that he was talking more for Juneboy's benefit than for mine. He had never talked to me like this, talking smart and sounding like a bigshot. The boy was trying to impress his cousin. So I just listened and didn't say nothing. Just let him talk on.

I looked at Juneboy. He was listening all right even though the television was still on.

DeSoto took out his Vicks chapstick and greased his lips. "I was just sitting there, driving my district, getting sicker by the minute listening to this turkey. You wouldn't believe the things he said!"

I had a plan. As soon as DeSoto took hisself home I said to Juneboy, "Juneboy, let's me and you go see Senator Cooper. He's one of God's children like the rest of us. He's ill and in our family we believe in visiting the sick. You member Grandmomma always visited the sick? I'm gon take him some flowers too."

He said he didn't want to go.

"Juneboy you spose to be a doctor. Maybe you can help that poor man. Come on!"

"Okay. I'll go with you but I'm not going as a doctor. He already has a doctor."

I called Senator Cooper's number and a woman answered. I told her my name and she went away and came back to the phone. She said just a minute the senator would speak to me. When I heard Dale's voice I told him I was on my way to pay him a visit cause he was sick. I apologized for not visiting him in the hospital.

When we got there, Dale's nurse met us at the door and introduced herself. Her name was Minnie. Then she took us in to see Dale. She showed him the roses then she took them away. So there we was in Dale's bedroom. He was sitting up in bed. He was trying to smile but Dale ain't never been one for much smiling. His jowls hung down like them kind you see on a bulldog. His eyes was muddy yellow and blue-looking. He looked tired, child, tired.

Juneboy shook Dale's hand and Dale ast us to sit a spell. Dale said he was moved that I wanted to come see him. He said he was sorry he had been rude to Renee in that television studio. I even think a tear came to his eye.

I told him never mind bout that. The important thing for him now was to get hisself well. I said I was sorry bout the death of his nephew.

"It was very sad to see a child die."

Juneboy ast him how the doctors at Grady diagnosed his illness but fore Dale could answer the nurse, Minnie, came back in with the pink roses in a silver vase, looking so pretty.

While Minnie was fussing with the roses, putting them with other flowers on Dale's nightstand by his bed, Dale started talking bout his sickness to Juneboy. He wont looking at me while he spoke so I figured he didn't think I could understand. I don't know. Dale can be funny like that. It's this class thing and education, you know.

Dale's a very, very proud man and it's always been hard for him to talk bout any weakness or something bad that done happened to him. I could see the strain in his face as he started trying to tell Juneboy the trouble. But after he said all he had to say, it came down to the fact that the doctors didn't know for sure what was wrong with him.

I said, "Listen to me, Dale. Juneboy here, you know, is a doctor and — "

"Now, Aunt Annie — "

"I only was gon — "

"You got any ideas about it, Dr. North?" ast Dale.

"None. I know only what I've heard and that's not much. It just developed suddenly?"

"Not as suddenly as the news had it. I remember it starting as an itch. The area got dry and the skin cracked. All of this happened in the span of, say, a week."

"Why don't you let Juneboy look, Dale? He might have some idea that can get you well. What you got to lose?"

"I don't mind."

Minnie turned from the flowers and said she didn't think it was a good idea, that Dr. Rivers and Dr. Selz wouldn't like it and that Juneboy be better off keeping outta it.

"Just calm down, Minnie. What they don't know won't — "

"I think she's right," said Juneboy.

"Ah, to hell with what those guys think of as their professional code of — "

"Okay," Juneboy said, "but it's strictly — "

"Sure, sure."

"I won't be able to tell you anything you don't already know, Senator Cooper."

"Fine. Minnie give him a hand."

Juneboy went and washed his hands and Minnie started turning the covers down and she took her sweet time slowly peeling off this big bandage. It was bout a foot long and wide. Dale kept saying ouch when she pulled the tape from his skin.

Juneboy came back with clean hands and waited for Minnie to finish. He ast her for gloves but she said she didn't have nothing but kitchen sink rubber gloves. He said never mind, then ast her for a flashlight. Dale told her where to find it and she brought it and gave it to my nephew.

Juneboy looked real serious or mad. Maybe both. I got the feeling he was mad at me for getting him into this.

The sore was on Dale's right side. I stood up so I could see it looking over Juneboy's back. I wanted to see for myself. Child, it was this big old red and puffy area but it looked like it was healing a bit. I didn't see no blood or white puss. It coulda been a bruise. I seen bruises like that from horse kicks. One time DeSoto was hit in the forehead with a rock and his head was all black and blue and swollen like that for a long time.

Minnie stood by me, just behind Juneboy. We both was watching. Her eyes looked as big as I guess mine was.

Juneboy went a long time without saying nothing.

"It's not skin cancer," Juneboy finally said. "I don't know for sure what it is but it might well be coreyox. Coreyox is this rare form of sickle cell. *The New England Journal of Medicine* just recently published the first results of experiments done on it. It was only isolated and defined last year."

Dale said he had been told of it and had already contacted them two doctors, Rineheart and Runes, who wrote the article bout it. He was planning to go to Harvard Medical School Hospital to see them.

Juneboy said, "For some unknown reason victims of coreyox tend to get the ulcerations higher on the body than with sickle cell, such as on the stomach or the buttocks. I heard of one woman in Boston who had them under her left arm."

Dale thanked Juneboy for taking a look. Then Juneboy ast Minnie to put a fresh bandage on Dale's wound.

★   ★   ★

When Juneboy and me got back we watched little old mannish Gary Coleman in "Diff'rent Strokes." I kept thinking Juneboy was bout to say something real strange bout the show, something to give me the jitters, but he didn't. He had done that some nights, you know. We'd be watching a show and suddenly he'd say something that didn't make a bit a sense to me. Like there was a scene in one of them police stories. All these peoples was in they cars lined up at a gas station. It musta been in California. One man drove in front of another as the line was moving. The man behind the sneak kept blowing his horn for the sneak to get outta line and go to the end of the line but the sneak wouldn't move. He just took out his newspaper and started reading it like nobody's business, ignoring the man behind him. This angry man got outta his car and went up to the car of the sneak. He took out a gun and shot him in the head. You know what Juneboy said when that happened? He said, "Unconventional norms in expression." Now, what kinda thing is that to say when somebody gets shot through the head?

I was still worrying in my mind bout poor Dale lying up there in his bed not knowing what was wrong for sho but you could see the man hadn't given up hope.

Juneboy went to bed round ten-thirty that Thursday night cause he said he had to get up and pack and get ready.

I stayed on watching the television. Some of the best shows come on on Thursday night. That night I saw a servant woman that spent her whole life working for this family, this servant ran the family affairs, bossy, you know, and kept her own man in line, too. Her missus fell sick and had to move to a warm climate. This poor servant woman took a job taking care of a vet, you know, a animal doctor, and she cooked his food and swept his floors and cleaned the office, all that kinda stuff. Then she just died. I didn't get nothing outta it. I was beginning to feel like television on this Thursday night was trying to work voodoo on me. I took it personally. I never seen such silliness. But I kept right on watching till I fell sleep.

19

First thing on "Good Morning Atlanta" there was Renee's opponent Senator Blackmore talking bout the Department of Corrections and what they wont doing right. I membered my phone conversation with him and wondered when he was gon get round to going public with his investigation. I wanted him to and I didn't want him. I was trying not to think bout my fear for Jeremiah and the rest of us if Blackmore came out with his evidence. And Butler and Renee might come out with evidence too. Lord, it was all too much all at once.

Blackmore said they don't reform the criminals. Hatton ast him bout the peoples he represents, if he thought he could represent a district with more blacks than whites. He got a little huffy. He said the days of racism are over in the South. What a laugh. He said we have to work from the "realities of a short budget," and do some "house cleaning." Hatton wanted to know what he meant and Blackmore said the House and the Senate had a lot of dead weight. Hatton ast Renee's opponent what he thought bout the high school teachers rallying for increased pay. He stuttered and said he thought they deserved more pay but that they should understand the economic problems. This man was talking hogwash, if you ast me. Hatton ast Blackmore bout police violence in Atlanta last week. Renee's opponent said he thought the police had a right to break up them demonstrators. I forgets what they was demonstrating gainst.

Taking my coffee with me, I went out in the backyard to see how the plants was doing. Morning time's the best time to see how much they growed through the night or if anything new done bloomed. There was six new yellow tulips had done opened up overnight. It was Miss Rhoda Belle Finn who got me started with tulips many years ago when I worked for her. This was after Bibb died and I was having a hard time. Miss Rhoda Belle was the best white lady I ever worked for. She never tried to work me like a mule. Matter of fact, she use to tell me to slow down. I did her wash and her ironing and cooking and some cleaning. She had another woman who came in to do the heavy housecleaning once a week so I didn't have much of that to do. She never ast me to clean no oven neither. And I didn't do no mopping, the other woman did the mopping. My work was what I said it was and I was pretty much in charge of everything since Miss Rhoda Belle was getting on up in age and her health was failing her. What energy she had she gave to her civic groups and to politics in her neighborhood. She was what we call a southern liberal. She cared bout colored peoples' rights. She donated lots of money to organizations helping the Negro peoples.

But she was some stubborn woman and I use to have to fuss at her and make her take a nap. She thought she had more energy than she had any right to think. You see, the doctor had told me bout her health and ast me to make sho she got herself some rest each day. So that's how I started with the tulips. I use to go out in the garden and cut a bunch of yellow tulips and put them in the tall pretty blue vase and take the vase to her room just to cheer her up while she was resting. She'd be there on the bed still in her clothes reading a book. The bright yellow color always made her smile and the blue right close to the yellow did too.

Miss Rhoda Belle told me what to do so I didn't have to worry bout having no more babies. The boys was still little then and I wont sho then if I was gon have anything to do with mens again or not. As it turned out, I didn't—cept for that one time I told you bout. But Miss Rhoda Belle sent me to her doctor who gave me one of them diaphragms. He showed me how to put it on and everything and gave me the little kit and the dispenser. But you know, I never once ever put that thing on again, cause I never had no reason to. I use to wonder if I got raped coming home from work what would I do. What if being raped got me pregnant? When I had thoughts like them I use to think maybe I was wrong not to be wearing the diaphragm. But I never got raped.

Well, the yellow tulips this morning made me member Miss Rhoda Belle. God rest her soul.

By and by, Juneboy got up. I was beginning to get nervous for him, what with him having to pack and get ready and that brunch thing at DeSoto's.

While Juneboy took his shower I warmed the coffee and watched the "Today" show.

When Juneboy came back to the back he was all dressed up in slacks and a summer jacket and he was smiling. It was round eight. I poured him a cup of coffee. I ast him if he slept all right. I always ast that. He said he did. He ast me how I felt.

"Fit as a fiddle!"

He sat hisself down at the table and gazed at the television screen while he sipped his coffee. Some man was talking bout "the blue collar vote" and the upcoming Republican Convention. Another man said Jack Anderson had found out some dirt on somebody and was bout to go public with it. Them his words.

I told Juneboy bout Senator Blackmore being on.

He just drinked his coffee and didn't say nothing. He kept on watching the screen.

Was he mad at me? I couldn't think of no reason why he should be. I guessed he just had the morning grumps. But just a minute before, when he came in, he was smiling. Maybe that was a pretend smile. Poppa use to be like that first thing in the morning, didn't want nobody to talk to him fore he got hisself together and sometimes that took till noon.

Then lo and behold, the local news came on and a man started talking bout the vegetable and fruit scandal. He said it was just like Watergate in that it was called the Greenhouse Tomato Conspiracy but it "involved" the whole market. Tomatoes was just a symbol, he said. He said Georgia greenhouse produce this year was expensive cause they wont making it due to some kinda disease. He said there was to be a official investigation and that Democratic candidate for state senate Mrs. Renee Hicks "led the probe which has opened the way for an investigation into whole-saler activity concerning all greenhouse produce."

I looked at Juneboy. He looked at me. I was wondering why they wont saying nothing bout Senator Blackmore's so-called investigation into the same thing.

Juneboy said, "If she succeeds with this, she won't lose."

"Everybody coming over behind her now."

"Have you heard any more about Senator Cooper?"

I hadn't and I told him. He still had that old sour face. I hadn't noticed him being like this before in the morning. Could it be he was sorry to be leaving?

The doorbell ringed. I went up there. It was Renee's little girl Jane with two of her rag dolls, both in one hand.

"Good morning, Grandmomma."

"Morning, Jane. You coming in or you gon stand there?"

"I'm coming in, Grandmomma."

Inside, she stopped.

"What can I do for you, little lady?" She looked so little and pretty. "Renee sent you for something?"

"No ma'am. I came to show you how my dolls can kiss."

She took one in each hand and forced they mouths together. I didn't know what to think. Something bout it looked to me like something a child her age shouldn't a been doing.

"See?" she said. "They know how to kiss. They love each other."

"Uh-huh. Come on in the kitchen and have a glass of milk and some cookies."

"Yes, ma'am."

Juneboy spoke to her and she said hello. I don't think she had too clear a sense of who he was, though she probably membered him from the night of Renee's dinner party. But when she saw Juneboy she came a getting just as shy as she could be. I lifted her up into a chair at the table and put a saucer in front of her. I got the cookies and poured her a glass of milk. I put a cookie on her saucer. I looked at the television. A woman was singing the blessing of microwave cooking. The bacon looked better than bacon had any right to look.

Jane was halfway through her cookie when the phone ringed.
I got up and got it. It was Renee. She said she couldn't find Jane,
that she had just disappeared. I told her to calm down, that the
child was here eating cookies and having a glass of milk. She
swore. Said she was gon skin that girl alive. How many times had
she told Jane not to wander off alone, even to her grandmomma's
house! Phew! She was whooping and hollering her anger something terrible. Said she'd be right over to fetch her.

When Renee got there she had calmed down some but she was
still all red in the face.

I made her sit down and have a cup of coffee. She said she had
already had three. I said have another one.

She sat down between Jane and Juneboy. She blessed Jane out
for a few minutes. Jane started crying. We talked bout the
tomatoes while Jane cried. Renee told us that Representative
Butler's life had been threatened by a anonymous phone call.
The police, he said, was planning to put a tracer on his phone but
at his own expense.

Then she told Juneboy that DeSoto told her bout him being
in Poland and Algiers and she wanted to know bout them places,
so while he told her I didn't listen cause I had heard all of it
before.

Then Jane started wandering round the room talking to her
dolls, then she stopped in front of the television and blocked my
view so I ast her to move. She moved on and stopped again. Again
she made the dolls kiss.

"Renee, look at that child. Ought she be making them gal
dolls kiss each other like that?"

"Momma, what's wrong with it?"

"Just don't seem right to me."

I saw her give Juneboy a look. He tried to not look back at her.
He pretended to watch the television.

Renee said, "I don't see anything wrong with the dolls kissing,
Momma. Jane's just playing."

I thought: Momma never woulda allowed it. One time
Momma caught me looking at myself down there and ast what I
was looking at and I told her at myself and she said that was bad,

nice girls didn't look at theyselves down there and nice girls never put they fingers down there cept to wash.

But I didn't say no more to Renee. She and her modern ways! She knowed how she wanted to raise her children and it was none of my business, but I couldn't help myself from noticing when she done it all wrong, like this thing bout the two gal dolls kissing.

Juneboy was talking to Renee bout her running. Cause I was watching Jane and thinking my own thoughts I can't tell you all of what they was saying to each other. Then the phone ringed and Jane ran to answer it. She is at that age, you see, when they is letting her answer they phones all the time. She loves it. I didn't like her doing this in my house, but cause I wanted to keep the peace with my daughter-in-law I didn't say nothing.

Jane came back and said the peoples hung up and that she had tried to call them back. The phone ringed again.

I went to it. The operator told me that my call to Alaska was ready now.

I said, "My call to Alaska?"

She said yes, she had just got somebody on the line trying to dial Alaska.

I thought, "Oh save me, Lord." I explained to the operator bout Jane.

I hung up. The phone ringed again.

I picked it up. It was my Dr. Limerick. I couldn't imagine why he was calling me. That is, not till he said, "The results of your physical came back. I thought I'd call you, Annie Eliza, to reassure you that you are — for a woman of your age — in excellent health. The arthritis is under control. You taking your medicine? Blood pressure is down. That's very, very good. No sign of liver damage, no sign of kidney damage. Your cholesterol is still a bit high but lower than before."

I kept trying to member when he tested me for all this stuff. I swear I couldn't but I didn't let on to him that I couldn't. I now figure it musta been bout a month fore Juneboy came down and I plumb forgot.

I thought bout Dr. Limerick. He was a happy fella. Musta been ten, maybe fifteen years younger than me. He was the kinda doctor who gets hisself invited to conferences in China and in Korea and in places I never heard of. He is a short man but stocky, and he has a lot of muscle. His eyebrows won't behave. When he called me this early in the morning on the morning Juneboy spose to leave I had a hard time listening to him. I member seeing Dr. Limericks' wife once in the office. She looked like a sad woman. She reminded me of my own Miss Rhoda Belle. That sad.

★ ★ ★

I hate it when the time drags and drags. I washed the dishes and dried them. Usually I let them drip dry but I had nothing else to do or didn't want to do nothing else. Fore I dumped the dishwater, I watched the suds pop. I counted them, the blue ones, the purple ones. Then I poured the water down the drain and watched it go down, leaving the sink with a sticky coating of dirty suds. I sprinkled powdered cleanser in and scrubbed the sink with the sponge. This wears the sponge out pretty fast but I didn't care. For a minute, I wont sure if I was really standing there doing that or dreaming I was doing it, I do it so naturally, without thinking bout it.

I could hear Renee and Juneboy back there talking and Jane playing. I was thinking bout what Dr. Limerick told me.

I went to the bathroom and looked in the mirror at my face. I didn't like to look at my own face much but I forced myself to do it. I won't never do it less my teeths is in. And I rather see myself in the mirror when I got my wig on but I don't go round the house wearing my good wig. I looked at myself. I was old all right. No doubt bout that. Old woman there in that mirror. But Dr. Limerick just said I was in excellent health. Then how come I felt so tired most of the time?

DeSoto wont gon show up till bout leven or so and it was a quarter to nine. Two hours. I didn't want to start dressing yet but I did get my things out and laid them out across the bed in the guest room. I put out my wig, my good blue silk dress, my black low-cut heels, my stockings, and my underthings. I looked at the pictures of the boys when they was little there on the dresser. This was they room. They looked so far away in the picture, like two little boys I knowed a long, long time ago way back in another life. I looked at Bibb's picture on the other side of the dresser. He was like a stranger. His face in the picture was a face I knowed only cause I knew I knowed it.

Time was dragging. I was shamed of feeling it, but I guess I wanted Juneboy gone. Just as I started scrubbing the area round the face bowl with cleanser, my telephone ringed.

It was Jeremiah. Right off I could tell he was in a bad way. He couldn't get his words to come out right.

I told him to calm down and talk straight.

He ast if Renee and Jane was here.

Yes, I told him.

He said something awful done happened.

Awful? What awful?

Jeremiah was crying. I could tell. He was crying. He said, "My friend Cherokee Jimmy just killed himself, Momma."

The minute he said it, child, I knowed why. Don't ast me how I know it but I knowed it had something to do with his shame at being mixed up in that Georgia Fruit and Vegetable Company scandal. But I didn't say nothing bout it right then.

"Go on, hush your mouth," is what I said.

"I'm not kidding, Momma."

"Jeremiah!" I was so scared for Jeremiah.

"He shot himself between the eyes. Held the pistol and shot himself between the eyes."

I heard Jeremiah blow his nose. Cherokee Jimmy was dead. I was still trying to get the thought through my head.

I said, "How you know this?"

"The mayor just called me. It's not in the news yet. George said his whole face was destroyed. It was like a—"

"Son, you come on over here right now—"

"All right, Momma. But you know Renee is still mad at me."

"Come on over here."

"All right, Momma."

"Come on." I hung up.

Jeremiah called back five minutes later and said he couldn't come over cause he had to go up to the police station.

A hour later he came walking in.

We was all there at the door to meet him.

He kinda pushed us aside and went on back to the back. We followed him back there.

I took the boy by his arm and took him into the room he use to sleep in when he was a boy. I ast him straight if Cherokee Jimmy was a investor in that Georgia Fruit and Vegetable Company and I made him look me in the eye and answer.

He said, "Yes, Momma."

Then we went on back to the back.

He looked like he was real tired. He sat hisself down on the couch like he was the tiredest man on earth.

Renee said, "Jerry, let's let bygones be bygones."

"Sure, honey. Glad to hear you say it." He looked at the floor like he was gon be sick. "I can't believe it. I just can't believe it. I, I, uh . . ."

"Jerry, did he say anything, leave a note?" Renee sounded real calm, like somebody talking to a mental patient.

His chin was on his collar bone. "Nothing. No note, no nothing. I don't get it. A close friend like this—"

Juneboy sat down.

Jane was watching—all eyes. She was watching all of us. It reminded me of myself when I was her age at times when the big peoples round me was unsure of theyselves. It always scared me. I knowed little Jane musta been scared just seeing all of us looking like we was looking.

Me and Juneboy sat down at the table. We was all quiet.

I thought of my brother Ruth. God rest his soul. I had dreamed bout Ruth shooting hisself. Had nightmares bout it. I didn't want to think bout it anymore.

Jane was turning the television channels now that she knowed we wont gon stop her. We was too interested in what we ourselves was doing. Children like that when they can get away with it. But outta one side of my mind and eye I was on to her.

Then Renee told Jane to go out in the backyard and play.

Everybody was sitting down waiting for Jeremiah to think of something to tell us. We didn't know what to think. And, child, you know, I was bout outta my mind already with all the other worry.

I looked at Jeremiah. His eyes was closed.

I looked at Juneboy. He was watching the television on the sly.

Seemed like I was the only body here who didn't know what to feel. I feeled kinda odd but I can't splain it.

20

Finally Jeremiah said, "Last week I had lunch with Cherokee and he was talking real strange, in parables almost. And I remember thinking how odd it was to hear him talking like a preacher but I didn't—"

Renee said, "Strange how?"

"He talked about when he was a kid. He went on about his discovery of himself, you know. It was the first time he had talked directly to me about his, well, you know, his homosexuality. It was like he *thought* something was going to happen to him, you know, the way people want to leave a record of themselves with a close friend. He talked about being fifteen. Told me about being two years younger than his sister. And about a boy named Sonny Lee. Sounded like Cherokee had a crush on this boy named Sonny Lee. Once in the toilet at his house they examined each other. I said to Cherokee, that's pretty common for kids to do—"

I interrupted. I couldn't help myself. "Disgusting, nasty thing!"

Jeremiah just stopped a minute while I blew off steam then he went right on talking this talk. He said Cherokee Jimmy had the strangest look on his face there last week at lunch in The Savannah Room in the Hotel Tower Place on Peachtree. Jeremiah likes to go there.

"He talked about his discovery of shame. I was a little embarrassed to hear him talking like that."

"Well," I said, "he had a right to be shamed of hisself."

Jeremiah ignored me. "He said the boys made fun of him because he could get into hot water jumping rope just as fast as his sister.

"Then he talked about being in college and his second sexual encounter. Said he was still a virgin by the time he was a second-year political science major at Spelman. I tell you, I was about ready to excuse myself. It seemed so blunt and personal. I'd never seen this side of Cherokee and it was disarming.

"You remember April Marie, Momma? He talked about going steady with her in college. He told me they didn't touch each other till their wedding night and the whole night was a disaster."

"Jeremiah," I said, "that will be enough of this kind of talk in my house. You hear me?"

"Momma, my friend is dead and . . . and I'm trying to understand why."

I said nothing but I didn't like it.

Renee said, "When I was a little girl I saw him and April Marie out at Stone Mountain Park holding hands and just walking along like the perfect lovers."

"Yeah." Jeremiah just looked at her.

"He told me about his mother too, for the first time. Said he used to listen to Jack Benny on the radio with her and that they were real pals when he was little. She was a high school teacher. You remember her Momma?"

I told him I did not.

"He told me he grew up ashamed of his father, who called himself an alderman but actually ran errands for local lawyers."

"Did he say what broke up his marriage to April Marie?" Renee looked like she was all ears.

"They just drifted apart. She eventually moved to Washington, D.C., and he got more and more into Atlanta politics. Politics became his whole life. Said he liked best the part of himself that was able to function in public life. Talked about his support of Martin Luther King. I tell you, it sounded like he was summing it all up. But why for me?"

I looked at Jeremiah. "Cause you was fool enough to sit there and listen like I'm fool enough to sit here listening to you going on bout what he said to you."

"Momma!" shouted Renee.

"All right, all right," I said.

"He talked some about Dale too. About their friendship. They met at a political rally for Jimmy Carter. He never said, uh, anything about an intimate relationship with Dale but his eyes got real soft and full of warmth when he talked about Dale. That was the most embarrassing part of the whole experience.

"He said Dale's father, like his own, had been a drunk and they had a lot of other things in common. He said Dale was the first human being he learned to trust. And, and — "

"And what?" I ast.

"And that I was the second one."

"But he didn't say anything about wanting to die?" Renee ast.

"No. Not a word." Jeremiah closed his eyes. Then he opened them. "But he did say something about Dale's condition. Something about if Dale kicks the bucket then most of everything for him would be over too."

I just wondered to myself if that lunch meeting Jeremiah and Cherokee had last week wont spose to be bout Georgia Fruit and Vegetable Company business and accidentally turned out to be bout all this other shameful mess.

Juneboy said he had to go get ready. He got up.

Renee got up right then like she was fixing to go with him. Then she walked over to him, like somebody bout to lay everything on the table, and gave him a big, big hug. I don't know why, but it kinda embarrassed me, child. I looked at Jeremiah but he wont paying no tention.

Then Juneboy left the room. But, you know, I think Renee and Juneboy had done got some sort of special magic going on between them. Seem like to me they changed each other for the betterment. I spect Juneboy was one of the first to express belief in Renee with this whole public office business. Don't ast me what she done for his spirits but it was clear to anybody with two eyes in they head that the boy was better looking than he was when he got here. He just looked a whole lot happier, especially when Renee was around. They seemed to speak the same language. You know what I mean?

I had to get ready too. I told them that.

Jeremiah went to the back door and called Jane. She came in and Renee picked her up. I walked them to the front door. Lord have mercy, I sho had a heavy heart.

★ ★ ★

DeSoto came for us at leven-thirty. He said Donna Mae had to go to her Elks meeting so she would be late. This was not the big annual meeting, just a local get-together near her house. Buckle was gon pick her up and bring her on out. DeSoto put Juneboy's suitcase in the trunk and we was on our way. I thought bout the Elks. Momma had been one for a while but she lost interest. Seem like every other woman in the world was a member of the Elks back in them days. I never could get interested myself. Donna Mae is a member of the Daughters section. They haves they big big get-togethers sometimes in Savannah or here in Atlanta or even in Memphis. They got a temple and titles for each other and secrets they not spose to tell nobody, leastways that's my understanding. The menfolks go to a lodge and the ladies go to this temple. But you know bout the Elks. Some colored peoples like it better than church.

Juneboy and DeSoto was talking they talk as we drove on through the city. It was a pretty day all right. The sun was most of its way up toward the top of the sky and there was the smell of dogwood coming through the gasoline smell.

DeSoto was telling Juneboy some more news bout Cherokee Jimmy but I wont listening cause I didn't want to know no more. I felt sorry for him but fore God he would be judged for his sins. That was all there was to it. God would handle him for his life and for the way he died. I didn't want to think bout it no more.

Whitney opened the door when we got there.

She looked real pretty in her summer dress all green and pink like a meadow.

DeSoto got hisself and Juneboy cans of beer from the icebox. It's a refrigerator but I still say icebox outta habit from when I was little and that was what we had in the house. Poppa used to bring a big block of ice home and put it in the top part. Sometimes the iceman would pull his old mule to a stop in front of the house and sell us a block and he would take it in hisself and put it in. That time when there was a lynching all the colored peoples went without ice for a week. Everybody's food rotted cause we was all scared to go outta the house to get ice, scared of the white folks. They still say over there in Monroe the boy they lynched didn't do nothing, he was just the first nigger they could get they hands on so they lynched him and he was only bout fourteen. I myself never saw no lynchings but I saw ashes. Poppa use to talk bout the lynchings he seen and he seen quite a few in his time. It wont no pleasant subject to have to listen to.

DeSoto and Juneboy was sitting at the dining room table drinking beer and Whitney was still fussing with brunch in the kitchen. She and DeSoto got a nice little two-bedroom house out in a mixed neighborhood. They been there five years. The neighborhood coming to be more black with each year but some of the whites say they ain't planning to move out. They got grape hollies all the way round the front yard and DeSoto keeps the grass cut real nice. In the backyard they got this big maple and a seedless ash.

Juneboy was telling DeSoto bout his feelings being back in the South now that he was leaving. He said the week he spent here was good for him. I was glad to hear him say it. He told DeSoto that it was real good for him to see us all again. DeSoto slapped Juneboy on the back and told him not to stay way so long again.

★ ★ ★

The TV set in the kitchen was on but I didn't want to get in Whitney's way standing there watching it. I went in the front and turned on the television to see what was happening to my soap peoples. Just as I done this, here comes Buckle and Donna Mae. I said to her I thought she had her Elks meeting and she said it ended and I said that that was quick and she said it had started at eight that morning.

She started asting DeSoto bout Cherokee Jimmy and I got sick of it and went back to the television. They all went back there

in the kitchen talking bout Cherokee Jimmy killing hisself. I
thought it a shame that this was the last few hours of Juneboy's
visit and they was talking this talk.

I heard DeSoto ast Buckle if he wanted a beer and Donna Mae
said no, he didn't. And everybody laughed. That is, everybody
cept Buckle. But the soap peoples was more interesting at that
moment so I concentrated on them.

Whitney checked on the biscuits. She was cooking biscuits and
bacon and grits. Everything was ready but the biscuits and she
was gon fry some eggs last. I went in and helped her bring the
food to the table. It sho smelled good. She cooked the eggs and
brought them.

We all started eating and kept right on talking. I ast Donna
Mae bout her work. Whitney and Juneboy was talking bout sickle
cell. And DeSoto was asting Buckle how his momma was doing
in the old folks home. The biscuits was real good, almost good as
my own. Buckle started pretty soon back on the subject of
Cherokee Jimmy. He wanted to know from DeSoto why if
Cherokee Jimmy was a queer why he was always seen with pretty
women on his arm. I membered the floozy he brought to Renee's
dinner party. DeSoto said it was just to throw peoples off. I said
let's stop talking bout that poor creature. Let God take care of
him.

Then, right in the middle of eating, Juneboy stood hisself up
and raised his glass to us all and in that old sweet voice said,
"This is to say thank you, Aunt Annie Eliza, Donna Mae,
Whitney, DeSoto, Buckle, for your hospitality. But you've given
me more without knowing it. Through you I've rediscovered
who I am and now I can go on from here. I love you all very
much."

Child, tears near bout come to my old tired eyes.

Then we ate on in silence for a while.

I noticed DeSoto was watching the little television on the
kitchen counter, looking over my head at the screen. There was
some kinda sports game on. It was turned real low. Then I heard
a lady in a commercial say you too could get rid of water weight
gain like she done with these little pills she depends on.

Whitney was telling Juneboy something bout one of her lawyers she worked for. Seems he got this case in where a man had a heart attack while watching a baseball game. He was trying to sue the television station that had the game showing. I thought to myself now this world done gone completely crazy.

Then the talk went on to Renee and her campaign. Donna Mae wanted to know if Renee had got to the bottom of that Greenhouse Tomato Conspiracy. But child, in my heart I was scared enough to die from the fear I was carrying like a basket of eggs. I told her the investigation was still going on. DeSoto said the mayor was now behind Renee and she couldn't lose with him like that. Donna Mae ast bout poor Betsy. I said I didn't know how she was doing. I ast bout Ballard. They said he was fine, at work as usual. My arthritis was beginning to bother me in the elbow of the right arm. DeSoto said Renee's friend Representative Butler had requested a police escort that morning but was told to go fly a kite. Buckle ast bout Jeremiah's ear. I told him to ast Jeremiah. Everybody laughed at me hushing up Buckle like that. I just didn't want to hear no talk bout Jeremiah. I was still mad at him. I could see him up in my mind standing there in his pulpit saying, "Make no mistake, there are Pharisees among us." Whitney said she had talked with Renee that morning, trying to get her to come to brunch, too, but she was too busy. Renee told her the kids had just found my girdle in the dirty clothes bin upstairs. I tell you, I never felt so embarrassed as I did that minute when Whitney said that right there in front of everybody. But I didn't hold it gainst her. She didn't mean no harm. Probably didn't even think bout it as something that would embarrass me. DeSoto made a big to-do bout it, asting me what my girdle doing in Jeremiah's house. Then I broke down and told them how the thing was killing me the night of the dinner party and how I went upstairs and took the blasted thing off. But I didn't tell them bout dropping my teeth.

I started feeling that big pain I felt the day Juneboy got here. But it was tiny right then so I didn't say nothing to them bout it. But it was the same pain all right. It didn't seem to be getting bigger and bigger. I kept right on eating. I done lived with more pain in my day than a whole battlefield full of wounded soldiers hold in they chests.

Now Whitney was asting Juneboy bout Poland and I turned the other way to try to hear something else. All I could hear was more talk bout Cherokee Jimmy coming from DeSoto's end of the table.

Well, when it was time for DeSoto to drive Juneboy to the airport we all got up and made a big fuss over him, hugging and kissing his cheeks and he was doing the same to us, me and Whitney and Donna Mae. Juneboy even hugged Buckle. We made him promise not to stay way so long again and to be sho to write sometimes and I told him to go on and marry that nice girlfriend of his, what's her name, and he said he was giving it serious thought.

Then him and DeSoto was gone.

I knowed it was the last time I would ever see Juneboy. I felt it in my bones. It was right there with the pain.

Then the phone ringed. I answered it for Whitney. She was busy with the dishes. It was Renee. The girl was crying something awful. Fore she said a word, I knowed what was coming. Jeremiah was on his way to hell and maybe he was taking her and the rest of us with him.

I ast God to help us.

21

Well, that is most of it and Juneboy left just yesterday, the hour Jeremiah was charged with conspiracy to fix prices.

Child, let me tell you, the minute Renee called like that at DeSoto's to tell me some mens done come to the house and tooked Jeremiah way and she said she thought they was policemens but they wore suits and not uniforms, you know, and they didn't tell her nothing, I almost nearly died right there in my tracks right in front of poor innocent Whitney.

But I never let on a thing, never said narry word to Whitney and got myself together and got outta there with Buckle and Donna Mae fore DeSoto could get back and tell by my face something was wrong. You see, I had to find out for myself. But like I said, I knowed what had happened already. Jeremiah was in deep trouble, just like Cooper and all them other peoples mixed up in that Georgia Fruit and Vegetable Company.

Well, right after they dropped me off, I drove straight on to the jailhouse uptown where I could just picture they had my son in handcuffs, and he was scared and needed us all there with him. But it wont like that, being as he was a respectable man and everything. They had him sitting in a chair by a desk and no handcuffs on him but there was a bunch of policemens round him and there was Renee standing by the door with her arms crossed and looking all red in the face like she done cried herself ugly.

These policemens was very polite mens, colored and white. One of them in a vest and with his tie just a little loose comes over to me when they done told everybody who I was and he says to me that he is delighted to meet me, the mother of a famous man, Reverend Jeremiah Hicks. And I could see Jeremiah sitting there looking all mad as the Devil hisself. I ast if I could talk to this old devilish son of mine. And the nice policeman told me go right ahead, that the secretary was typing up the charges gainst him and nine other men. They let me and Jeremiah and Renee go into one of them little rooms by ourselves. Even sent a gal in with coffee for us. They was all real nice folks. I said, "Son, tell me everything." Renee stood. She wouldn't sit down. She was snorting like she wouldn't never believe nothing that came outta his mouth nohow.

I said, "Talk to me. If you can't talk to your own mother you can't talk to nobody."

Then he looked at Renee giving him this dirty look.

I said, "Y'all stop this fussing and being divided right now. This ain't no time for a family to be divided gainst itself." Then I turned back to Jeremiah.

But it was Renee who burst out with all this stuff bout what was happening. "Senator Blackmore handed in to the police all this stuff he dug up on the operations of GFVC. Just think, Momma, I was getting to the same point—"

She was real mad. She cursed. I won't repeat the word. The girl started acting real crazy, walking all over the room and throwing her arms and turning red in the face.

I looked at Jeremiah. "I got good lawyers, Momma. Don't worry."

Renee said, "Don't worry, Momma," mocking him. Then she came over to me and said, "He's got good lawyers, all right. No doubt about that. They were just in here, Momma, and we were in this very room and they talked to him. You know what they told him?"

"What?"

"They told him that he's going to be charged with defrauding the public and he's going to be prosecuted. You hear me, Momma? Your son, my husband, the respectable spiritual leader of East Point!"

Jeremiah said, "Renee, just calm down."

But she went on, "His precious lawyers, both of them, told him that one Sam Kingston of GFVC's Board of Directors

declared himself and nine others as having been involved in
price-fixing and is on tape, taped by Senator Blackmore, saying
that your son, the great man, was one of those ten. Because of
Kingston's confession, Kingston is going to get a lighter sentence
and these other turkeys—except for Cherokee Jimmy, of course,
who got himself out of it—all nine of them are going to rot in
prison. You hear me, Momma? Rot in prison."

"Calm down, Renee," Jeremiah said. "You don't know what
you're talking about."

"I certainly do. I was right here and I heard everything they
told you. The prosecutor these guys are getting is one of the
toughest in the state. Now, tell me, Mr. Preacher, they didn't say
that?"

Jeremiah shook his head like he thought Renee was a fool.

But I was listening to the child cause I figured I was gon get
more outta her than outta my own son.

"And selecting the jury," she said, "is going to be tricky cause
these three niggers—your son, Cooper, and the dead nigger,
Cherokee—are the only niggers on the Board of Directors. The
other seven, Momma, are white men of great respectability. Now,
Jeremiah's lawyers are white."

"Renee," he said, "I wish you would shut your mouth."

"Oh, do you, now. Don't you think your mother has a right to
know what's going on, what might happen to her son?"

I told Renee to tell me what the lawyers said.

"They said conspiracy itself is a crime and that if they are lucky
they might be able to get the racketeering charges dropped but a
whole lot depends on how the other defendants plead. They said
the State of Georgia, as the plaintiff, don't really have a defined
position except in the sense that these turkeys are being brought
to trial. And another thing they said, Momma, was that in these
kinds of cases they've had a lot of jury tampering in Atlanta lately,
so this thing could drag out for months and who knows, years.
The lawyers will be the only ones who will get anything out of it.
They didn't say that, but you and I know that. So they're planning
extensive cross-examinations of the twenty-three grand jury

members and the same for the regular jury if there is a trial—and there will be."

"Renee, you talking to Momma like she's some kinda fool."

"I am not! You just don't want her to know."

"Go on, Renee."

"Momma, he's ruined my chances at a senate seat! And we might be looking at selling the house, all our stocks and bonds, savings, the cars, and going into bankruptcy," she said. "And just to pay the lawyers to save this nigger—this dumb nigger!—from prison."

I said, "I guess I just don't understand the charges. What did Jeremiah do wrong?"

"Momma, conspiracy can be a killer or a loophole. They said your son might walk out of that courtroom a free man or die in the dungeons. They were trying to get Jeremiah ready for everything. They asked him if he bought something with a guarantee that it was worth what he paid for it and it turned out to be worth far less, what would he do? And Jeremiah said he would try to get his money back. They said, exactly. That's what the prosecutor is going to say to him. And the prosecutor is going to say that Atlanta's consumers want their money back and since he caused the breach of trust, it is up to him to redress them.

"Your son was buying goods—that's what the lawyers called them, goods—and was paying the vendors what they were worth in Mississippi and Florida then bringing them to Georgia and selling them at prices for state produce in this neighborhood, locality, state. Now, that was what they told Jeremiah he was facing. The prosecutor is going to attack him with this and he better be ready with an answer."

Jeremiah had turned away from us and had his eyes closed.

"One of the lawyers told Jeremiah that a sticky point could be that a lot of their purchases were made on credit from those two out of state markets. There's something in the law about credit purchase that's different from cash purchase. I didn't get the whole point but it had something to do with the delivery of goods in good faith at quoted prices. These guys could roast for reselling the goods at the prices they sold them at, if conspiracy can be proven. Momma, that is essentially what your holy boy is facing."

Jeremiah was still looking away. Then he got his tongue back from the cat and said, "Momma, if goods are sold and if those same goods are delivered without anything being talked about regarding the prices then there is—"

Renee cut him off. She said, "Good faith is what the prosecutor is going to try to nail him and his buddies on, Momma."

"He wont acting in good faith?" I sho didn't mean it as a question cause I already knowed he wont. I knowed the expression from TV.

Renee said, "Georgia state law says no sale is binding when based on misrepresentation. Misrepresentation of a product whose real value is intentionally concealed is punishable by Georgia state law. It's that simple, Momma. Conspiracy."

I said, "Okay."

Somebody knocked at the door and Renee opened it and it was one of the nice policemens. He said Jeremiah had posted his bail and he was free to go home.

Well, I called DeSoto but a friend of his on the force had already told him and he was so depressed he didn't want to talk. Jeremiah went on to their house but Renee came with me. She said she knew Jeremiah was gon get drunk and she didn't want to be there. The children was with the sitter somewhere. I called Ballard and told him and he just grunted like I knowed he would. He said he would tell Donna Mae. Then I called my sister Kathy but she wont in, probably in church. Then I called Dale. There wont nobody there. That worried me.

"Well, it's done. We just got to find a way to live with it," I said to Renee, who was just sitting back here at this table looking all depressed.

"But, Momma, it makes me look like a fool, for one thing. I'm out there investigating some crap that my own husband is up to his neck in. God!" She shook her head and tears started again. "How could he do this? How—how could he?"

"The Bible say—"

"Don't tell me what the Bible says, Momma."

"It's the word of the Lord, child. Somewhere in the Gospel of Luke, Jesus say something bout he come not to bring peace on earth but division and he go on talking bout families divided gainst each other, three gainst two, two gainst three, father gainst son, son gainst father, mother gainst daughter, daughter gainst mother, mother-in-law gainst daughter-in-law, daughter-in-law gainst mother-in-law. Now is the time we need to stick together, Renee, learn forgiveness."

"But what made him get himself mixed up in this mess, Momma?"

"Greed."

"He's ruined his life."

"Don't put the cart fore the horse."

"But we didn't need it."

"My son, a teacher of the Word, done forgot the Word hisself."

"He's ruined everything. This is one mess he won't be able to worm his way out of. I feel it, Momma. I'm really scared."

"Jeremy forgot that life, honest life, is more important that material things."

She took out her handkerchief and blew her nose then looked at me with them red eyes. "Momma, I—"

The telephone ringed and I got up and went up the hall and picked up the receiver. I thought it would be Donna Mae.

It was the mayor. I said, "How do, George."

He spoke back to me, then ast what I knowed. I told him I knowed bout as much as they let me.

"Annie Eliza," he said, "I just talked with the district attorney. He's seeking a grand jury indictment against the individuals on the Board of Directors of the Georgia Fruit and Vegetable Company. Jeremiah and Dale are named in the indictment."

"I was just at the jailhouse, George."

"Oh, so you know something about this already. Of course you would, but what you might not know is that this D.A. will get what he wants, Annie Eliza. Things don't look good for your boy and Dale. I warned these boys a long time ago they had to keep their noses clean if they hoped to last in public life, but no, they wouldn't listen to me, wouldn't follow the example set by Mitch. They just let their eyes get bigger than their stomachs."

"Can't you talk with the D.A.?"

"I did. I couldn't ask him to do anything illegal, you know that. It's not my way. And, besides, he wouldn't even if he could. I called you, Annie Eliza, to tell you that the worst that can happen will be that Jeremiah could get between three and five years in prison and, if a miracle happens, he might get a five year suspended sentence. But don't count on it. I've already talked with Dale."

"I wish you'd talk with Jeremiah."

"I plan to, but the timing has to be right. He's already got two of the best lawyers in Atlanta, Stock and Thiel. If anybody can get him a suspended sentence, they can."

I membered the way Jeremiah looked sitting there in the police station and my heart almost broke while I was listening to the mayor trying to tell me things.

"You know this means it's all over for Renee."

"Why you say that?"

"Nobody would ever vote for her now. She can just forget a career in politics. I'm going to ask her to withdraw."

"But Jeremiah might go free."

"Don't matter. It's over for her even if he goes scot-free."

I did begin to cry just a little bit. "She's in a bad way. She's back here in the back."

"I won't talk with her on the phone. I want her to come up here and see me tomorrow. I can't see her today. Tell her to call my secretary and make an appointment."

"I'll tell her."

"The district attorney plans to ask Jeremiah and Dale to plead no contest. There might be some trouble, he feels, getting them to agree. It's their only chance. They got to show some remorse, otherwise they got about as much chance as a snowball in hell. Well, Annie Eliza, I got to get back to work. The city budget is in a mess and you know how it is, if you don't do a job yourself it just won't get done the right way."

I thanked George for calling and hanged up.

Me and Renee talked some more in the back.

"George is going to ask me to drop out of the race."

"Will you?"

"I don't know, Momma. I just don't know. A reporter called me just before I went to the station. He was calling from the *Constitution*. Wanted to know what I thought about my husband being charged with racketeering and conspiracy."

"You didn't say nothing, did you?"

"Sure, I did. I told him nothing has been proven yet."

"Good."

"Then he wanted to know what I would do if Jeremiah was found guilty. Would I still run for office."

I waited for the child.

"Then he asked me a question I got to find an answer to. Since I was investigating this thing, he said, it didn't appear that I knew my husband was one of the crooks. He said crooks. So would I go on supporting the investigation, take the side of the law against my own husband."

"What'd you say?"

"All I could say, Momma, was I had to be for what was right. I couldn't say anything else. How could I?"

"You didn't have to answer him. He might quote that in the newspaper."

"Even if Jeremiah is cleared, the scandal will ruin my chances anyway. George is going to tell me that. He might be right. I just don't know. But if I make a show of sticking up for my husband and not for what I was trying to uncover, everything I told people I stood for will just be undermined and destroyed worse than I could ever face."

"Oh, child —"

She looked at me and sniffed. "Deep down, I'm so mad at Jeremiah I could kill him. I'm not kidding you, Momma."

"Don't talk like that, child."

She lowered her head. "But I could. I really could."

"You must pray for his and your own forgiveness."

Me and Renee went over to her house and sho nuff Jeremiah was
down in the basement at his bar drinking. I told Renee to stay
upstairs. I went down the dark steps. He was fixing hisself a
drink. You could tell he already done had two or three. I leaned
myself gainst the pool table and crossed my arms and just looked
at him. The phone ringed and Renee upstairs answered it.

I said to my son, "Jeremiah, talk to me."

"About what, Momma?"

"Bout yourself."

"I don't know what you want me to say, Momma."

"Yes you do, son. Talk to me."

"I know you disappointed in me. I'm sorry, Momma. You want
me to say I'll be a good boy and I won't do it again."

"That might be a start. But I'm not going to talk with you bout
this mess again so you better talk with me now."

He drunk some more of that old nasty stuff. Scotch I guess.

"I'm waiting, Jeremiah."

"I'm sorry, Momma. I truly am. I didn't mean nobody any
harm. None of us thought we were doing wrong. Everybody
cheats a little, Momma."

"I never cheated nobody in my life," I told him.

"You're different, Momma."

"Why don't you try to be just a little different yourself? Why
don't you ast that God you preach to everybody about to show
you how to live by his rule?"

He looked shame of hisself. He couldn't look me in the eye.

I wont feeling as sorry for him as I thought I would. Somehow
he wont the little boy I knowed who needed me. He was beyond
that. And I thought of Juneboy. I turned to leave, then turned
back and ast, "You build the church with Scoop's money from
gambling?"

I saw Jeremiah's eyes fix on mine. I saw the alarm. I saw the
sadness at having to lie again. I already knowed the truth, long
buried, buried so long I couldn't member where it came from. I
knowed the answer but wanted him to speak, speak for the good

of his own soul, right now, fore it was too late, if it wont already too late.

"Yes, Momma. I built the church out of Scoop's bones."

I felt my face smile but it didn't feel nothing like no smile. "Then," I said, "you owe Juneboy."

"Owe him what?"

"His father's bones."

Then we went back upstairs.

★ ★ ★

Bout a hour later DeSoto showed up. Whitney was with him. He wont feeling too good, you could see that right off.

Renee and Jeremiah was upstairs in they bedroom talking. A couple of times I heard her scream at him and one time there was a loud crash. But we didn't go up there.

DeSoto started walking round all moody and wouldn't talk to nobody, hardly had anything to say to his own wife. She was worried bout him and she took me off to the kitchen to tell me so. She said, "Momma, DeSoto is really depressed. He can't sleep nights. I'm concerned. He won't eat either."

I figured DeSoto knowed bout all of this fore it come out in the open. He had been carrying the fear for his brother longer than I had. Not sleeping, not eating.

I said, "Whitney, child, he'll get over it. He's always been like that bout his brother. Don't you worry yourself and make yourself sick. You listen to me. Send DeSoto back here and I'll give him a talking-to."

And sho nuff she sent him and he came in the kitchen with me and I made him a cup of coffee and just looked at him.

I said, "DeSoto, you got to pull yourself together. You can't go on like this, not sleeping, not eating. Are you drinking?"

"No."

"Are you going to work every day?"

"I missed a couple of days."

"You don't want to mess round and lose your good job."

"I won't, Momma."

"Jobs are hard to find."

"Don't worry about me, Momma."

"All right. Just treat your wife right. Don't make her worry herself sick."

★ ★ ★

Back at home I called Dale and got that nurse. She didn't know if Dale could talk with me. He was resting and she had to see if he could talk.

Then I heard Dale say hello.

I ast him how he felt and he said, "Well, Annie Eliza I'm still kicking. That doctor from Boston is here in Atlanta. He put me through three hours of tests today at the hospital. He thinks it's just what your nephew said it was: coreyox. But the tests will tell for sure. You know, I've reached the point where it doesn't much matter. That whole trial business and being back in the hospital just about did me in for good."

I waited, not saying nothing.

Then he told me, "If it's coreyox it's not the worst disease in the world. Dr. Rineheart says I might live twenty or thirty years with it. But I won't ever have much strength. And, on the other hand, I could die tomorrow."

"But Dale, that's the way it is with all of us. We never know. Only the Lord knows."

"How's Jeremiah doing?"

"I ain't been able to bring myself to say much to him. Did they arrest you too?"

"My lawyer posted bail for me this morning while I was in the hospital. Annie Eliza, you got to forgive Jeremiah. He hasn't done anything that other people don't do."

"That don't scuse it."

"Put it behind you. Talk to you son."

"I talk to him but there ain't nothing to say."

"Well, just let him know you still love him."

"He knows that." I watched the blue light coming in through the hall window. "You gon have to be confined to the house?"

"Mostly. I don't mind. I'm tired of the world out there anyway."

"I know what you mean."

"Is Renee still running?"

"She ain't said she won't."

"She just might do all right. Give her my best. I wish I had some way to apologize to her, but—"

"Call her and—"

"I suppose I should. I owe it to her."

★   ★   ★

Well, that is all of it and now, child, I tell you, I don't know if I have the heart and the strength to go on but we're waiting now for the trial. And for Renee, too—and I personally think she's gonna win just cause peoples nowadays don't let something somebody else done wipe off so strongly on somebody else. And I guess the news is out all over the country this morning, even way up North. Esther probably knows by now. Juneboy too, there in Washington, D.C.

All we can do is hope for the best and pray, pray real hard. I think back and member how many hard times we got through and somehow I just have to believe that this one ain't much worse than the baddest we ever faced.